A Hire Love

Candice Dow

Dafina
BOOKS

KENSINGTON PUBLISHING CORP.
http://www.kensingtonbooks.com

DAFINA BOOKS are published by

Kensington Publishing Corp.
850 Third Avenue
New York, NY 10022

All Kensington titles, imprints and distributed lines are available at special quantity discounts for bulk purchases for sales promotion, premiums, fund-raising, educational or institutional use.

Special book excerpts or customized printings can also be created to fit specific needs. For details write or phone the office of the Kensington Special Sales Manager: Kensington Publishing Corp., 850 Third Avenue, New York, NY 10022. Attn. Special Sales Department. Phone: 1-800-221-2647.

Dafina Books and the Dafina logo Reg. U.S. Pat. & TM Off.

ISBN-13: 978-0-7582-1938-1
ISBN-10: 0-7582-1938-5

First Kensington Trade Paperback Printing: February 2007
10 9 8 7 6 5 4 3 2 1

Printed in the United States of America

This book is dedicated to my niece and namesake, Candice Taliah Dow, born March 2, 2006. I made a commitment to myself to finish this book before you were born. Thanks for arriving two weeks late and granting me an extension on my self-imposed deadline.

Acknowledgments

I would like to thank God for the abundance of blessings in my life. I am ever so grateful for His goodness and mercy.

All good things come in threes, and I can't believe how time flies. Just a year and a half ago, I was a first-time author, biting my nails, anxiously awaiting feedback on my first book, and how I prayed that at least one person would like it. For some reason I thought those jitters would go away with subsequent books. Guess what? They're still here, but I believe it is what makes me humble and drives me to write stories that you will enjoy. To my lovely readers: It is your love and support that keep me afloat. Your words pull me through and you make this journey worth the ride. To all the African-American book clubs, thank you. You are our backbone, and I appreciate you keeping it tight for us. So much love and gratitude goes out to you.

To my wonderful literary agent and friend, Audra Barrett: When you proposed the idea for this story, I remember you thought you'd have to sell it to me. Before you could even finish your pitch, I knew it was something that I'd be honored to write. Thanks for trusting me enough to be the surrogate mother to your baby! You are brilliant and I couldn't ask for better representation.

To my mother and father, thanks for over-nurturing me and making me believe that anything in this world is attainable. To my sister, Lisa, where would I be without you? Auntie's Angels: Morgan and Macey, keep making me proud. You are everything and everything is you! Thanks to all my family for being there and loving me despite my frequent absences from the family meetings. We are bound together with chords that cannot be broken! Special thanks to the family promo-team, especially Danece "Down for the Ride" Sykes, Tara "Just Tell Me What I

Gotta Do" Collier, Nia and Little Kevin, Sonia Harrison, Malik and The Twins.

Anika, you always know exactly when to push and when to pull. I am so blessed to have you to share my triumphs and successes, as well as my failures and mistakes. To the "Sex and the City" crew turned "ANS Street Team." Just when I thought you girls were too commercial for the grind, you stepped up the game in a major way. Nicole Dehlitsch, every writer needs to have you in her life, and I'm so glad you're in mine. Julian Brown, my lifelong friend, thanks for actually listening.

To my fellow authors and friends: Darren Coleman, thank you so much for your guidance and assurance as I try to figure this literary industry out. I wish you continued success. Daaimah "Everyday I'm Hustlin'" Poole, you are my girl! I am intrigued by your drive and determination. You deserve the best, and I wish you all the success in the world. Lissa Woodson aka Naleighna Kai, I can always trust that you are promoting me even when I'm not promoting myself and I thank you.

To the other authors who have blessed me on this journey with a smile, an encouraging word, a laugh, or a listening ear, I just want to tell you that I appreciate you: Janine A. Morris, Brenda L. Thomas, Victoria Christopher-Murray, Mary B. Morrison, Kendra Norman-Bellamy, Karen Quinones-Miller, Carl Weber, RM Johnson, La Jill Hunt, T. Styles, Nikki Turner, Joel McIver, Yasmin Shiraz, Yolanda Buick, and so many others—much success.

To the TriCom Publicity team, thank you for all of your hard work. Many thanks to Robilyn Heath, Heather Covington, Shunda Leigh, and Nakea Murray.

Thanks to the entire Kensington staff, especially Latoya Smith for holding down the fort. Jessica McLean, you are the best and I'm so blessed to have you.

If I forgot anyone, blame it on my mind and not my heart. Until next time, I'ma keep rhymin' and keep writin' and you will always be my reason . . .

With love,
Candice

PROLOGUE

Mounds of makeup-soiled tissue sat on the pew separating my sister and me. My mother was on the other side with her Southern church hat cocked to the side. Spit bubbles lined my lips as I asked, "Why?"

With her left arm wrapped around my shoulders to settle the jitters, my mother wiped my face with the ball of her right thumb. My sniffles stuttered as I fought to catch my breath.

When we fell in love, I thought to myself, this is too good to be true. As the pastor did the eulogy, our life flashed through the lenses of my Chanel sunshades. He was the man of my dreams. Why couldn't this be a dream?

With my arm stretched to the picture that sat atop the casket, I rocked back and forth wishing that I could touch him just one last time. It was a blow-up of the *Black Enterprise* magazine cover when he was featured: *Hip-hop pays off for young entrepreneur/writer*. He began the first magazine geared toward financial independence for young artists in the game, profiling rappers who'd gone bankrupt, along with those who made their money work for them. His life was dedicated to changing the minds and pockets of those who were pimped by the industry.

In the middle of the eulogy, his voice rippled through the church: "Fatty-Girl." Chills ran through me. My head swung around. Again, he called for me: "Fatty-Girl."

In the doorway of the church, he stood. The glare around him forced me to squint. Still, I could decipher the vision before me. I smiled as he strolled toward me. Dressed in what he wore into the office the day he was rushed to the Emergency Room: Black Prada shoes; Seven Jeans; Armani button-down. I bolted from the pew and into his arms. His cologne filled my nose. I didn't care how he got here or the mix up as to his death; I just wanted to hold him and forget about ever losing him.

People in the church gasped and some even snickered. I could give a damn about what they thought. All that mattered was that he was here with me. I kissed his cheek. It was cold and hard. I tried again. It was even colder. I rubbed his back and he evaporated in my embrace.

Everyone in the church pointed and laughed at me as I stood alone in the aisle hugging myself. Why didn't they help me? I just lost my husband and they found my desperation a big joke.

When my alarm clock interrupted my recurring dream, I sighed slightly as the "Hot 97" morning show host giggled in my ear. Damn it. This is no *Deliver Us from Eva*. This is my life. I'm in my king-size bed without my king.

My legs kicked wildly. As if this day was different than any other, I huffed because I didn't want to get up. Why can't I just lay here forever? Piles of manuscripts were scattered on the floor beside my bed. Derrick would always straighten up after I fell asleep. The disarray forced me to cover my face.

I stretched and rubbed sleep from my eyes hoping for a miracle. When I looked around, the papers remained. I sucked my teeth. *I need help.* All editors need an assistant at work and at home.

When I heard Whitney Houston's voice come through my speakers, I rose up.

"If tomorrow was judgment day . . . and I'm standing on the front line . . . and the Lord asked me what I did with my life; I'd say I spent it with you."

A smile spread across my face as I sang the lyrics to Derrick's favorite song. My head bobbed side to side. I felt his presence. The dream. The song.

He was my inspiration to peel out of bed. I two-stepped into the bathroom and mimicked his silly robot dance. *My love is your love and your love is my love.* When the song ended, my grouchy mood was gone. Derrick stopped by to cheer me up. He always did have perfect timing, if you don't count that he croaked too soon.

Scene 1

FATIMA

I scrounged around the house stuffing papers in my bag. When I reached the front door, I realized that I hadn't had my caffeine. I rushed back into the kitchen and opened almost every cabinet. Where is it? I just bought some yesterday. After a five-minute search, I noticed the huge Pathmark bag on the kitchen table stuffed with bags of coffee. It was too late to even consider, so I rushed out and I peeked in the mirror over the dining room table. My wedding portrait on the opposite wall was reflected in it. Derrick smiled at me. Just as I do every morning, I took a deep breath and smiled back. His voice vibrated through the room: "Chill out, Fatty."

I frowned at him through the mirror. He continued, "You can't take on this world by yourself. You need help. It's that time."

With my hands propped on my hips, I rolled my neck. "Time for what?"

The silence left me wondering if I were hallucinating. Here I am speaking to myself and hearing him. *Maybe it was time.* It was time for me to get my butt to work.

After sprinting up 138th Street to Adam Clayton Powell, I stuck my arm out and hopped into a gypsy cab. I exhaled, "Fifth Avenue. Between Forty-eighth and Forty-ninth."

This, of course, would be the day that someone would want

to play me. I wiped the moistness forming on my nose. Then, I asked him to repeat the amount I thought he stated. "How much?"

With a strong West African accent, he said, "Twenty dollar."

"No, fifteen."

He demanded, "Twenty dollar."

"I catch a taxi everyday from here. It's fifteen."

He continued to drive. "Twenty."

"Whatever. Fifteen—or I'll get out first."

This bastard called my bluff, as he had the audacity to pull over on 125th Street and pop the trunk. What could I say? *No, you're going to take me to work for the right price?*

Instead, I flung the door open and contemplated cursing him out, but I chilled. My mobile office was in his trunk. Five dollars wasn't worth losing the possible bestseller that I was reading.

He said, "Six dollars."

"P-lease!"

As I rushed to the back of the car, I spit obscenities. Why this morning of all mornings? When I looked up and saw Starbucks, I was thankful. It's hard to cope without coffee. Derrick learned early in our relationship that I was addicted. He would have it ready for me by the time I got out of the shower. He'd always brag that that was the key to our happiness.

Derrick spoke to me again, "Fatty, you need a hug."

I do not need a hug. I just need some coffee and I'm twenty steps away.

"You need someone to take care of you."

I can take care of myself. The last person that offered to take care of me retired early, so I'm not interested.

"Yes, you are. Maybe you should start dating."

Dating? Do I look like I have time to date?

"You have to make time. I'm dying watching you battle this world alone."

Ah! I think you already died. It's a great thing that everyone in New York is crazy, because no one questioned my conversation with the sky. I rushed into Starbucks and ordered my medication. As I stood there waiting for it, Derrick made sense.

When the caffeine circulated through my blood, I woke up. Why am I acting like I'm dead, too? I am young and vibrant. How long am I expected to be the mourning widow? *You're right, Derrick. It is time.*

It was as if all I ever wanted was his permission, because I was suddenly eager to get on the dating scene. I rushed out and hailed a taxi. Again, I told him where I was going. He nodded. I asked, "How much?"

"Fifteen."

I nodded and rested my head on the cracked leather seat. I called my home girl, Mya. As the phone rang, I giggled about how Derrick used to call us C1 and C2. That stood for Country One and Two. She grew up in Mississippi and I'm an Alabama girl and we met first day of freshman year at NYU. We took pride in our country nicknames. Guess that's the Southern happy side of us, but over the years we've become more Northern than Southern. She answered, "Hey, Tima. What's up, lady?"

"Hey, C2."

"Haven't heard that one in awhile. What's going on? I tried calling you last night."

"I was reading."

"The story of your life."

"Pretty much. Anyway, girl, I had that dream that Derrick is still alive. You know the one where he comes to the funeral . . ."

Although I don't believe it was intentional, she sighed impatiently and confirmed that she recalled which one. Her familiar snicker told me her thoughts. She thought I was insane. Considering the circumstances, I do damn good. Imagine marrying the man of your dreams at the age of twenty-two and he ups and kicks the bucket by the time you're twenty-five.

"Well, why did my alarm clock come on and his favorite song was playing? I mean I just felt his presence."

"Really?"

"I feel like he wanted to tell me that I'm free to date again."

She laughed. "*Again?* You've *never* dated. He is the only person you ever dated."

"I did date."

"Who?"

"Remember freshman year, I went out with . . ." I paused. "Um . . ."

"No! I remember you interning at *Vibe* magazine freshman year and becoming Derrick Mayo's assistant." She chuckled again. "And he scooped your young, tender, country butt up."

"I didn't get that internship until May. What was I doing before then?"

"Being a nerd."

"All right. Whatever. I think I want to start dating."

"Tima, are you sure?"

"Yes, I'm sure."

Apprehension rumbled in her sigh. "Tima?"

"Mya?"

Time had ticked away so rapidly. It took almost two years to get over the shock. He drove me to work. I kissed him good-bye. He said, "Kiss me again, Fatty." I kissed him again and he asked, "Do you love me?"

Though he should have always been stressed, it was never evident in his face. But that morning, his forehead was wrinkled. Dark rings formed shadows under his eyes. There was a cloud over him as I voluntarily leaned in for another kiss. "Of course I love you, honey."

"See you at seven."

"Where are we eating?" I laughed. He'd worried me all night about going to get ice cream. I said, "Ben and Jerry's?"

He chuckled. "We'll hit BJs after dinner. I'll call you after lunch."

I hopped out of the car and that was our last exchange, our last words. The phone call that came wasn't from him, but his secretary. He was rushed to the hospital and pronounced DOA. For two years, I waited for the punchline. This last year, I've just been trying to stay afloat. It wasn't until he mentioned it this morning that I internalized my loneliness. I swore if Derrick wasn't reincarnated, I would be single forever. Hey, some things are easier said than done.

As my mind reminisced on our last encounter, the phone sat glued to my ear and the taxi driver asked, "Left side or right?"

I sputtered, "Right."

Mya was still on the other end, explaining why she thought I wasn't prepared for the dating game. "Mya, maybe you're not ready for me to date?"

"I guess. It's just a dog-eat-dog world out here. I don't want you to have to deal with that. See, I know what's out here. I think you'll be shell-shocked."

"Whatever. Maybe we can go for a drink later and discuss the pros and cons. I have to go. I'm at work now. What's your day like?"

"I have a casting at one. Depending on how many good actors come out will determine how long my day will be. I'll call you and let you know."

I sighed. "Oh the life of a casting director."

"Tell me about it."

Shortly before one, Mya called. Surprisingly, her first question was, "Are you sure about this dating thing?"

"Yes."

"Okay, if you're really serious. I guess I should do my part to help you out."

"Yes."

She suggested I use a dating service. My lips curled. "Girl, please. Only desperate people use services like that."

She laughed. "See what I mean? You don't know anything about dating. Remember, that romance stuff you edit is fiction. Real people are on the Internet, using services, and anything that works."

"Whatever? I know *some* people use those services, but not me."

As she rushed off the phone, she did her best to convince me why I needed to go to an upscale dating service. "Although it's just a date, he needs to be handpicked." She snickered. "Okay, so I made you an appointment with the Black Love Agency."

My nose wrinkled. "That sounds like a porno agency."

"See, you are so outdated." She paused. "Now, would I send you to some sketchy place?"

"I guess not. When is the appointment?"

"This evening at six."

"What?"

"Yeah, I just sent the email with all the details."

"Wait—"

"I figured we should do it while you're pumped. Tomorrow might be too late. Who knows? Derrick may drop by tonight and tell you he changed his mind and he doesn't want you to date."

"You are such a smart-ass."

"Love me or leave me alone. I got to go. Hopefully, we'll talk before you go. If not, we'll hook up after your meeting."

My mouth sat open and my heart pounded, as I held the phone. Kia, my editorial assistant, stood in the doorway and interrupted my thought process. Her timid smile greeted my confused look. My eyes shifted left and right. Hers returned the gesture. As I motioned for her to enter, I laughed.

Unaware of the joke, she laughed too. I asked, "Kia, would you use a dating service to find a date?"

"Uh, a dating service?"

I smirked. "You're single, right?"

She nodded as I tried to recall my last question. "Yeah, you're single or yeah, you'd use a dating service?"

She covered her smile with her right hand. "Both."

"Would you?"

She nodded, and I asked, "Really?"

"Yeah, if I could afford it."

"So, is this what people do?"

"Yeah, some people. Most people will try anything at first."

Her confidence surfaced as she became the expert and I, the rookie. She continued, "It's just another way of meeting people. That's how I look at it. You never know where you'll find love."

Love. Technically, I've already had my shot at love, a love that would be impossible to replace, so I am just searching for a date. She giggled as my mind wandered off.

"I don't know." I lowered my chin and said, "I have an appointment at Black Love this evening."

"That's great, Fatima. I heard of people meeting nice guys through that agency."

Her excitement settled the doubt blustering in me, I blushed. "Really? So you think I should go?"

"Yeah, tell me how it works out for you."

"I certainly will."

After I changed from my stilettos into my loafers, I dodged to the subway to make my appointment on time. While I sat on the train, I took note of all the people without rings. It would be interesting to take a survey of how many people would be willing to go through an agency. When the train approached my stop, I daydreamed. Derrick's voice yanked me from my seat and before I could rationalize, I stood in front of the building.

Do I really have to stoop this low? As I debated the purpose of an agency, my cell phone rang. Mya shouted in my ear, "Go ahead, Fatima. Go in."

"How do you know that I'm not already inside?"

"Because I know you."

After looking around to make sure no one recognized me, I grabbed the door. "Whatever. I'm already inside."

"No, you're not. I can hear all the traffic on the street. You can't fool me. I know you too well."

"All right, all right. I'm going in now."

"Okay. Call me as soon as you're done."

Just as a matter of accuracy, I checked the directory for the suite. When I noticed only the initials BLA on the plate, I thought that was suspect. Why didn't they want to publicize that they were the Black Love Agency?

Before getting on the elevator, I took a deep breath. Inside the elevator, I took another deep breath. As the elevator went higher and higher, my reasons increased: *You can't be single forever. An occasional date to accompany you to professional engagements. A nice guy to take you out to dinner. And after a three-year drought, an occasional lay probably wouldn't hurt either.*

I stood in front of the young receptionist and smiled. "Uh . . ."

"Good evening. Do you have an appointment?"

"Yes. My name is Fatima." As I was about to state my last name, I felt like I was committing adultery. When I looked at the twenty-something black chick across from me, I wanted to bee-line out of there. Most people who knew people knew Derrick Mayo. How could I use his last name at the damn Black Love Agency?

"Fatima Barnes?" she asked.

My eyes expanded and my smile stretched even wider, because Mya was clever enough to book the appointment using my maiden name. I felt pumped again.

The receptionist handed me a clipboard with a stack of papers. "If you could just fill these out and give me your thousand-dollar deposit, we can get started."

Can't I appraise the damn prospects before they want to take my money? I leaned onto her desk, "So, do you think it's worth it?"

She shrugged her shoulders. "A lot of people say it is. Many of our clients have gotten married."

"So, usually how many dates do most people go on before they find what they're looking for?"

"Well, we charge a thousand per month and you get unlimited dates. So, it's hard for me to say. I mean most people stay with us on average three or four months." Trying to whisper, she added, "You know, depending on their personality, some are with us longer."

"This is the first time I've ever done anything like this."

Her smirk assured me that she thought I was lying. "Yeah, I understand."

"Do you have any tips?"

She chuckled. "Only pick men who are new to the service."

"Thanks." I checked out the nameplate on her desk. "Sha-kee-me-a. Did I pronounce it correctly?"

"Yeah, most people get it wrong. That's amazing."

Being that people often mispronounce my name, I know how

important it is to get it right the first time. "Yeah, I hate when people say my name wrong."

She nodded. "I know. I blame my mother though."

I laughed and plopped into one of the chairs in the waiting area. "Uh-huh. Me too."

We giggled a bit about the name game before I began filling out the stack of papers. As I plowed through the pages, I became apprehensive. There were too many clauses. They're not responsible if someone kills me. They will not refund for loss or damaged property. This is ludicrous. As I disputed everything on every page, I scribbled in my address, my name, my expectations, my signature, and damn it, I signed my check.

I stepped back up to Shakemia's desk and handed her the clipboard. Before I gave her the check, I asked, "Are you sure it's worth it?"

She nodded. "Yeah, we have a good selection of men. You'll be happy with our services."

"Okay."

She winked. "I'll look out for you."

I covered my chest with my hand. "Really?"

"I gotchu, Ms. Barnes."

"Thanks."

"No problem. Someone will be out in a second to take you back."

A middle-aged lady opened the door, came out, and smiled. My insides frowned. How is she supposed to help me find someone with the right combination of street and intellect? I crept toward her, "Hi."

Her quivery voice said, "Hello, Ms. Fat-a–mah."

I smiled at Shakemia, and corrected her, "Fa-tee-mah."

"Yes, Fat-a-mah, I am Gertrude. C'mon back."

As we walked back to her conference room, she went over what I was supposed to have read. "I'm sure you know that I've been doing this informally for over thirty years. The business has been in existence for about ten. I'm really good at what I do. I help you handpick all of your dates. I do a full psychological profile before the first date."

"We have to do this tonight?"

"It depends when you'd like to go on your first date. Are you in a rush?"

"Oh no, I'm in no rush to date."

She snickered. "No, honey. I mean are you in a rush this evening?"

I checked my watch as if I had more to do than read manuscripts and she waited for my response. I shook my head and she invited me to sit at the conference table.

"Okay, we'll profile you this evening."

The dysfunctional connotation associated with profiling rattled my nerves. "How do you profile?"

"You take a series of quizzes."

"Are they open book?"

She didn't respond. Her fifty-something maturity didn't find me at all humorous, so I reverted to intellect. "So what do you conclude from these quizzes?"

"They give me an idea of what you're looking for. How you expect to be treated. What type of person you'd be most attracted to."

"So, when do I get to the pictures?"

"Well, you'll only see pictures of men that you're compatible with."

"So, how long does it take you to grade the quizzes?"

She chuckled and pointed to the computer workstation. "Your answers will be analyzed immediately. Then, our database will be automatically searched for matches. And you and I will analyze the results. How's that sound?"

"Sounds good."

As I sat down at the workstation, she gave me basic instructions. I raced through the series of questions that had nothing to do with me going on a date and became irritated. Why Mya thought this made more sense than online dating perplexed me. The nine hundred and eighty dollar per month overhead charge for this fluffy office was the only difference I could identify. If nothing comes of this, I swear Mya is giving me back my money.

When I finished the useless profile, I walked to her office and smiled. "All done."

As she looked at her computer screen, she motioned for me to have a seat. "A widow, huh?"

No matter how often I hear it, the word makes me cringe. "Yes, my husband died three years ago."

"He really took care of you, huh?"

Yeah. Yeah. Yeah. Get to the point, lady.

She smiled. "I'm just analyzing your results."

"I thought you said the computer does that."

"Well, Fat-a-mah."

I curled my lips. She continued, "We have a large database of professionals and it's rare that you come up with no matches. So, when that happens—"

"Are you saying I don't have any matches?"

Her lips folded and she nodded. "I usually go back and analyze the results myself."

Just friggin' great! When I decide it's time to date, the damn computer says there are no men out here for you, Ms. Fat-a-mah.

"So what does your analysis say?"

She turned from the computer and folded her hands on her desk. "When did your husband die again?

"Three years ago."

"It appears he was a lot older than you. How much?"

What did my new date have to do with me and Derrick's age difference? "Seven."

"He practically did everything for you."

"No. He did what a man should do for his wife."

She chuckled. "I hate to tell you this, but your expectations are out of this world."

I snatched my neck back. She nodded. "Based on what you've written, I don't think anyone can make you happy right now."

Thanks lady. Thanks a whole lot. Can I get my damn check back? I raked my fingers through my hair and her jaw dropped. "You still wear your ring?"

As I peeked down at my three-karat princess-cut diamond solitaire, I clasped my hands together.

"I'm sorry. I don't think we can help you. You can get your check back from Shakemia. Maybe you need some more time to get over your husband."

I don't need to get over him. I don't want to get over him. Still, her conviction aggravated me. "So, you're trying to tell me that you don't have anyone that fits my criteria?"

She shook her head, and I pleaded, "I mean, it's just a date."

"People are searching for spouses. One thousand dollars a month is a pretty penny if you're just looking for a date."

I said, "Money is not an issue. I'm just looking for quality guys to date. If there's nothing you can do for me . . ."

When I stood, she motioned for me to sit. "This is against the rules, but I'll let you view a few profiles and we'll charge you one hundred dollars per date."

With both thumbs up, I said, "Okay, let's do this."

"Don't tell anyone I did this for you."

"You've got my word."

We moved back to the conference room and she selected a few profiles. She said, "You like the bad boy, huh?"

"No. I like the professional with an edge."

She laughed. "Most women these days do."

After searching through about eleven profiles, I selected two: One guy was a thirty-year-old business owner; the other was a twenty-nine-year-old banker.

The next step was to contact them and let them see my profile. If they were interested, she would make the connection.

Scene 2

FATIMA

In less than twenty-four hours, Gertrude called to say that one of the guys was interested. When I called Mya to tell her about my probable date, she teased, "Tima's going to talk to a guy! That's so funny."

I chuckled. "It *has* been a long time."

"It's been an eternity. Do you even know what to say?"

"Girl. Hopefully, he can lead the conversation, 'cause I don't know what to say to a guy."

"Tima, that is messed up. Personally, I don't like to talk a lot before I go out with a guy. If you talk too much and you meet him and don't like him, you feel obligated to explain. If you just briefly discuss the details of the date, you don't owe him anything if you don't like him. Trust me. You remember all the times I had to tell a guy after the first date that me and my old boyfriend got back together."

"Why did you lie?"

" 'cause I had sat up on the phone with the person, telling him that I was ready for a relationship. When I met him and didn't like him, I had to say something." She giggled. "For the record, do not tell anyone that you haven't dated since your husband died. You should always have a recent old boyfriend or have a friend that you see off and on."

As I was schooled on the rules of the modern world, I laughed. "That is ridiculous."

"Play or be played."

"That's a shame."

"Love is a game, baby girl."

My cell phone rang as I jotted down mental notes. When I didn't recognize the number, I said, "Mya, I think that's him."

She shouted, "Don't answer!"

"Why?"

"Because you want to hear his voice first. Then, you call him back. I can tell from a guy's voice if he's someone I want to talk to. What if he sounds like Steve Urkel?"

"Mya, you are making this way too complicated."

"Whatever—I'm just looking out for my girl."

"So, when do I call him back?"

"After we listen to the message."

"We?"

"Yeah. We're in this together. You aren't skilled enough in the screening process yet."

I called my voicemail and linked it with Mya. As I waited for the new message to play, I twiddled with my wedding ring. There was a short pause before he spoke:

"Hey, Fatima. This is Damien. Looking forward to talking to you. You can hit me back on . . ."

Mya said, "Well, at least he sounds sexy."

"Yeah, that's a plus. So, when am I allowed to call him back?"

"In ten minutes, but remember, get the details of when and where you'll meet and get the hell off the phone."

"This is so silly."

"Trust me. You'll thank me in the end."

"One last question."

"I'm listening."

"Do I really have to take my ring off?"

"Is Derrick still wearing his?"

I laughed. "You know what? I need to find better friends."

"Sike, I'm just playing, but it's time to take it off. Your husband is gone. He can live in your heart forever, but no man will ever take you serious with another man's ring on your finger."

"I'll think about it."

"Baby, it's your world. You can do what you want, but would you want to hang out with a man still wearing his wedding band?"

"You're right. Let me get ready to call this guy back."

Before I called him back, I went into my bedroom and searched for my ring box. When I sat the solitaire and the wedding band in the box, I felt naked. To appease myself, I slipped the diamond band on my right hand and tucked the solitaire away in my special drawer that contained a bunch of sentimental gifts from Derrick.

When I returned Damien's call, butterflies floated in my stomach. A piece of me prayed for his voicemail, but as I prepared my message, he answered.

"Hello."

I stuttered, "H-hi. Ah. Damien?"

"Yes. Fatima?"

"Hey, how's it going?"

"Everything's good. How are you?"

"I'm fine."

"That's good."

"So . . ."

I searched for something, anything to say, but he relieved me. "So, when would you like to hook up?"

Boy, did he get to the point fast. This divide-and-conquer method to dating is no fun. When Derrick first called me, we chatted for nearly four hours. Do people do that anymore?

I said, "Uh, whenever."

"Maybe we could catch a movie on Saturday."

"That's cool."

"Where do you live?"

I thought it over and said, "In the city."

"I'm in Brooklyn."

I certainly wasn't anxious about inviting a stranger into my hood, so I offered to meet him in his. He promised he'd give me a call before the end of the week with the movie times. Just like that, my inaugural speech was over.

On Saturday, I stuffed some reading into my large Louis Vuitton satchel. While I sat on the train headed to Brooklyn on a first date, I got antsy. Didn't want to read. It was like I was fourteen again. What should I say when he walks up to me? *Hi. Nice to meet you. Good to see you.*

At two-fifteen, I was still standing in front of the movie theater in Prospect Park for my two o'clock date. My blood pressure escalated. How the hell can you be late for a first date? My weight shifted back and forth on my four-inch heels. I tossed my hair behind my ear and called Mya. "Do you know this clown isn't here?"

"Tima, don't get all up in a bundle. Maybe something came up."

"He has my cell phone number."

"He'll be there. Just be cool."

I looked at my watch. "Whatever. I'm about to leave. I don't have time for this."

"Dating is not easy."

"Well, you've given me that whole spiel before. Isn't that why you sent me to that jackleg dating service? Wasn't that supposed to guarantee a quality guy?"

I curled my lips and waited for her to respond. She laughed. "No one told you to have unreasonable expectations."

I laughed too. "Whatever."

"This is the dating game. It's hit or miss."

Standing on a corner in Brooklyn on a Saturday afternoon wasn't exactly my idea of dating. Shit! I could have sat home for another weekend. Mya said, "He's almost twenty minutes late. Do you want me to come down there and go with you?"

"No, I'm leaving now. I'll call you when I get uptown."

Damn it. This is not worth one hundred dollars a pop. I want a refund. I could go to any bar for this kind of treatment. Damn if I'll pay for irresponsible men.

Just as I stormed up Prospect Avenue, my phone rang.

He sighed before speaking. "I'm so sorry, I couldn't find my keys, but I'm on my way."

I checked my watch and contemplated if I should even wait. Hell, I spent forty-five minutes traveling here. I've stood for thirty-five minutes waiting for this loser. At least, I should get a free movie out of this.

When he showed up, it was ten minutes to three and I was livid. He leaned in for a hug and I retracted from this caveman. Okay, I did request a guy with an edge, but his edges were ragged and he was rugged.

Either the untamed weeds sprouting from his face camouflaged the fine guy with a five-o'clock shadow that was on his profile, or I had been bamboozled. As he began to explain the lost key fiasco, my mind was already on the train back to Harlem.

"I had to go to my mom's job to get her key," he said.

Lawd, please don't tell me this man lives with his mama. He continued. "She went in her purse to get her keys and she had my keys."

I cringed. That damn Black Love. There is no way in the world he is paying a thousand dollars a month. The organization must be a cover-up for some sort of drug-trafficking. Although the date was over before it began, I decided to engage him slightly.

"So, you and your mother live together?"

He nodded. "Yeah."

"So, what kind of business do you own?"

"Is that what my profile says?"

I nodded. As he snickered, I looked around. Is there a comedian performing? He doesn't have a job?

"So, do you pay for the dating service?"

"Nah. If you aren't doing the selecting, you don't have to pay."

My mouth hung open. "So, I take it, you're not selecting."

"Oh, hell nah. I ain't paying for no dates."

Was that a double negative or a triple negative? Whatever the case, he was a quadruple negative. Late. Lives with mama. No job. And more important, no tact.

Mya is in for it and so is that damn Gertrude from Black Love.

She tried to act like her matchmaking was something special and that she had it down to a science. What a joke. Not that I expected my first date to be love at first sight. Duh! That only happens once in a lifetime and I've had my turn, but are there any respectable men out there that are cool enough to just hang out with?

Neither of us said much from that point on. My body language told him this was our first and last date. His carelessness let me know that he was just a random flunky that Black Love hires to go on dates with desperate women.

Scene 3

FATIMA

Black Love refunded my one hundred dollars on the spot. Mya endured my bitching and complaining all day for two days. When she called to make sure that I at least got my money back, I said, "This is ridiculous. They should have quality men."

"Fatima, baby, you're tripping."

"If I'm paying, at least give me quality service."

"Looking for a quality man is like looking for a needle in a haystack."

"I don't believe it."

Mya smacked her lips. "Have you just been ignoring me for the last nine years or what? Remember all I went through before meeting Frankie?"

"I guess."

"You're going to have to manage your expectations or you're going to be upset a lot."

"Oh well, let's just forget it."

"You can always go the traditional route."

"The traditional route?"

"Yeah, join some organizations, meet new people, and develop relationships like that."

"I may as well run a damn marathon, too. That could take forever."

"The problem is that you want what you want when you want

it. Just because you decide you're ready to date, what, five days ago. You think it just happens?"

"Yeah."

She mocked Gertrude from Black Love, "Sorry, Fat-a-mah. It might take awhile."

"I just need to meet someone that's cool. He doesn't have to be perfect."

"Your definition of cool far surpasses most women's definition of perfection."

"Mya, I don't want to talk to you anymore. You're making me feel worse."

"That's not my intention, honey. Maybe you should try some of the online sites."

"Now that's what I pay you for. Suggestions, not discouragement."

"Okay, I forgot. You'd rather be lied to."

Instead of defending myself, I laughed off the discomfort of her accusation and got the 411 on Internet dating. While I listened to her strategy, I logged onto the first site she suggested. She recommended I post my picture.

"Mya, I can't. What about the whole anonymity spiel?"

"They don't know who you are. They just know how you look. You don't have to give them your phone number. They email you through the website. So, they don't have your direct email. It's just a picture. All the people in New York, no one will ever recognize you." She chuckled. "My picture was out there for three years and no one ever approached me and claimed they saw me. If you don't put a picture out there, you'll be wasting your time."

I performed a search as if I were a man searching for a woman. As I paged through hundreds of profiles, I was amazed at the competition. There were beautiful, successful women sprawled all over the site. You've got to be kidding me. If they weren't embarrassed, why should I be? Before I realized it, I was on the Kodak website uploading photos of me and deciding which one to post.

By the time I got off the phone with Mya, I had written my personal statement and selected what I wanted in a man.

This was much cooler than Black Love. I could select color, height, job description, salary. This is great for us superficial folks just out for a date. When the results returned, my mouth hung open. Several attractive men appeared.

In thirty minutes of posting my profile, over ten guys already emailed me and dozens had cyber-winked. As flattering as their messages were, I wanted to take control and select the men that I wanted to correspond with. While I sent several "thanks, but no thanks" messages back, I chuckled. There is just something about feeling desired, even if you're not interested.

This was my source of entertainment during the entire day at work. I can't remember when I'd had so much fun flirting. It was the coolest thing. Immersed in my online rejection correspondence, I pushed today's deadlines to tomorrow.

Of all the men in my search, there were only two that I was compelled to approach. Something in their profiles stepped off the pages; whether it was the fine smile, salary range, and the arrogance to title his profile "Young and Successful" of one, or the sexy picture and the poetically written personal statement of the other. My enthusiasm slightly diminished when neither had responded and I noticed they both had been online.

When I got home, I checked again, but my inbox was loaded with junk from a bunch of ugly ducklings. What's up with that? This is just another hoax to play with people's emotions. Fine men post their pictures just to have their egos stroked. *Hi I read your profile. I thought you were so gorgeous.* In reality, they know they're not having trouble finding dates. It wouldn't surprise me if one of them compiled all the emails he had received in a book and titled it, "The Words of Desperate Women."

It pissed me off that I had subscribed to this. That is, until I walked into the office the next morning to an email from "Young and Successful." Kia stood in front of me explaining something as my ego was resuscitated. *Thanks for expressing interest. I loved your profile. You're beautiful. It looks like we have a lot in common. Tell me more about the life of an editor.*

Kia posed and waited for me to stop gloating. When I glanced up for her to finish, her eyes danced in her head. I smirked. She quickly altered her expression. "So, what's up?"

She repeated herself as I planned my email response. She asked, "What do you want me to tell her agent?"

Clueless of whom or what she was talking about, I said, "Tell her . . ."

"I'll come back when you get settled."

"That would be good."

I replied promptly. After a few emails, he asked if we could instant message. After consulting with Mya, I downloaded Yahoo! Messenger and BackInAction chatted real time with YoungAndSuccessful. By noon, I knew that he lived in Brooklyn, worked for Morgan Stanley, no kids, never married. If he was actually the person in his photo, he was also fine. We even discussed the death of my husband. Our correspondence was loaded with thought-provoking topics. By the end of the day, he asked if it would be okay to have a real conversation.

After consulting with Mya, I agreed. He told me he would call around ten and he kept his promise. I picked up like I'd known him for years. "Hey, Young and Successful."

"Ms. Fatima. Please call me Nate."

Our real chat was equally as enticing as our cyber-chat. We disregarded the divide-and-conquer rule and talked for over an hour. His appealing voice made me eager to meet him in person and we agreed to meet for drinks the next evening.

Mya willingly accompanied me on the date with "Young and Successful" just to provide real-time coaching with managing my expectations. When we arrived at the empty happy hour, I realized I'd picked the wrong club on the wrong evening. The techno-music attacked me the moment we entered. We had fifteen minutes before he arrived, so we ordered drinks to take the edge off. He walked in at seven-thirty on the dot, and Mya nodded.

His tailor-made suit impressed me and his nice teeth added to the package. He introduced himself and appeared distracted by Mya's presence. I said, "Nate, this is my girl, Mya. I asked her to tag along. I hope you don't mind."

"I don't mind. It's cool. I don't know about you guys, but this music is driving me crazy."

Mya said, "It's killing us, too."

"Why don't we get out of here and go somewhere else?"

We shrugged our shoulders and followed him out of the club. He paid for the ride to the next spot, but it didn't appear he gave the driver a tip. Then again, maybe I'm just suspicious.

We found a loveseat to accommodate all of us and I conjured up a discussion about love and relationships with hopes to gain insight on the male perspective. He touched my leg occasionally as he spoke. As my body became reacquainted with the touch of a man, I realized how much I missed it and how much I longed for it. Mya and I exchanged approving nods throughout the conversation. The game isn't so bad. After two dates, I met someone that I could definitely consider seeing again.

When the check came, I looked at it. Mya looked at it. Nate didn't as much as glance at it. Mya put her credit card inside the folder. I clutched my purse. Nate seemed unfazed. The waiter asked if we were ready. Mya said, "No, not yet." She leaned over me and dangled the folder in Nate's face. "Did you see the check?"

"Fatima's going to take care of me."

I smiled. Mya's neck rolled. "No, she isn't, because I'm taking care of her."

He repeated, "And she's taking care of me."

I giggled while he kidded with Mya. She rolled her neck again. "I know you better be joking."

"I paid for the taxi over here."

Mya said, "Are you friggin' kidding me?"

My knee tapped his knee. "Stop playin'."

"You can get me tonight. I'll get you next time."

My blood pressure began to elevate. Did he really believe there would be a next time if I took care of him tonight? There's no way in the world he was serious. I said, "You're funny."

Mya huffed and puffed in my ear. When the waiter came, she handed him the check. Up until the waiter carried the check away and Nate didn't chase him down, I thought he was a prankster. Turns out that Mr. "Young and Successful" was more like a wankster.

Mya and I sat with our arms folded, waiting for the waiter to return with the receipt. He had the audacity to tug on my arm. "What's wrong?"

If he didn't know, damn if I planned to offer him an explanation. He asked, "Would you like to dance?"

"Do I look like I want to dance?"

"What happened?"

Mya chimed in, "You."

"For real, Fatima. Tell your girl to mind her business."

Mya stood up and said, "Get my card. I'll meet you downstairs."

When she stormed away, he said, "Your girl is trippin'."

"Am I missing something here? Did you just eat and drink and not offer a penny? Now, my girl that paid for everything is trippin'?"

"I asked you to take care of it."

My eyes rolled in my head. "But I didn't say I would."

"Well, it was obviously not what I thought it was."

"I just met you. What are you talking about?"

He sucked his teeth. "I mean, you approached me."

I sat stunned. Words to dispute his claim never came. Anger percolated in me as I thought about spitting in his face. The waiter returned with the receipt and Mya's card in just enough time to save me from being hauled away in handcuffs. I signed Mya's name and stomped away.

Mya stood by the door, pissed. She cursed his existence as we hailed a taxi. I apologized and offered to pay for his portion. "You don't have to pay for that loser. Bad enough you wasted your time getting cute tonight."

"Yeah and just to think, he was this close to a second date."

"He's obviously gotten away with that kind of behavior, because he looked at us like we were out of touch. Women must really be desperate."

I laughed. "You ain't lying about that. It's really rough out here, huh?"

"Uh, yeah."

"Men don't have standards anymore and women are just accepting it, huh?"

"Basically."

"I quit."

She laughed. "You have to stay in the game or you've already lost."

"What's the purpose if everyone is a loser?"

"There are good men out here. It just takes time. It's like searching for the perfect dress. You know?"

I pouted. "A dress can't eat and drink and not pay the bill."

"Silly, you know what I'm saying. Sometimes you have to try on a lot of dresses before you find what you're looking for. And sometimes, you go right in the store and the perfect dress is right there, but you can't take for granted that it'll always happen that way." I sucked my teeth and she stroked my hair. "It'll get better."

Scene 4

FATIMA

When I got home, I removed my profile from the dating website. Mya called when I got to work to see if I'd really thrown in the dating towel.

"Tima, you just have to be patient. It might take awhile."

I laughed. "It's not like I'm looking for a husband. All I need is a damn stand-in. Is that asking for too much?"

"A stand-in?"

"Yeah. Someone who can be emotionally supportive. You know, the way Derrick used to be."

"Sweetie, Derrick was sprung. You're not just going to leap out here and find that in one week." She sucked her teeth. "The only way you can guarantee that is if you write a damn script and get some starving actor to play the role."

She laughed hysterically. The great idea siren alarmed in my brain. A big smile splattered across my face and my large eyes shifted. "Mya, you're brilliant."

She sucked her teeth again. "Girl, please."

"No. That makes perfect sense. I need to write a script."

"Fatima, don't play." She chuckled. "I was just being facetious."

"No, but it's the best idea you've come up with this week. I'll write the script. You can call your agency contacts to get some actors to come out for an audition."

"Stop joking, girl. I'd lose my job playing games like that."

"Why? I'll pay them the appropriate scale. This is a professional job."

"Whatever. You shouldn't have to pay for love."

"That's just it. It's not about love. I just need a handsome man around that treats me well and can help make the everyday hustle a little easier. Someone to take out the trash. Someone to bring me flowers."

She added water to the seed fermenting inside of me. "Someone who knows how to treat a woman."

"See, it's the perfect plan."

Clearly she thought I was bluffing as she egged me on. "You definitely should write a damn script, because men up here have no clue as to how a man should treat a lady."

"I *am* going to write it."

As if she was distracted by something, her voice lowered. "You're crazy."

"No, we're crazy, because you're going to help me."

"Whatever."

As we sat on the phone, I jotted down some important characteristics of my leading actor. I pulled up my StoryWeaver software. Under the character description I entered RN for the main character's name. I giggled at my homemade abbreviation for real name. Didn't want any slip-ups at the wrong time. Could you imagine the scene? I'm at a banquet with my hired partner and I erroneously tell someone his name is Jacob. We're pretending we're in love and one of my business associates interrupts the scripted scene: "Hey, Jacob." My partner doesn't answer to the given name or his response is delayed. Nope, he always has to be on point. As I typed the script, Mya cleared her throat, "What are you doing?"

"Okay, listen. He has to always, under all circumstances, treat me like a princess. He has to be over six feet tall. Two-hundred-twenty pounds to two-hundred-forty. And more important than the physical, he must exemplify the four key characteristics that constitute a good man."

"Oh, so now there is a science to a good man?"

"No, not a science. More like a blueprint."

She howled. "Trust me. There is no blueprint that can separate a man from a good man."

"Patience, respect, understanding, and honesty. Those ingredients create the perfect recipe for the perfect man."

Just as it exited my mouth, I titled it, "The Perfect Script."

"That sounds like something straight off the pages of one of your little novels." We laughed and she said, "Did you not hear me when I said that I was just being facetious when I suggested this?"

Ignoring her reluctance to consort with me, I continued: "He'll be a successful entrepreneur who dabbles in real estate and a diverse set of other lucrative investments."

As I spat out the requirements, I imagined her rolling her eyes in her head. "Fatima. Maybe you should go out with a shrink and not a man."

"Whatever. I don't think this is crazy at all."

"That's even more reason why you should see a shrink."

"Stop!"

"You should stop. I think the whole idea is selling yourself short."

"No. I'm just hiring help. My heart belongs to Derrick. No one will ever add up anyway. Don't you get it?"

"Fatima, I'm not telling you it's easy, because dating is one of the hardest things you'll have to do, but you will find love again."

"How many times do I have to say I'm not looking for love? Can you at least try to understand where I'm coming from? Please."

"I guess." She chuckled. "Let me go, sweetie, I have some work to do."

"Okay. Promise you'll think about my script."

She sucked her teeth. "Promise me you'll refill your Prozac."

"That's busted. Talk to you later."

Although I had tons of work to do, I was submerged in developing this script. Each time I would attempt to shut the screen down, something else would pop into my head. I created scenes around frequent events, such as dinner dates. I listed my favorite restaurants. His part of the script was to play the man who knew me so well, he ordered my food.

> *RN and Fatima are at dinner at a four-star restaurant. RN has just pulled out Fatima's chair.*
> RN (speaking to waiter): We'll have your most expensive bottle of Merlot.
> WAITER: Would you like water?
> RN: She'll have water, no ice with lime.

I gave guidance on what to do when planning dates, giving gifts and being supportive.

> *Fatima is at work and receives a gift from RN, handwritten sentiments are her favorite. She opens the gift and calls RN to thank him.*
> FATIMA: I wanted to thank you for the gift, but, more important, the note.
> RN: Sometimes words describe my feelings best.
> FATIMA: Don't make me blush.
> RN: I'll try my best.

While I stroked away at the keyboard, Kia came in and startled me. "Hi, Fatima. You have a meeting in fifteen minutes."
"Okay. I'm coming."

> *Mornings*: Coffee should always be brewed. He should never forget to tell me to have a great day.

When I noticed Kia's silhouette in the doorway, I huffed. She smiled and sang my name. I rushed to write an afterwork scene.

> *Fatima is in a taxi after a long day at work and RN calls.*
> RN: Hello, Fatima. How was your day?
> FATIMA: It was hard.
> RN: Baby, we can talk about it at dinner tonight.

After saving my script, I rushed from my office. While the marketing team discussed strategies for one of next month's releases, I scribbled in my notepad. What to do when Fatima's sad? How to act with her family? What kind of dates does she enjoy?

RN and Fatima are walking through Central Park after a date. The night is breezy. Fatima folds her arms. RN takes his jacket off.
    RN: Here, put this around you.
 FATIMA: I'm okay.
    RN: Please, I want you to put it on. You seem a little chilly.
 FATIMA: Thank you.
    RN: I have to take care of my baby.

Before the meeting was done, I'd filled up two pages. As I perused the notes, I shook my head. Well, what matters most is that I'm paying for this service, so maybe I can get what I deserve.

Fatima is having a bad case of PMS and she asks RN to get her pizza at 3 AM. RN smiles.
    RN: Whatever the little lady wants.

By the time I met Mya for drinks four hours later, my script was near completion. I handed her the printout of the first draft. "Read my script."

She looked at me from the corner of her eye. "Didn't I tell you to take your medication?"

"Stop! That's not funny. You know that stuff almost made me crazier than what I am."

"If that's the case. You're right. Maybe you shouldn't take it." She flipped through the pages. The excitement on her face didn't complement her monotone voice. " 'Cause you're really going off the deep end with this."

I propped my elbow up on the bar as I watched her become

engrossed in my words. The rapid pace in which her eyes shifted confirmed that if nothing more, it was a good read. As her body language mellowed, I knew she had fallen victim to my plot.

"So, you're really serious about this, huh?"

"Yeah. Are you going to help me?"

"How long is the gig?"

"Um, just until this lonely feeling goes away."

"That could be a long time. How long are you willing to pay for love?"

"For company."

"Shit. If you're paying scale, I'll be your company."

My nose wrinkled. "Um, if this is a twenty-four-hour-a-day job, what is the appropriate scale?"

"I just don't think anyone is going to take this serious."

I yanked her arm. "Just tell me."

"It's kind of hard to explain. Scale is based on the type of work: TV; commercials; film. And film is broken up into three different levels: low-budget; mid-range; full-budget." She took a deep breath. "I just don't know where this falls in."

"So, you're interested?"

"I mean. It sounds fun, but I'm wondering how we work the contract. Will anyone take us seriously?"

"Okay, we'll draw up a six-month contract and rate it like a low-budget film." As I watched her slip deeper into my drama, I scooted up in my chair. "What do you think?"

"You're looking at about three hundred dollars a day." She used the calculator on her cell phone. "That's about fifty-five K for six months. You're crazy."

"That's the money I get from Derrick's estate. That's not even touching the insurance money."

She giggled. "Well, hell! Let's go for it. We could make this a reality show."

"No, I'm not down for that. We're not going to have me all posted up on network TV. I have a reputation to uphold."

"Hey, we may as well get paid for it."

"Whatever. How are you going to cast the actors?"

"Oh, hell no! I'm not casting anyone. You are," Mya said.

"How am I supposed to do that?"

She sipped her drink. "I'll have a call out for men that match your description tomorrow. For the guys that I like, but don't make the cut, I'll tell them about this opportunity and see how many of them are down. You can set up your own casting. You know what you're looking for better than me."

I put my arm around her neck. "What would I do without you?"

She gyrated her slim hips like Lil' Kim and chanted, "Who gon' love you like I do? Huh? What?" She raised the roof with her hands and her large bangle jingled to the melody. "Who gon' treat you like I do? Huh? What?"

Scene 5

RASHAD

Trying to become an actor should be described as the test of a man's humility. Things I swore I would never do, I find myself willfully submitting to on my quest for stardom. An Asian lady stood over me, waxing every strand of hair growing from my torso. I squinted to avoid screaming as she ripped out the follicles. How many men would tolerate this torture?

When I walked into the casting for an underwear commercial, my question was answered. I wasn't the only buffed, hairless Black man in the room. As I surveyed the competition, I was confident about my chances. Though I long to one day have a respectable role in a major film, it seems directors love me more the less I have on. Often I want to scream, "Damn it! Does anybody see that I really have talent?"

When I auditioned, I thought for certain I'd nailed it from the expression on the casting director's face. Her large hazel eyes pierced through me as if she wanted to indulge in me for dessert. I sat in the waiting area for the first-round decisions. Several guys walked out with their heads hung low. As a matter of habit, I always give my competition a head nod.

When I was called into the room, I entered stoically. It will take more than rejection to destroy me. The casting director sat alone in the room. I searched for her cohorts. She chuckled and twirled her finger in her naturally curly sandy brown Afro. "It's just me. I'm Mya."

"Please to meet you, Mya."

I grinned in celebration. Her face elongated and her high cheekbones protruded as she took the regretful deep breath. My confidence fizzled, before she said anything. "You will not be proceeding to the next round."

This part always bothered me, because the constructive criticism was never constructive. It was always that you're just not what we're looking for. How can a man improve when no one can say what's wrong?

After her thirty-second pause, I stood and extended my hand. She obviously had no advice. She continued, "Have a seat."

She covered her face. "This is so embarrassing."

Don't tell me this lady wants to sex me up after seeing me in my underwear. She was much too slim for me, but still I smiled. "Go ahead. Say what's on your mind."

"Okay, I have another opportunity that you might be interested in."

I scooted up in my chair. This was my kind of criticism. She explained, "It's kind of out-of-the-ordinary, but it's still acting. The pay is equivalent to the base scale for a low-budget film."

"Really?"

"Yes, it's a six-month contract, subject to renewal."

"What film? What company? Tell me all the details."

"It's sort of like reality-TV."

"That's cool."

"If you were to get the part, you would be playing the boyfriend of a young lady who is tired of dating losers."

I chuckled. "Okay. Will it be aired? What's the object of the show?"

"Well, it's kinda like reality-TV without the cameras."

"Get out of here."

She shook her head and grabbed a folder. "She plans to cast sometime this week. If you're interested, let me know and I'll get you on the schedule. And please, do not discuss this with your agent or any other actors." She winked. "This is a side job where you make all the money. I've hand-selected you, because my instincts tell me that you're a really cool guy."

"I appreciate this. My lips are sealed."

This job sounded like a dream come true. Get paid for reality. Who could beat that?

When I got home and opened the folder, I flipped through the script. I was convinced that the main lady was the casting director. Had the dating scene gotten so bad that beautiful women now had to pay men to act like their man? Sadly enough, I wouldn't know. I'd been out of the mix since my last girlfriend gave me the ultimatum of choosing her or my acting career. My mother raised me to believe that a man should take care of his woman and knowing that I wasn't in the position to provide for a woman like I should, I let her walk. No woman should have to sit around and watch a man dream. Nor should a man sacrifice his dream to be with a woman. If he doesn't have his stuff together, he needs to be alone.

The scenes outlined how the man should react to various situations. Most of these things should be second nature. Before I buried myself in the remainder of the script, I called Mya and told her to put me on the schedule. I said, "You can tell everyone else to stay home."

She chuckled. "I'm sorry. I'm not at liberty to do that."

While she gave me the details, I scanned my closet and planned for attack. She told me that the main character, Fatima, would like to be referred to as Ms. Barnes during the casting. I asked, "Is Fatima her real name?"

"Yes."

I prayed this young lady was as cute as her name. Her adorable little comments in the script made me anxious to meet her. The thought that she felt deserving of this treatment intrigued me more.

Scene 6

FATIMA

Mya scheduled five actors to meet me at a midtown restaurant thirty minutes apart. I sat alone reading over the portfolios of the prospects. Even I had begun to think this was a ludicrous idea, but it was too late to reconsider because Number One was about to walk on stage.

Before I pulled out my makeup compact, I took a deep breath. As I powdered my nose, I frowned at my reflection. *What the hell are you doing? He doesn't have to find you the least bit attractive.*

I gave the host a heads-up that I'd be here for awhile. While I sipped on a glass of Merlot, I drummed on the table.

When I saw the host direct Pee-Wee Herman to my table, I choked the stem of my wineglass. I ducked down and peeked over my shoulder. Is there any way I could hide out until Number Two arrives? I bit my bottom lip. Then, I realized this is no blind date where I have to sit here and smile at some poorly dressed man. My script dictates what I like my man to wear and he was out of character. By the time he reached the table, my expression should have shooed him away. He extended his hand and I scrutinized his outfit. A plastic replica Prada belt sat inches below his chest and strangled the waist of his straight-legged slacks. Dense collections of lint were scattered all over his shirt. He should have vacuumed it.

We shook hands and he raised mine and planted a kiss on it. "Please to meet you, Ms. Barnes."

I nodded, but didn't tell him that I was pleased as well. When we sat, I flipped through my copy of the script and ignored his icebreakers. I found the section on *Attire and Style* and turned the paper around so that he could see. "Did you read this section?"

"Yeah, I noticed you specified a stylish guy, but it says only dress shirts in the blue family or white." He curled up his nose. "That's not so stylish. I figured I'd break out with a little pastel. You know, embellish a little."

Did he just pop his collar? He needed to bring it down a notch, one collar at a time. I stared through him.

"See, I'm a Metrosexual. I felt like that's what the script was asking for."

Maybe we were from different metro areas, because around my way, there was nothing metro or sexual about him. I squinted. "Can you read?"

"Yeah."

Through clinched teeth, I said, "That's not what I asked for."

"Nah, I've heard directors like to see you put a spin on things."

I laughed. A spin is one thing, but he'd spun out of control. Would the fashion police please escort this clown away from my table? I extended my hand. "Thanks for coming out."

As he continued to defend his fashion violation, I nodded. "I understand, but I'm really looking for something specific. I'm sorry. Thanks for coming out."

He departed with a smile after kissing my hand. I raised my glass to the waiter. I had fifteen minutes to gulp down two glasses. Even when you write explicitly what you're looking for, dating is a challenge. I rolled my eyes in my head. I'm paying for them to follow instructions and they still want to do it their way.

I looked up and saw Number Two approaching with a crisp electric blue dress shirt and nice fitting black slacks. When he extended his hand, I glimpsed at his nice cuff links and exhaled.

He raised my wrist and planted his soft lips on my hand. "Good afternoon, Ms. Barnes."

"Good afternoon . . ." I shuffled through my papers to find his name.

He asked, "Would you like a Sante Fe Salad?"

The intensity in his eyes charmed me. When the beautiful Hispanic waitress got the same intense stare, my eyes tried to recruit his back in my direction. He was so entranced that he didn't notice the disgust on my face. Finally, he turned and smiled at my frown. He reached across the table. His fingertips grazed my forearm. "You look beautiful today."

Aside from his wandering eyes, I thought he was attractive. He was obviously ambitious. He had several noted gestures in the script down in less than twenty-four hours. Another waitress passed and his head tilted while his eyes stripped her naked. Does this man have any self-control? Just as he was about to be dismissed, the waitress returned with our salads. He might as well have winked at her.

I said, "You've fallen out of character three times in ten minutes."

He acted surprised. "When?"

If he wasn't conscious of it, he must be a pervert. I extended my hand. "Thanks for coming out, but I don't think you're the guy for the job."

His chest collapsed. His eyebrows reached up to form a temple in the middle of his forehead. "C'mon. Give me a chance."

"I did. Thanks for coming out."

His head drooped as he stood. *Next*. Puddles formed in my eyes as Number Three approached. Don't even ask what he had on. My watery eyes were too glossy to notice. My nose burned. Did the script say bathe in cologne or wear cologne? My mug questioned the scent as he neared. Is it Brut? Is it Musk? It stunk and he stunk. I rubbed my eyes. Somebody, help me.

As he extended his hand, my lips flipped up to protect my nose. I nodded, but did not speak as he greeted me. He asked, "Are you okay?"

Here we go again. I'd pretty much reached my threshold. My eyes twirled rapidly in my head. "What kind of cologne are you wearing?"

"It's your favorite."

"Oh, no, it's not."

He smiled. "It's Acqua di Gio."

"Not Giorgio Armani's version."

Even if he bathed in it, he shouldn't smell like that. As we debated about his cologne, he jumped and pulled his cell phone from his pocket. It vibrated in his hand. He flipped it open.

After checking his phone, he smiled as if to say, "So where were we?"

I asked, "Are you expecting a call?"

"No."

"So, why did you feel the need to look at your phone during your audition?"

He gasped. "Ah, c'mon. I mean this is so informal. You know?"

What happened to always respecting me and the job? I cleared my throat. "Thank you for your time."

I didn't extend my hand, nor did he. My forehead fell into my helpless hands. Convinced that I should cancel the next two appointments, I called Mya.

"How's it going?"

When I didn't respond, she said, "You didn't like my picks."

"They were all nice looking, but they were all losers."

After explaining to her how they'd all misinterpreted the script, she laughed hysterically. "Now, can you see why my job is so stressful?"

"Girl, I feel for you now. It's one thing to read a manuscript that you just don't like and send a rejection to a faceless person. But it's entirely different when you tell someone exactly what you're looking for and they sit in front you and do something totally different. Then you have to smile when you tell them that they misinterpreted you."

"You got it down in just three auditions. That's what I go through everyday."

"I guess that's why you're so blunt."

"After all this time, you finally understand me."

I laughed. "You're silly. I'm about to leave. Cancel the next two guys."

"No! You have to go through with it now. It won't be so bad. You only have two left."

"I don't feel like it."

"The best is yet to come. Be patient."

"Mya, Number Four should be here. I'm leaving."

"Tima, you are rotten. You better not leave after I put my job on the line for you."

"Don't patronize me. You didn't put your job on the line."

She laughed. "Sike. Can you just calm down, though? I'm sure he'll be there. These guys are looking for work."

I sighed. "No wonder he's looking for work. He can't follow directions. He'll still be looking in thirty seconds."

"Have you checked to see if Paxil will work for you? That seems to be a milder alternative to Prozac."

"Screw you."

After our quick laugh, I hung up and put an X across his resume. Tardiness will not be tolerated was the note I placed beside the name. The waitress walked over with a new bottle of the same sixty-seven dollar Merlot that I had just emptied. I raised my hands. "No, thanks. One bottle is enough."

She smiled. "The gentleman at the bar sent this over to you."

A milky brown brother with that deep red undertone strolled toward me. His clean shaven face exposed the true dimensions of his features and it appeared that the claymaker shaped everything to perfection. He was a work of art and I wanted to purchase the sculpture with no questions asked. When I finally caught my breath, I looked him up and down. Now he'd put a spin to the script that had my head spinning. He wore a khaki designer blazer, with a crisp white shirt. Jeans. Cowboy-inspired brown shoes and a brown leather belt. He grabbed the chair and asked, "May I?"

I nodded affirmatively. Was he technically late even though he was at the bar? Hmmm. Let's see. He was much too gorgeous to reprimand. My inquiring mind concluded he was about six-two and around two hundred thirty pounds with ten percent body fat. I extended my right hand and his brown skin fused with my brown skin. We were a perfect match. My nose inhaled the pleasurable scent of my favorite cologne. His deep set eyes gazed into mine, as his soft lips melted on the top of our grip. When he sat down, I crossed the fingers of my left hand under the table.

He asked, "Awkward, huh?" I nodded and he continued, "Yeah, I'm sure this is pretty hard. I've been sitting here watching the competition."

"So, what did you think?"

He laughed. Was he showing his sense of humor or was he laughing at my unconventional method in finding a date? I raised my eyebrows. "So?"

"Well, I don't like to bad talk my opponents. I like to let my skills shine through and allow my director to discuss the others' talents at his—" he nodded toward me—"or her leisure."

"Makes sense. Um . . ."

He waited patiently as I organized my thoughts. "So, how long have you been acting?"

"Practically all my life . . ."

"Really?"

"Yeah, my mother was a stage mom. I did several commercials as a kid. A few little kids' shows."

"'Romper Room?'"

He chuckled. "Yeah, I was actually on a few episodes. I did a gang of stage plays in my teens." He took a deep breath. "I've always loved performing, but then I went to college."

"Why did you say it like it was a death sentence?"

He shrugged his shoulders. "Not a death sentence, just a dream deferred."

"What school did you go to?"

"H-U."

"Which H-U?"

"Don't play—the one and only, Howard U."

I shrugged my shoulders because I'm not hip to the whole HBCU civil war for supremacy.

"So, I take it that you didn't like school?"

"Oh, I loved school. It was corporate America that I had a problem with," he said.

My dancing eyes questioned what he meant and he explained: "Work made me miserable and I regretted putting acting to the side for school, because I felt like it was too late to go back to what I was put here to do."

"How old are you?"

"I'm twenty-seven." He sighed. "You know most actors were building their resumes while I was in college. I was way behind the eight ball."

"So . . ."

He laughed. "One day I caught a taxi to work and my stomach balled in knots. I told the driver to take me home and I set my sights on acting. I stopped worrying about my resume being good enough and focused on my talent and the drive in my heart."

"How long ago was that?"

"Two or so years ago."

"How has it worked out so far?"

"It was pretty steady at first. No big breaks. Several low-budget commercials, stage plays. Enough to stay afloat, but over the last few months things have almost come to a halt."

"What field did you work in when you—"

"Accounting." I raised my eyebrows and he added, "I'm much better at acting, I mean, auditioning than I am at accounting. I'm an audition expert."

I laughed. He shook his head. "I'm good at what I do."

I laughed harder. "I believe you."

"Nah, you think I'm joking. I can audition my butt off, but the decision is subjective."

"I feel you." I reverted to the script. "You know that good money management is a requirement. You can't make sound investments if you can't handle money. Right?"

He whipped out his Palm Pilot and turned it around for me to see. "I believe the exact wording was to be continuously learning about investing and money management."

"Well, you get the point, right?"

His humble smile collided with mine. We chuckled.

"What did you hate so much about work?"

"The lack of creativity. See, creative people can't thrive in corporate America. It robs us of our soul and for me, it wasn't worth it."

"I do understand."

"I believe in following your heart and that's what I'm doing."

"What will you do if it doesn't work out?"

"Have you ever heard that what you believe is your destiny? I'm a positive man."

"Yes, but you also have to be a realist. You should always have a backup plan."

"A backup plan is a submission to defeat. Your heart will give you the okay when it's time to give up, but not until then should you consider a backup plan. Backups distract focus and unconsciously make you conform. Conformity seems too close to comfort for me. Comfort steals your drive and settles your hunger. I have to put it all on the line. Blood, sweat, and tears."

He smiled and his philosophy made me smile. Though I could have interpreted his speech to say that he planned to be a starving actor for the rest of his life, I decided to assume that this was a man with strong faith. I shrugged my shoulders. "It makes sense. So, did you live in New York prior to pursuing acting?"

"Born and raised. What about you?"

"Alabama."

He blushed. "I love Southern women."

"Why? Do you think they can cook?"

He laughed. "I used to, but I noticed that the script says the only thing that you can make are reservations."

I smiled. He said, "It's okay. I love to cook."

I should have just told him that he was hired on the spot. Instead, I decided to be fair and finish the auditions. Thirty minutes didn't seem long enough. If I didn't account for his tardiness, twenty minutes was too soon, though it was long enough for me to decide that he would likely be my leading man.

Smiling, I said, "That's good to know. I'm quite impressed. I'll give you a call to let you know my decision."

He gazed into my eyes. "And you didn't even allow me to get into character."

"Yeah, I understand, but I have more auditions."

"Really? I thought for sure you'd found your guy."

We both chuckled. He smirked and noted, "Confidence was in bold print."

"I know. You clearly have that mastered."

"Do you promise to call?"

My heart fluttered and I paused before I spoke: "Yes, I promise."

"And I promise you that I'm the man for this job."

When he stood, he delicately gripped my fingertips. As he kissed my hand, his eyes pierced through me and summoned me to stand. *Just hire him Fatima!*

"Thanks so much. We'll talk soon."

He smiled. "I'm holding my breath, so don't take too long."

His chest inflated with air and mine deflated. He was clever, funny, handsome, and the guy for the job. I pulled out my cell phone to get Mya's input on my selection. When I looked up, Number Five strutted in, and I slowly closed my phone. A platinum chain hung from his neck. His plaid Polo shirt was unbuttoned all the way, exposing the seven-inch crucifix dangling on his white T-shirt. Aside from the flamboyant jewelry, I couldn't have created him better from scratch. He made me hold my breath. While I disregarded his attire, I absorbed him. He was at least six feet four. Caramel brown. Dark features and a fabulous smile. His pec muscles reached out to me as he approached. I squirmed in my chair. Hmmm. My mouth watered when, unlike the rest of the actors, he reached for a hug. Awkwardly, I stood. My, my, my! I felt protected.

My interview questions escaped me. As I cleared my throat, he smiled at me. "Would you like some water?"

"No, actually, I'm okay." His concern flattered me as I confirmed, "I'm good."

He grabbed the pitcher on the table and began to pour water into my half-full glass. A triple-tier platinum bracelet dangled from his wrist. Though his looks and appeal had me floating, those jewels were sinking the odds. Finally, I sipped the water and smiled.

"See, I knew you needed water."

"So, how long have you been an actor?"

He shrugged his broad shoulders. "Acting actually came to me. I started out as a model."

His defined bone structure was definitely what I wanted to see on the cover of a magazine. I took a deep breath. Unconsciously, my head nodded.

He smiled back. "Yeah, so I got a few acting gigs and found this to be more lucrative."

As I critically examined the bling he flossed, I teased, "I can tell."

He didn't catch the joke. If he is hired, I'll stress the dress code then. For now, I decided to get acquainted with his personality. Sike. Not really, it was one of those instances when attraction defeats intellect, because I heard nothing this man said.

He was funny. *I think.* He was clever. *I guess.* Just as I was about to say cut, he said, "I bought tickets to the Alvin Ailey performance tomorrow, would you like to go?"

I had to decline because Mya and I had tickets for tonight. "Did you already have the tickets or did you purchase them because the script said that I never miss the company when they're performing?"

"The latter."

"How'd you get tickets so late?"

"eBay."

I asked, "eBay dot com?"

"Yes."

Hmmm. He's fine and computer-literate. Every thug needs a lady. Okay, okay. I interrupted whatever he was saying, "I should be making a decision soon, so I'll give you a call."

"We're done?"

"Yeah, I've had a long day, but thanks so much for coming out."

His head bowed. "Thank you."

I sat there alone and sipped more of the wine that Number Four had bought. How could I not be sure if I wanted Four or Five? I was physically attracted to both, but something about Five connected with my body. Then, on the other hand, Four had it all, but he also seemed too arrogant to become fully immersed in the script. Since this script was about me, I needed someone that I could mold, like Number Five.

Mya called as I compared their pros and cons. While I tried to explain the dilemma, she interrupted me, "Duh? Have another audition."

I huffed. "When do I have the time to do this?"

"Have them meet us at Lotus after the show."

"Tonight?"

"No, next week."

I laughed. "Okay, I'll give them an hour apiece."

"It sounds like a plan. See you at six."

"Thanks, Mya."

"Don't mention it."

Mya would never understand my rationale for wanting Number Five. So, I planned to have him arrive at eleven and have Four come at twelve. Maybe she would be slightly convinced by the time Number Four got there.

Scene 7

RASHAD

When I walked into the restaurant, my mouth nearly hit the floor as I realized that Fatima was the Fatima Barnes that I had found on the Internet, the widow of the ex-CEO of *Droppin' Dimes* magazine. After Mya confirmed her name, I figured I should do a little research, like I would any other leading lady.

When I entered her name, tons of pictures appeared under the Images tab. She had the same cheerful expression on each photo. I was immediately captivated by her beauty and not to mention her thin-but-thick body. She glowed on the pictures and even more in person. Idle emotions were resurrected in me, as I smiled at her smile and translated her antics. She questioned by batting her long lashes. Her button nose wrinkled when she was uncertain of what to say next. If she doubted what I said, she sucked her cheeks in and pursed her full lips in an adorable juvenile-like manner. Her evenly arched eyebrows rippled when I didn't respond expeditiously. She was something special and something in her resonated with me. It could have been the humble undertone to her surface-level confidence, but whatever it was I had all the inspiration I needed to fight for this job.

She propped her elbows on the table and I took note of the large Tiffany bangle that hung around her small wrist and the Cartier watch on the other. The diamond band on her right hand blinded me and I tried to defer my attention from her jewels to focus on her beautiful brown eyes. Her long hair swept back and forth over her shoulders and complemented her contemporary chic attire. She wore jeans and a black top that hung low enough to imagine cleavage, but mostly it was her bare contoured chest that was exposed. A large green Juicy Couture leather bag accentuated her basic outfit. She was the epitome of effortless class.

I didn't doubt that she would keep her promise to call. There was just something there. You know that thing when you know the other person finds you just as attractive as you think they are? Still, it was hard for me to pry myself from the seat, because I wanted to find out more about her. She stood when I kissed her hand. Even with high, high heels on, her head met my chest. If she picked me, I planned to reaffirm what she already knew a man should do for a woman.

Not that I am a slacker by any sorts, but if I were going to hang out with Ms. Fatima and her Cartier watch, I needed to Will-Smith-up my attire. That's the process by where you add designer pieces into an average wardrobe. I headed over to Macy's and splurged with the assumption that I would receive my first check in a couple of weeks.

After tossing nearly a rack full of clothes over my arm, I looked in the ladies' department for things I thought would look nice on Fatima. I planned to woo her. She wouldn't know what hit her when my tenure was done.

On my way home, I stopped at the florist and bought my mother fresh flowers. It had been awhile since I surprised her. As I continued my previctory celebration, I grabbed some dinner for the only lady that's down for the cause in my life.

When I opened the door to the apartment, I called out, "Hey, lil' mama."

She waved to me as she walked from the bedroom talking on the phone. Her strong accent implied that one of her sisters was on the other end. When I handed her the flowers, she said, "This boy. He thinks he can give me flowers for rent."

I bent down and kissed her cheek. "Hey, Ma."

"What is this?"

I put our food on paper plates. "Where did you get this Roti from, boy?"

"Your favorite place."

"This boy."

That was her way of saying she was happy. She continued cackling on the phone as she ate her food. I sat in the living room and studied my script. My mother said, "All you do is read these scripts. When is someone going to hire you? You're too handsome to be out there looking for work. They should come get you. I know you're tired of waiting tables."

As she spoke to me, her sister talked loudly on the other end. "Your auntie asks, 'What is wrong? Why you don't have no woman?'"

"Women take up too much time and cost too much money."

As they found joy in my inability to land an acting role and lack of love, I shook my head. Those voids were in the process of being replaced. I pretended to laugh hysterically, "Ha-ha-ha!"

"Don't get cute with me, boy."

I stood and headed to my room. When I grabbed the over-stuffed shopping bags, she asked, "Anything for me?"

Speaking into the phone, she said, "I don't know where he get money from, but he stay sharp as a tack."

After I put my new clothes away, I knelt down and prayed. When I got up, my cell phone rang and the caller ID stated PRIVATE CALL.

I anxiously answered. Fatima's sweet voice trickled through the line: "Hi, it's Fatima."

I gasped. "Now, I can breathe again."

"Not so fast. I'd like to invite you to a second audition."

"Give me the time and place and I'll be there."

"I'd like to meet you at Lotus tonight."

Lord, you sure answered this one on time. "I'll be there."

When I hung up, I jumped up and sifted through my closet. I was going in for the kill. Everything had to be right. I rushed out for a shape-up on my already freshly cut hair. The barber re-shaved my face and I was ready to sweep Fatima off the dance floor.

Scene 8

FATIMA

On the way to the theater, Mya and I discussed the two that made the cut. She accurately recalled them both. She imitated Number Five's stance. "He's like WHOA. You know I saw them in their underwear."

"Stop playing."

"How'd you think I narrowed them down?"

The taxi driver peeked in the rearview mirror. My eyes asked Mya to hush. She shooed her hand. "Whatever. I'm not thinking about him. Anyway, like I said, I picked them based on their . . ."

We burst into laughter. "Did I say I was having sex with them?"

"Uh, there was a scene in the script labeled *Sexual Encounters* and you asked that they consent to an HIV test."

"Shhh . . ."

"Why are you worried about what he thinks?" She frowned at the back of the driver's seat. "Sex! People talk about it. And most adults are having it." She laughed, adding, "Just because you haven't had it in three years!"

"Three years, two months, and thirteen days."

"Dang, Tima. That's like an eternity."

"Time just slipped away."

I got quiet as I thought about my last sexual encounter. Mya interrupted me, "Well, anyway. I hooked a sister up. You'll be satisfied with either of them."

"You're bad."

"You need some bad."

"I need companionship, damn it."

She waved her hand. "Whatever."

By the time the performance was over, it was nearly eleven o'clock. We rushed to the club and Number Five was already there. I pointed him out. "There's Five, right there."

Mya squinted. "Where?"

"Right there in the white tee."

Her face crumbled. "In the white what?"

"Tee."

"Not the one with that huge-ass cross around his neck?"

I nodded. He strutted toward us and gave me a hug. Mya looked like she could yank my hair out. In between giggles, I reintroduced them. She pointed at him without shame. "You weren't wearing all of that when I . . ."

"Nah, I was just wearing my boxers. Remember?"

We laughed. Mya didn't. He asked, "Would you guys like a drink?"

We nodded and told him what we wanted and he walked to the bar. Mya frowned. "He looks like a thug."

"He's fine though."

"Okay. Did the script say that it was important that the main character's real personality reflect some of the basic characteristics or what?"

"Girl, we can fix what we don't like."

"Trust me. I do this everyday. Acting is just acting like yourself with guidelines."

"So what are you trying to say?"

"If you pick him, you'll have a thug on your classy arm." She paused. "Isn't that why you got rid of the dude from the dating service?"

Before I could explain that he was so much finer than that guy, he walked back toward us, holding our drinks. He said, "I got an Apple Martini."

As I reached out for my drink, he handed Mya hers. We nodded approvingly. He got a checkmark for taking care of me and my girl. Just like Derrick used to do when we were broke college students. I winked at her and she winked back.

Number Five grabbed my hand and pulled me to the dance floor just as the music slowed and Mary J.'s "Be Without You" blasted through the speakers, then he pulled me close to his chest of steel. I laid my hand on the left side and leaned my head on the other side. He felt good. This felt good. We were on the same beat. As my body began to enjoy this type of closeness, the hands on my watch glowed in my eyes and our bond was disrupted by the stroke of midnight. I backed up and told Number Five that this portion of his interview was over. Though he was reluctant to leave, he was delighted to know he hadn't been totally dismissed yet. After a few close hugs, he said his good-byes.

When I walked off the dance floor, Mya was in the same place I left her, shaking her head no. I smiled. "What?"

"You know I used to envy you finding Derrick when you were nineteen, but not anymore."

"Why?"

She rolled her eyes. " 'cause you must still be nineteen if you're even considering him."

"Whatever. He's a sweetheart. We're going to change his clothing."

"A thug is a thug."

"Derrick was a thug."

"Thugs don't launch their own magazines. Thugs don't teach people how to invest. Do you need me to continue?"

"No. I get where you're coming from."

Why is she being so uptight about this? She nudged me. "Isn't that Number Four?"

Mya grunted. "Now I would pay him any day to play my boyfriend."

"My companion. Damn it!"

She waved her hand. "Yeah. Yeah. Yeah. I'd pay him. That other character looks like a slickster. He'll mess around and take your money and never . . ."

She was interrupted by Number Four's presence. As we hugged, he gave me a quick peck on the cheek. He looked at Mya. While he expressed his gratitude to her for presenting this opportunity to him, he tightened his grip on my hand to assure me that though he looked and spoke to Mya, I was still the center of his attention. He wore a fitted rose-colored button-down that accentuated his muscular torso. Though his face was completely bare, his eighty-five degree angular jawline gave him a no-nonsense stance. It wouldn't surprise me if I found out that he wore foundation even off the job, because there was not a blemish on his skin. As I stood there entranced by the way his fuller bottom lip opened and closed and only partially revealed his smile, it dawned on me that ten minutes had passed. Don't even ask what we talked about. When five more minutes passed, his appeal crept down the Richter scale, because no one had a drink in their hand. I smirked at Mya. She laughed at what she knew was bothering me.

When he asked me to dance, I said, "I need a drink to dance."

"Okay. Apple Martini, right?"

I nodded. He walked away without asking Mya what she wanted to drink and I teased, "See, at least the thug asked you if you wanted a drink."

"Girl, men nowadays aren't into taking care of your home girls. Things might change once you start paying his ass. At least he looks the role."

"He is fine. Who was working with the most?" I asked.

"I'm not telling you. They had on boxers. I couldn't tell the exact size anyway."

"C'mon. Tell me. It was Number Five. I know it."

"I'm not telling."

"I know."

"You think you know."

I grunted. "I felt it."

We laughed. "A'ight then. You don't need me to tell you."

Number Four came back with two drinks in his hand. When he handed Mya a Cosmo, she thanked him and rolled her eyes at me. He had obviously read the scene: *When hanging out with me and my best friend*. I smiled. Either he was a damn good actor or he was technically my type. I wasn't sure.

After I took a few sips of the drink, I sat it on a bar table. Finally, we stepped onto the dance floor.

Instantly, our movements synchronized as we grinded to the same beat. He sang the words to every song in my ear. We bounced, we dropped down, we leaned back, and we rocked with it. Our transitions were continuous and unrehearsed like we had been partners for years. Through it all, his suave composure was never compromised. With those skills, he could be paid above scale.

As our batteries began to die, we swayed together. He looked into my eyes and wiped my forehead with the ball of his thumbs. My body went limp. Before I allowed him to dance into my heart, I swerved off the dance floor. This is a job interview. I have to stay focused.

When we walked over to Mya, her smile stretched the width of the club and I rolled my eyes in my head. Our expressions conversed, as she obviously thought Four should be hired. He rested his arm around my shoulder; goose bumps appeared and the hair on my arms stood. My heart fluttered. I wanted to suppress the reaction, but I all I could do was get away, fast.

After I overexaggerated my fatigue, the three of us left the club. He stepped into the street and hailed a taxi for us. Mya winked at me. I ignored her and gave him a hug before I got in.

Mya folded her arms. "If you don't hire him, I may hire him as a backup."

"Shut up!"

"I'm serious. You're fooling around with 50 Cent and you got a man with class that you'd possibly like without paying him. You're crazy."

"That's the problem. I'm not supposed to really like him. I'm just supposed to like having him around."

"Tomato, tom-a-toe."

"Mya, I'm not trying to get caught up. He's just an actor and I'm the director. This is not real."

She sucked her teeth. "So, who are you going to choose?"

"I don't know. It's harder than I thought."

"It really ain't. I think you're being silly. You need to have another audition."

"For what?"

"To see who you're about to hand a ten thousand dollar advance to."

When her comment struck me over my head, I agreed, "You're right."

"Hell, you might need three or four more."

"Now, you're pushing it."

"Honestly, even actors can act only for so long. Although, this is a real nontraditional role, you want someone with integrity."

Her knowledge seeped in as I began to plan for the final round. I asked, "Where do you think I should meet them?"

"Somewhere neutral where neither guy is in his element."

"How about Central Park?"

Her smile and nod approved of my location. I said, "You think that's good."

"I think it's perfect. It will help you to see the real person. And this time, give them several hours."

I scheduled the auditions two hours apart. Number Five arrived at 110th and Lenox. *On time. Right location.* At least he was a punctual thug that followed directions well.

The brim on his New York Yankees cap cast a dark shadow over his fine face. Of course, he wore the thug uniform. A white tee and jeans. He handed me a bouquet of lilies. I sniffed them and swallowed my desire to ask him why he consistently wore white tees when I specified designer T-shirts: Nike; Giorgio Armani; Sean John. *C'mon, man, get with the program.*

He hugged me. The strong guns surrounding me were his lifelines. We walked down close to the water. My fellow bench buddies, who usually smile when I walk up, seemed to be tense as we approached.

I smiled at an older white guy. He waved rapidly. What's up

with that? The lightbulb went off after my middle-aged white girlfriend changed benches when we sat near. Oh snap! They were afraid of my companion. Uh-oh. *Bad sign.*

When he asked if we could go somewhere else, I realized that he'd sensed their reaction too. I stood and fake rolled my eyes at the people treating him like hired help. That microsecond of a gesture distanced me from him by almost twenty steps. Hold up! What happened to the part where you're supposed to stand and wait until I'm ready? As I trotted after him, I was nearly tackled by a Hispanic chick with a stroller. I paused to grant her right-of-way. When I looked up, it appeared he was even farther.

The girl called out: "Manny! Manny!"

You've got to be kidding! I picked up my pace just enough to be a few steps behind her. She yelled, "Where the hell you been, Manny?"

Manny looked like he wished he could disappear, while I was amused by the episode. Do people really act like this? Her neck rolled a mile a minute. "You told me you were going to get the kids this weekend. What happened?" She pointed her finger at him. "You're a damn liar. Where you been?"

As I casually slipped passed them, I wondered if this was a setup or if this was a mere coincidence. If it was the first reason, he didn't want the job. If it's the second, damn if I want him to have it. I ran my index finger back and forth across my throat. *Fired.* **No Baby Mama Drama** was another thing in bold letters. He was fine, but his jewelry and his baby mama didn't fit into my script. I dropped his cheesy flowers in the nearest trash receptacle. See, I tried to help the economy out and be an Equal Opportunity Employer.

With two hours to kill, I walked up Lenox to 120th to Settepani Bakery. As I devoured my cheesecake and made updates to my script and the contract that I planned to give to Rashad, I laughed. Did I really have a choice? Hopefully, he wouldn't do anything stupid. Though I feared the tingle he gave me, he was pretty much my only choice. This was too much work. I didn't have enough energy for another round of auditions. If he screws up, the script idea is over and I'll keep my money in my damn pocket. Or better yet, I'll buy a damn robot.

I walked back to the meeting location around two. My head throbbed as I stood on the corner without a companion at ten minutes after two. I took a deep breath and called Mya.

I said, "My pressure is up."

"What's the problem now?"

"Don't act like I'm getting on your nerves."

"But you are."

I laughed. "That's a shame. What are friends for?"

"Girl, you have overstepped the boundaries of friendship this week."

"Shut up. We're making up for three years of dating all in one week. Plus, the Bible says you're supposed to help me."

"Fatima, don't play with me. Nowhere in the Bible does it say I have to help you find a man and then listen to you complain about every little thing."

I snickered. "But it says that you should take care of widows and orphans."

"Don't play on my sympathy. Let you tell it, you're not a damn widow, your husband just died. So what, are you an orphan now?"

"You make me sick."

We laughed for a minute. She said, "Honestly though, what's going on?"

"I'm on the corner waiting for Rashad. He was supposed to be here—"

A taxi pulled up in front of me as I chatted. Rashad opened the door. He gestured for me to get in with him. Caught in between telling Mya that I had to go and trying to explain that I wanted to stay in the park, I hopped in. When I sat inside the taxi, I scoped his outfit. His navy and white Polo shirt fit perfectly. His jeans were loose, but not baggy. There's a fine balance and he had it. I said, "Um, I asked you to meet me in the park, because I wanted to stay in the park."

"I know, but you also asked me to plan something interesting here."

The taxi pulled up to the horse carriages. He walked to the attendant and gave his name and we were loaded into a carriage. His arms surrounded me as we snuggled. After the horse began to trot, he said, "We have an extended ride."

"How long?"

"Forty minutes." He peeked at the paper sticking out of my bag. "So, you come here to read?"

I nodded.

"What are you reading now?"

"Romance . . ."

"Okay. You want to share."

Since most men are repulsed at the thought of romance novels, I twisted my lips. "No, that's okay."

He tugged at my bag. "C'mon, sell it to me like you'd sell it to your sales team."

"How do you know about that?"

"I know a little bit about everything. So, tell me. What are the heroine's issues and why is the hero the chosen guy?"

I giggled. "You are so funny."

"At least tell me their names." He paused. "Let me guess: Fatima and Rashad."

I giggled harder. "Okay, it's a historical romance that occurred during the Civil War. A black soldier."

"And the heroine."

"She's his general slave."

"What?"

"Are you joking or do you really care?"

He stroked my hair. "I'm an actor, baby. I love a good story."

I gave him a brief outline of the story. He flattered me with his interest in my interests. Just as I was about to tell him that he would be the hero in my script, the carriage slowed in front of Tavern on the Green.

He helped me from the carriage. Someone opened the door as we walked toward the restaurant. The doorman said, "Good afternoon, Ms. Barnes."

I blushed and looked at Rashad in amazement. The hostess smiled when we entered, "Mr. Watkins, right this way."

He guided me by putting his hand on the small of my back. We were escorted through the maze of corridors into a room with the best view of the park. An expensive bottle of Merlot was on the table. Seconds after we sat, our entrees were delivered. This was unreal. *Oh yeah, I forget. It is unreal. It's scripted, Fatima!*

Rashad was clearly the man for the job. If not for the food on the table I would have pulled out the contract. Instead, I smiled. "The job is yours if you want it."

"Thank you."

"We'll go over the contract after lunch."

"That's fine with me."

He poured the wine and raised his glass. "To the perfect script."

"Yes, to the perfect script."

After we swallowed, he asked, "Is it okay for me to ask how you got to the point you wanted to write the script?"

I twirled my wine and bit my lip. "Well, I was married."

"What happened?"

I took a deep breath and rested my back on the chair. "He died."

He squinted. "How?"

"He had a heart attack."

"Wow, that's serious. How old was he?"

"Thirty-two." I looked down at the china on the table. "So, I didn't date for a long time and when I started dating, the quality just wasn't there. And I thought it would be a good idea if I gave future dates guidelines. And most people don't follow rules unless you pay them."

He chuckled. "Would you consider yourself a control freak?"

I gasped and covered my chest. He said, "Okay, I'm just saying. The more I know about you, the better equipped I am to give you everything you need."

"It's all in the script."

He leaned toward me. "Fatima, I like to go over and beyond the call of duty."

He sensually licked the crumbs from his lips. My eyes lowered as I fantasized about what he insinuated. Then, he restarted the interview.

"There's nothing in there about your family. Do you have any?"

"What do you think?"

"I'm just saying. Everything isn't in there."

"What do you want to know?"

"Do you have siblings? Parents?"

"Uh, everyone has parents somewhere."

Rashad smirked at my silliness. "You know what I mean. Are they living? Are they together?"

"Are your parents together?"

"No. My mother is here and my father is in Trinidad."

"Is he from Trinidad?"

"Both of my parents are."

"Did you say you were born there or here?"

He laughed. "I was born here."

"Was your father ever here?"

"He got homesick." I twisted my lips. He smiled. "Honestly, he went back when I was four or five."

"Were they married?"

He lowered his head and mumbled, "They're still married."

Since he seemed to be embarrassed by this, I shrugged my shoulders. "Hey, that's how it is sometimes."

"You still haven't told me about yourself. Is your name really Fatima?"

I batted my napkin at him. "Stop."

"Hey, I don't know."

"Okay. My parents are still together. They live in Alabama and I have one sister, eight years younger than me."

"Are you close?"

I shrugged my shoulders.

"You know if you're close or not," he said.

"When I left for college, she was ten and you know . . ."

He shook his head. "No. Tell me."

"I guess we never had a bonding period." I pushed my glass toward him for a refill. "I almost immediately got into a serious relationship and I guess I didn't do all the things big sisters do," I said as I took a sip.

"What do you mean?"

My eyes lowered and I played with the stem of the wineglass. "Well, like, I guess I should have gone home more often when she was in her teens. That way I would have had more influence on her and there wouldn't be such a social gap."

"What is she doing now?"

"Just hangin' out in Alabama."

"Do you think it's too late?"

I huffed and he noticed my frustration. "You don't have to discuss it anymore. Are you close to your parents?"

"We're close. I just don't talk to them all the time. You know, with work and all."

"So, you just came to New York and disowned Alabama."

"Can we talk about something else?"

His fingers intertwined with mine. "As long as whatever we talk about helps me learn more about you."

Scene 9

RASHAD

You would think I'd be flattered to sign a contract for fifty-five thousand dollars to be distributed over six months, with a ten thousand advance. My coworkers hustled around me and made my date extraspecial. Their hospitality secured my chance of getting the role.

But when she announced that the job belonged to me, I suddenly felt like a damn male prostitute. Why would this beautiful woman across from me feel the need to go as far as paying for companionship?

"So, Rashad, are you close to your parents?"

My stomach rumbled. I didn't want to explain to her that I lived with my mother. I quickly reread the portion in the contract that stated she would only need my address for emergency purposes, but most scenes would occur in her house. While I contemplated my response, she tilted her head. "Did you hear me?"

"Yes, I'm very close to my mother."

"What about your father?"

I hesitated before I spoke. I hated that my father and I were estranged and I hated that it was my mother's fault. She convinced me that he was a loser and if he was a man, he would have stayed in this country and provided for his family. It wasn't until I came to my own revelation that I finally understood him and his stance. He was a humble man and being here for the love of money could not replace the beautiful sands in his country.

She squinted. "Are you close to him?"

"I wouldn't say close because we don't talk often, but I've definitely grown to have respect for him."

"Did you have a relationship with him growing up?"

"Yeah, my mother shipped me to Trinidad every summer."

We laughed and she said, "So you didn't always have respect for him?"

"I didn't understand him."

"Meaning?"

I laughed. "Now, who asks all the questions?"

"I answered your questions."

"After I nearly begged you to."

Her expression softened. "Well, I'm begging you."

I laid the contract on the table and took a deep breath. "When my father left the States, he gave up the promise, that's what my mother said. He went back to Trinidad to work construction and play in a calypso band in the evening. When I was young, I thought that was quitting, now I think it's living. Everyone isn't motivated by money."

She looked down at the contract. "So, you're not motivated by money?"

"I'm motivated by happiness and, unfortunately, in this country, money provides a pathway to happiness."

She snickered. "I was curious if you were interested in doing this for charity."

If I had other gigs lined up, her beauty would have forced me to say I would do it for free. Instead, we both laughed and I didn't say anything. I looked back at the contract.

She pursed her lips and her blinking eyes contemplated as she studied me studying the contract. "Do you have any questions?"

As I filled out the direct deposit information, I joked, "You're not going to take my routing number and suck all the money out, are you?"

Her eyes zigzagged. I said, "Just playing, baby. So, as long as I stay in character around you, I can live my life?"

"As long as I'm happy. That's the most important part."

My smile got wider and wider as I read the last lines of the contract. I had a few questions but nothing I wanted to bring up before I signed. If I fall for another woman, I have to resign immediately. Does that mean I can still see other women? Of course, I have no plans of dating anyone until I get another gig that pays as well as this.

I was partially tempted to run it by my agent, but I am much too proud to reveal to anyone that I'd succumbed to this. When I looked at Fatima, her hair lay flat on her full breasts and I scribbled my signature on the contract. To hell with it! What could she do? Rape me.

"Your name *is* Rashad, right? That's not a stage name or anything?"

"How did you know I had a stage name?"

"Huh?"

"Yeah, I used to be a stripper."

She dropped her head. Her eyes fluttered when she finally looked up. She leaned her elbow on the table and massaged her temple as if to say, *now you tell me.* I went for it: "My stage name is Microwave."

Her expression cursed me. I said, "I get it hot, fast."

"Tell me you're joking."

As I grazed the fine hair on her forearm, I said. "Didn't you ask for a sense of humor? I'm just playing."

The air trapped in her lungs escaped. We both laughed. I said, "This is the closest I've ever come to selling myself."

"Rashad, do me a favor. Now that you've signed that contract and once the direct deposit goes into action, I don't want to discuss our arrangement. I want you to make me forget that I'm paying you. Got it."

"Got it."

Our waiter, my homeboy José, came over with her favorite dessert. Her chestnut eyes danced with excitement.

"You're such a sweetheart."

As we stood to leave the restaurant, she patted her belly. "My stomach is falling out."

"Your stomach is fine."

She looked at me inquisitively, probably curious if my compliment was scripted or sincere. I resisted the urge to tell her it was really me and not who she was paying me to be.

Scene 10

FATIMA

We left the restaurant and walked hand in hand to Staples. I was really enjoying his company. Now I consider myself a smart girl, but this had to be the brightest idea I'd had in all my life. Who really has time to go through the get-to-know stage?

When we entered the copy center, it dawned on me that I was really about to hand over a ten thousand dollar check to a complete stranger. Although Mya claimed she would make sure he never worked in this town again if he ran off with the money, I suddenly felt the need to protect my assets.

He voluntarily whipped out his Staples card and stuck it into the machine. I smiled and asked, "Can I get a copy of your license also?"

He slipped it from his wallet. I glanced at his address and was happy to see that he lived ten blocks away from me. That should make his commute easy.

"I don't know if you'd like to take care of this all today or if you'd prefer to do it tomorrow. I'd like to get another form of ID, like a social security card and/or passport."

"How do I know this is legitimate? You could be trying to steal my identity."

"Whatever. I need it for my protection."

He reached out his hand. I looked down at it and raised my eyebrows. "What?"

"Give me your hand."

"If I'm going accept this job, you have to trust me."

"Still, I like to . . ."

"Shhh. I got you. I'll let you copy my social security card."

"Thank you."

I turned to operate the machine and the instructions blurred as the screen displayed a digital replica of his handsome face. He put his hand on my shoulder. "Is everything okay?"

If you stop touching me, maybe I can handle this. After I gained my composure, I copied his license and we left the store. Suddenly, I was unsure of what to do next. We both appeared awkward. I shrugged my shoulders. He did the same. "So, when do you want to start?"

He placed his hand on my shoulders. "I started when I signed the contract."

"Oh, yeah. Okay, so you're my man now."

He laughed. "Yep, I'm your man."

"So . . . you want to go shopping?"

He nodded. "Sure."

Then, I remembered that Mya and I planned to meet to discuss my final decision. "You want to have drinks with me and Mya?"

"Whatever the little lady wants."

I batted my eyes. He stole that right from the script. Still, it flattered me. "Thank you, honey, but you don't have to do that." I winked. "Girl talk. I'll get up with you later."

"That's cool. I know y'all have a lot to discuss. Let me know if you need me to meet you somewhere later."

"I certainly will."

He stepped out into the street with me and opened the taxi door. I was tempted to stay in the middle of the street with him. His warmth invited me to stand up Mya and go home with him, but I recovered and got into the taxi. Even his good-bye wave welcomed me.

My heart still rumbled from his touch as I called Mya. "Girl, let's celebrate."

"So, I guess you picked Rashad."

"He signed."

"You are lying."

"No, actually I'm not. I got a man."

She laughed. "Yeah. We definite have to celebrate. I'm thinking Sangria."

"I'm thinking a whole pitcher."

"I'm headed uptown, so I'll meet you at Pio. Are you on your way?"

When I walked into our favorite Peruvian restaurant, she was already there. The hostess directed me to where she was seated. A pitcher of Sangria was already on the table. Before I could sit, Mya gave me a high-five. I giggled. "This might be the silliest thing we've ever done."

"I don't believe you sold this to me. The bad part about it, I'm more excited than you. If this goes over smoothly, I swear I'm going to start a business."

"Girl, who are you telling? This is brilliant."

While we gloated in our brilliance, I realized that I wasn't so bright. "Oh my goodness. I was supposed to get his HIV and drug test results before he signed the contract."

Mya shook her head. "Whatever. You haven't given him a check yet. And positive test results nullify the contract. Don't worry. Just get it tomorrow."

"Where can we go?"

"There's a clinic not too far from your office."

"I'll call you tonight for the details."

We rocked to the Latin music and sipped more Sangria than either one of us could handle. She pointed at me and I pointed at her and we praised each other over and over again. "You're a genius."

"No, you're the genius."

By the time we left, we were two pissy-drunk geniuses. Though this intoxication could hardly compare to the one I felt when Rashad's face crept into my mind. Boy, I wish I could bottle him up and sell him. His deep set eyes still pierced through me from hours earlier. As I prepared my nonchalant speech, I dialed his number. I used the divide-and-conquer method to avoid inviting him over. By the time I got in the house, I was tempted to call him back, but I couldn't even stand up straight, so I did the smart thing and fell asleep on my couch.

Scene II

RASHAD

When Fatima decided to hang out with Mya, that was my get-out-of-jail-free card. Though I had thoroughly studied the script, I was rather rusty on the investment requirements. If I'm going to do this, I plan to be the best. I chuckled to myself as I reaffirmed my father's words of wisdom: "If you're going to pick up trash, I want you to be the best damn trashman you can be."

I stood in Barnes & Noble searching for books on investing, home improvement, and real estate. When I paged through some of the home renovation books, it surprised me how much I already knew. My summers laying concrete and putting up Sheetrock in Trinidad would come in handy for something.

I proceeded to the investment and real estate sections. The two topics seemed to correlate. Buy low, sell high. Real estate was the primary focus in the investment section. As I flew through the pages, it was like reading a good script and I was inspired to play the investor.

Though I was tempted to call Fatima and spit out verbatim what I'd just absorbed, I resisted. Instead, I spent my last three hundred bucks on books. Is it inappropriate to ask when do I get my bonus? I trotted home excited about finishing my reading.

When I entered the apartment with a goofy grin, my mother looked up inquisitively. I bent down to give her a kiss. She asked, "Why are you so happy, boy?"

"I got a gig."

"What kind of gig?"

"Well, it's like an assistant to a movie director."

"So, you aren't going to be in the movie. You'll just be running around for some director, buying coffee, getting lunch, and kissing his behind?"

"Exactly, but they're paying well."

"I guess that's a start." She snickered. "My son, the asswipe."

"Ma, why do you always have to go there?"

"Because I love you. I send you to college and you have to kiss some director's ass. That's not fair. They should see how good you are."

She acted as if I were the only man in New York trying to get a job. Did she ever think about the competition? I know she wants the best for me, but damn. She called one of her many phone buddies and I heard her talking: *Why can't that boy just work a regular job? Do you know he graduated magna cum laude? He's just like his father.*

She lived in the past and it troubled her that I have yet to amount to her expectations. It hurt me to hurt her, but ultimately I have to be happy. It's one thing to try and fail, but I couldn't live with myself if I didn't commit at least five years to this. I pulled out a book and plopped on the bed. I folded a pillow around my ears to drown out my mother's negativity.

Fatima called around nine to say she would see me in the morning and to remind me that we forgot to get the HIV test. Considering I haven't had sex since my last test, I wasn't worried about the results.

When my alarm clock went off at six-thirty in the morning, I rolled back and forth. Damn if I wanted to get up just to get coffee. After a ten-minute internal debate about whether I could really be a servant, I got up, showered, and was out the door in fifteen minutes. As I stood in line at Starbucks, the aroma refreshed my excitement. My heart raced as I anticipated knocking on the door. What do I say?

She opened the first of the double doors. *Action.* The second door swung open. I hugged her and inhaled her freshness. "Good morning. You smell good."

"Thank you. I just got out the shower."

Her peach terrycloth robe was drawn tightly and accentuated her hourglass figure. She looked to be just a little over five feet with her heels off, yet she sashayed like a model even in her fluffy slippers. Something about her long ponytail flopping up and down made me less intimidated. She spun around to the sound of my chuckle. "What?"

"Nothing. I'm just admiring how adorable you are this early in the morning."

She reached for the cup of coffee. "Thank you."

"Certainly."

When she plopped down on the couch, she kicked her feet up on the coffee table, which was covered with tabloid magazines. Before I sat, I picked up this week's *inTouch*. "Don't tell me that you read this trash."

"Every day."

As I flipped through the pages, I shook my head at her. "This stuff doesn't change. It's the same thing every week."

"Well, I still like it. Actually, I'm addicted."

"Addicted?"

She nodded bashfully. "It's like a good soap opera to me."

"You're like the girl on MTV."

She impersonated the commercial and pretended to cry: "Jen and Brad. Nick and Jessica. Paris and Paris. Where do broken hearts go?"

I laughed. "That commercial cracks me up."

"The bad part about it is that I really get all involved in their lives just like that. I can't tell you how many nights I sit here pissed about something I read in a magazine." She poked at a picture of Paris Hilton. "This chick does something every week to make me mad."

"I don't believe you."

"I guess it's because I haven't had much excitement in a long time."

Her body stiffened after she revealed her vulnerability. I

wanted her to understand that I understood so I massaged her knee. "Hopefully that will change soon."

She stared off into space and I wondered what had abducted her. The "Today Show" entertained me while I awaited her return. My eyes toured her spacious, modern apartment. Her eclectic style gave me deeper insight into Fatima. It takes a special personality to coordinate gold, purple, and red and pieces from different eras. The décor depicted a person that was adventurous, explorative, and fearless. Suddenly, I remembered that she didn't always live here alone. Was this style Fatima's or her husband's?

As I wondered about him, he stared down at me. Their poster-size wedding portrait on the opposite wall disrupted my observations. I froze. What am I doing here? Why am I in this man's house? As my ego fueled my apprehension, her husband's pupils trailed me. When I leaned left, they followed. When I leaned right, they darted in my direction. As I played peekaboo with the portrait, Fatima nudged me. "What's wrong?"

"Nothing."

"You sure? You seem uncomfortable."

"Nah, I'm okay."

How could I explain that her husband was harassing me? She smiled. "I'm going to get ready. I'll be back," she said as she walked downstairs.

"I'll be here." When she left the room, I whispered, "I think." I frowned at him. *If this bastard stops staring at me.*

His smile flatlined and his nose flared. I pleaded with him and my sanity. *Look dude, I'm not here to disrespect you. Your wife is paying for my company.*

After a thirty-minute dispute with her husband, Fatima's high-heels clicked up the stairs. Her tight pink business suit suffocated all of my indecision. Like what could he do? Jump off the wall and attack me. I stood up and smiled. "You look nice."

"Thank you. I meant to tell you that you do, too."

I looked down at my long-sleeve Armani T-shirt and loose fitting jeans and shrugged my shoulders. "Thanks."

Seconds passed as we stood speechless. Finally, she ended

the hypnosis. "Weren't you supposed to bring me something today?"

My eyes shifted as I came down from Fatimaland. What was I supposed to bring her? C'mon Rashad. You can't mess up this early in the game. Apparently recognizing the distressed look on my face, she sang my name. If she was smiling, it couldn't be too serious. Her breast grazed me as she stepped closer. "Your social security card."

Mentally wiping the pool of sweat that I assumed had developed on my forehead, I sighed and whipped out my card. When she grabbed it from me, our fingertips flirted. Her lips curled seductively as she untangled our connection. "I'm going to make a copy. I'll be back."

I admired her thickness as she strutted into her home office. Her freshly curled hair hung down her back and bounced with her bounce. The definition in her calf muscles captivated me. When she returned, I stood in the same spot, paralyzed by her movements. She handed the card back to me and I tried to engage her with my touch again, but she pulled away.

"So, are you able to meet me at my office around lunchtime? There's a clinic not too far . . ."

While she proceeded to give me all the specifics, I nodded. Did she realize that I was at her disposal? As long as she was paying me the negotiated salary, I am wherever, whenever she wants me to be. I asked, "Do you mind getting tested?"

When her neck snapped back, I realized that it may have been offensive. Just because a woman claims she hasn't been with anyone in three years doesn't mean it's true. Prepared for her opposition, I poked my chest out and peered into her eyes like, "What?"

When her shoulders sagged and she blushed, I knew she appreciated my stance. "It doesn't matter. I'll get a test."

Scene 12

FATIMA

As I waited for my copier to scan Rashad's social security card, I bit my nails. *What the hell are you nervous about?* Though I wanted company, I didn't expect to be smitten with the hired help. When I looked at the photo of Mya and me on my desk, I could hear her saying, "Don't be scared now."

When I walked back into the living room, Rashad's gaze warned me that we needed to get out of the confines of my house, fast. Either the heat was on ninety or he had me hot and bothered. While we worked out the specifics of the HIV test, I fanned myself. When I agreed to be tested also, an appreciative smile spread across his face like he expected me to resist. "Teem."

Teem? No one had ever used that as a nickname for me, and I liked it. Hell! I liked him! He continued, "I think this is going to be good for the both of us."

I exhaled, "I agree."

In the middle of my living room, I floated away. When I inadvertently landed, I felt faint. *Is he using magic on me?* When I refocused and checked the time, I snapped out of his spell. "I have to get out of here."

I scrambled around the living room moving fast and doing nothing; he stood patiently like he admired my scatterbrained hysteria. Finally, he asked, "Do you need me to get anything?"

I actually thought about what he could do. "Uh." I looked under the magazines on the table and searched for what, I don't know. "Um." Then, I rushed over to the dining table. "Let me see."

After realizing I was wasting more time for the hell of it, I told him not to worry as I convinced myself that I had everything I needed. I headed for the door and he followed.

Out on the steps, he grabbed my bag. As I flopped down the stairs, he tagged behind. My mind was already at work as my pressure began to rise and my eyes danced in my head. When I looked back at his lackadaisical stride, I became irritated that I was on the curb and he was on the next to the last step. When I began to walk toward Adam Clayton Powell, I said, "C'mon."

"Calm down."

I insisted, "This is every morning. I'm always leaving in a rush."

When he caught up to me, he said, "Work isn't going anywhere. It will be there when you get there. Calm down"

"I have meetings. I'm sorry. I just don't like to have people waiting for me. Do you know what I mean?"

"I feel you."

His response confirmed that he knew nothing about dependability or time management. As I rushed up the street, he strolled, but somehow we covered the same distance. It frustrated the hell out of me that I was out of breath and he looked like he was on a moving sidewalk.

Before I got into the taxi, I handed him a business card. "Meet me at my office at twelve." Praying that his tardiness would somehow disappear, I huffed, "Be on time."

"I'll be there."

"Rashad, do not be late. I usually don't have long for lunch."

"I'll be there."

His confident tone calmed my heartbeat. Suddenly, I wasn't concerned about getting to work on time. My mind shifted to counting the minutes before I would see him again. I turned around and watched him through the back window of the taxi. He strolled up the street like he didn't have a care in the world. As soon as we were separated by multiple blocks, I slid down in the seat and exhaled.

Scene 13

RASHAD

Instead of allowing time to control me, I've made a habit of enjoying each moment in time. People consumed with time seem to have more stress. What does that tell you? Worrying about being on time will have you in the grave in a timely fashion. When I stood outside of Fatima's office at five minutes to noon, even I was shocked, and the look on her face when she exited the building confirmed she felt the same. To mask her smile, she curled her lips, but I could tell she was happy to see me. I leaned in for a hug and she swished by me. "C'mon. We have to hurry."

My body swirled around in the direction of the breeze she generated. Why does this girl rush like the world is coming to an end? Partially offended that my affectionate gesture was ignored, I strolled behind. She strutted ahead of me and I called out to her, "Fatima."

With her eyes squinted and using her hand as a sun visor, she asked, "What?"

When I caught up to her, I bent down and stole my hug. My goal was achieved when she paused momentarily to breathe. After just one quick breath, she relapsed. "We have to hurry. I have to get back to work."

I shook my head at the back of her, amazed as she jogged up

the street. When we went into the clinic, she put our names on the list and we sat in the waiting area.

"Are you having a rough day?" When she nodded, I patted her knee. "I'm sorry."

"It's not your fault." She bumped her shoulder into mine. "I'm sorry I made you sorry."

Her corniness made me shake my head. They called us individually and neither of us appeared nervous. It's always a good feeling knowing you haven't done anything stupid since your last test. I strolled up in there like I'm just here for my papers. It took all of one minute for the both of us to give blood samples. Our results would be back in two days. On the way out of the clinic, she tugged my arm. "Are you nervous?"

"Are you?"

"No. You may as well say I'm a virgin."

Though it is obvious that she's not, it aroused me to imagine that she was damn close. As my mind wandered off, she tickled my lower back. "You never answered my question."

"What question?"

"Never mind."

With my arm around her shoulder, I bent and whispered in her ear, "No."

As if my closeness invoked a sudden chill, she folded her neck and snatched it away. We laughed for no reason. She was with me and I was with her and her job was somewhere on another side of her brain as we took our time getting back to her building.

Before she went in, she said, "You're a free man until the results come back."

Her words crushed me as I looked forward to sharing the evening with her. I frowned. "You mean to tell me that you don't want to see me before you see the results."

"Why waste time getting all into you, if you're infected?"

How could this Southern girl be so witty? As I tried to contain my laughter, I shook my head. "You are a trip."

"I'm serious."

"I know. That's the funny part."

"Same place, same time, two days from now."

Though I was happy that the time off would allow me a few days to catch up on my prerequisites, a part of me enjoyed just being in the midst of her feistiness. As she disappeared into the building, I watched my reflection in the glass doors. What have you gotten yourself into, Rashad?

Scene 14

FATIMA

From the second I waltzed into my building after leaving him, I wanted to talk to Rashad, but I had to stay strong. If I start going back on my word too early, then he'll think he can manipulate this situation. A day later, I sat alone in my living room; my irrational justification no longer made sense to me. I picked up the phone thirty-three hours and sixteen minutes after I told him I would see him in forty-eight hours. As I reprimanded my pride, he picked up and chuckled. "Teem."

"Hi, Rashad."

"You know it broke my heart not to talk to you."

"Why didn't you call?"

"I didn't want to be a pest and I didn't know if you decided to hire someone else."

"Whatever. Give me more credit than that. If I'm going to fire you, I'll let you know."

"I bet you will. I forgot who I was dealing with."

"You better recognize."

"You crack me up. But for real, you balled up my heart and threw it in the middle of Fifth Avenue."

"Well, I'm just trying to protect mine."

"I want to protect it, too."

His comment left me speechless. I couldn't write his lines

better. How does this stuff just flow so effortlessly? Does he have a magnifying glass over my heart?

"I'm sorry if your feelings were hurt, but I just—"

"Want to be safe. I understand."

In less than three days, he finishes my sentences! Isn't that supposed to take years? Oh yeah, I forgot. We're on an expedited schedule. Still, something felt authentic about our connection. I prayed that his test checked out because I enjoyed his flirtation, his humor, his smile, his body. Hell! Just about everything about him was downright intriguing.

I asked, "So, what did you do today?"

"I had a few castings. What about you?"

"Work."

"Do you like your job?"

"It's okay."

"How do you feel when you get there? Are you happy to be there?"

I laughed. "I mean I feel like most people feel when they go to work."

"And how is that?"

"Never mind."

"Why do you always say never mind? Do you think I won't understand?"

"Do you think you're a psychiatrist?"

"Why would you say that?"

" 'Cause you ask a million questions."

"Do questions make you uncomfortable?"

I huffed. "You're stressing me out."

"Fatima, I didn't mean to stress you out. If it will help, can I offer you a massage as an apology?"

"Not if you're going to ask a bunch of questions while you're supposed to be helping me relax."

"I promise. I won't talk. I'll just listen."

"So when can I take you up on this offer?"

"When you open the door."

"Just ring the bell when you get here."

My buzzer startled me. Still holding the phone to my ear, I rushed to the door oblivious to what I was wearing. His phone was still pinned to his ear, as we talked face-to-face on the phone.

"How did you get here so fast?"

"I wasn't too far away when you called."

"So, what made you come over?"

I finally closed my phone and he followed. I glimpsed at my risqué attire. I had on black boy shorts with *Sexy* written in rhinestones across the booty and a black tank top. I folded my arms across my chest, while he explained. "When you called, I just started walking this way and hoped that you wanted to see me as much as I wanted to see you."

"Don't you think you should have warned me? At least, I could have been prepared."

"You look prepared to me, sexy."

"Don't play. What's in there?"

"Massage oil."

"So, you already had this planned?"

He put his hand on my shoulder and laughed. "No, I thought I would give you a massage tomorrow. You know, when the test results come back." Knowing that comment deserved a laugh, he paused. "But it just all fell into place tonight."

I watched him make himself comfortable as he walked into the kitchen. He looked up over my cabinets, where I keep my overstocked bar. "What's your favorite wine?"

My head hung, as I pointed to the Yellow Tail Merlot.

He climbed onto a chair to get the bottle. "I thought you liked to drink expensive wine."

I waved my hand. "That's just a front. I surely can't ask for Yellow Tail when I'm out. Can I?"

He jumped down. "That's cute, though."

"What? That I like cheap wine?"

"No, that you know how to let your hair down when you're home."

He lifted two plastic cups from the top of the refrigerator. "So, these, or do you want glasses?"

"Hey, it's Yellow Tail. It doesn't seem right to drink out of Mikasa."

While I revealed my Southern etiquette, he shook his head in admiration. He filled the cups and raised his twenty-ounce Solo Red. As our plasticware collided for a toast, we giggled. He said, "To being hood on Strivers' Row."

After I took a long sip, I said, "To taking Yellow Tail to the head."

As if he was about to accept the challenge, he put the cup to his mouth. Then he shook his head. "Nah, some things just aren't meant to be taken to the head."

"It all depends."

As we stood in the kitchen, sipping and searching for other things to talk about, he said, "I think I came here for a reason."

"Okay, is anybody stopping you?"

He laughed and washed his hands. "It'll probably be best if you lay on the chaise." Before I sat down, he said, "Go get a towel or a sheet or something. You don't want any oil to get on the chaise."

When I returned with a large towel, the digital cable was tuned to the *Sounds of Nature* music channel. He had lit the oil burner. I raised my eyebrows. "Is that the scent that I had in there or—"

"It's black coconut. Do you like it?" I nodded and he said, "Lay on your stomach."

While he fumbled around in the small bag he came in with, I squirmed, and he asked, "Are you okay?"

He rubbed his hands to heat the massage oil and caressed my shoulderblades. As he began to knead the muscles, he said, "Teem, you're stressed. We have to make sure you don't get like this anymore."

"I know."

My stress disintegrated in the palms of his hands as he sedated my body. Waves crashed ashore and I drifted away.

He climbed on top of me and pushed my hair to the side. His tongue caressed my neck and I moaned. As he struggled to slip my tank top over my head, he whispered, "I've wanted you from the second I saw you."

I turned to face him. "I wanted you, too."

We kissed passionately. His hands touched my face and I stroked his head. I had succumbed to his seduction. We panted anxiously and our bodies grinded vigorously. As he pulled down my shorts, I grabbed his shirt and it ripped from the collar. He groaned like my aggression aroused him more. While he cupped the back of my head with one hand, he unbuckled his pants with the other. Captivated by the muscles bulging all over his body, I yanked his jeans down to his knees. My heart throbbed in my panties as I begged for him and he granted my request. I nibbled on his neck to muffle the sounds howling in me. While he gently loved me, I ran my hands over his smooth skin. As I whined in appreciation, cool air and chirping birds woke me from my dream. I lay alone on my chaise, fully dressed with my hands between my legs. My heart plummeted as I hopped up and looked around. How embarrassed would I be if he had witnessed my wet dream? Oh no. I took a deep breath, hung my head, and called out for him. When he didn't answer, I tiptoed around. After I confirmed that he was gone, I still sat up rocking back and forth. At what point did he leave?

As I stood on the elevator to meet Rashad, I rubbed my hands together. I took a deep breath and stepped out of the building. He smiled. "Teem."

My eyes shifted. A question mark covered my face when he said, "I had a good time last night."

My eyes opened. He asked, "Did you?"

He grabbed my hand and said, "What's wrong with you today?"

I shrugged my shoulders and pretended that I was preoccupied with work. "We just have to hurry 'cause I have to get back."

During the jog to the clinic for our results, I decided not to stress the possibility that he witnessed my porno skit. As long as he didn't mention it, I wouldn't mention it.

I then began to wonder how I would react if he were positive. My stomach began to swirl. Thankfully, my jitters were unwarranted as we exchanged our results. He hugged me and sealed our agreement. He is my man and I am his lady until further notice. Out in the middle of the busy street, our emotions escaped and we kissed like we were distant lovers.

He jogged with me back to work. Since I planned to work late, I told him to come by in the morning to get his bonus check. Not to mention, I was nervous that my dream might come true now that I had his results in my hand.

Scene 15

RASHAD

Following the same routine as I did the first day, I stopped at Starbucks and was on Fatima's doorstep by seven-fifteen. When she opened the door, she rolled her eyes. "Why are you always late?"

"I'm sorry. There was a backup at Starbucks. It must have been a new guy, because . . ."

"All right, you can save it."

As she swished across the living room floor in her robe, I didn't want to debate with her. She walked into the kitchen and my eyes followed. "So, what did you do yesterday?" I asked.

"Work."

She didn't ask me, so I offered, "Yeah, I went to the gym after I left you. Then, I went to Barnes & Noble for about four hours."

She brushed passed me and made me feel an inch tall. "It must be nice to chill all day."

The sting traveled through me and I fantasized pushing her down the stairs. When she reached the bottom of the stairs, I stumbled into a chair and struggled to swallow her disrespect.

My head pounded while I attempted to watch the "Today Show." As the reality of this situation weighed heavily on my morality, I dozed off. Her heels trudging up the stairs woke me.

As I stood to walk her out of the house, she pulled a folded check from her suit jacket pocket and handed it to me. She opened her arms for a hug and I took it as her request for for-giveness and we left the house without much to say to each other.

As soon as she hopped into the taxi, I glanced at the fortune burning my hands: *Ten thousand dollars.* Until this moment, I thought I was a star on a special starving actors' edition of "Punk'd." Somebody pinch me!

My largest advance ever burned in my pocket, as I literally jogged to the bank. Who gives a damn what she says out of her mouth? It's what comes out of her pocket that matters. If I man-age this money correctly, I would be a prostitute for only six months tops.

As I sat in my bedroom with books and newspapers scattered around the floor, my agent called to ask if I'd be available at noon for an audition. I glanced at my clock and gasped, "So, in an hour."

"Yeah, one of my other clients isn't feeling well."

Maybe my recent deposit was why I wasn't inspired. Normally, I'd be jumping around the room with one leg in my jeans. As I reminded myself that my real character will probably not deal with the constant humiliation forever, I agreed and she faxed me the script. I was forced to study it and be on the train in thirty minutes.

When I rushed into the audition about ten minutes after twelve, I walked up to one of the screeners and introduced my-self. He cleared his throat. "What time were you told to be here?"

"Uh. I just got the call at eleven because—"

"We were expecting you at twelve."

"Look, man. Am I too late?" I looked at my watch. "Man, it's only—"

He looked at his clipboard and pointed to the waiting area. "Have a seat, Mr. Watkins. I'll see if the director still wants to see you."

As I sat in a stiff leather chair, I wished I could turn back the hands of time. I'd already blown my chances. Why does it seem that my agent intentionally puts me at a disadvantage? I decided to review the last-minute script in my hands. At least I could have da bomb performance.

They finally called me in after two hours. When I entered the studio, I projected confidence as I smiled and gave eye contact to the panel of directors. My heart thumped as always. Finally, I was told to read a section in the script and was delighted to discover it was the portion that I'd thoroughly studied during my wait. Holding the script in my hand, I acted out the role of a disgruntled crackhead. Their comments slightly distracted me. *He's much too muscular. He looks too polished. I don't think he has what we're looking for.*

My performance gave me chill bumps, yet the decision-makers looked at me like I wasn't good enough. When I was done, I was surprised when one of the directors asked me to read another part.

I anxiously flipped to the section. Again, with every nerve in my body, I read the script. Over and over again, they had me read different portions of that role. They even requested I read for a different role. Toward the end, I was convinced that maybe they liked me. That was before they told me that I was a great actor, but not exactly what they were looking for.

As I left the studio hanging my head because I'd yet to land an acting gig in six months, it dawned on me. Damn it! I *have* an acting gig that I am slipping on. I pulled out my cell phone and called Fatima.

Her assistant put me on hold for nearly fifteen minutes. Finally, Fatima got on the phone.

"How do you plan to fit your two daily phones calls into fifteen minutes? I get off at five."

A bad taste formed in my mouth, but as I thought about the money I now had in the bank, I swallowed the irritation. "I was just calling to say I'll call you back in five minutes."

She didn't laugh. So, I tried again. "Nah, I had an audition that lasted all day."

My ideal woman would ask how it went, but Fatima said, "So, that's your excuse?"

"Not an excuse, just an explanation. I'd like to meet you for dinner. Is that possible?"

"I guess."

"I'll meet you on Forty-second Street and Ninth. There's a French restaurant I'd like to take you to."

"Okay. What time?"

"Six?"

"That's fine. I'll see you then."

By the time I arrived at the restaurant, Fatima called to say she was running a few minutes late. The hostess asked if I wanted to be seated while I waited for my date. Desperately needing to unwind, I agreed. It is no wonder I stopped dating because I felt like I was working three jobs.

When the waiter checked on me, I ordered a shot of Cuervo and a bottle of wine. Immediately after I downed my shot, I began to sip on the wine. When I looked up and saw a beautiful silhouette in the door, it seemed worth the stress. She was gorgeous even after a long day of work. She strutted over to the table. As I stood to pull out her chair, she smiled. "Hi, Rashad."

When she sat down, she noticed the candy and card addressed to her. Her composure softened. "For me?"

I handed her a box of chocolates, her eyes filled. As I adored her appreciation, she blew a kiss at me.

"So, how was your day?"

"Stressful."

Scene 16

FATIMA

As I sat across from the perfect man for the perfect script, I couldn't believe how easily he had fallen into character. I glanced at the handwritten sentiment inside the card and batted my eyes at him. The words on the card forced me to forget his sentiments were out of obligation: *Fatima, you are a beautiful woman. The few hours we've spent together have already made me want to be a better man. I found myself smiling today, anticipating seeing you this evening. I hope this makes you smile, because I love when you do.*

As a silly grin played on my face, he reached for the wine bottle. "Would you like some?"

After he poured the wine, he raised his glass. The waiter came with two small salads and interrupted our toast. I raised my eyebrows. "Did you order already?"

When I noticed there were no menus on the table, I answered my own question. He lifted his glass again: "To Fatima, for letting me take control."

"Whatever."

He pulled back his glass when I tried to tap it with mine. "Stop, Rashad."

"Do you want to keep controlling everything? Or are you going to let me do my job?"

"Shhh . . ."

He looked around at the invisible people my twirling eyes implied were eavesdropping. We burst into laughter.

"Fatima, I was just talking about my job as a man, not as . . ."

Nearly jumping out of my chair, I reached over and attempted to cover his mouth. "Shhh. People might hear you."

Why did it tickle him that our arrangement embarrassed me? Again, he snickered, "Teem, you're funny."

"Well, I'm not trying to be."

"Okay, why don't you make the toast?"

Just as I was about to speak, he cleared his throat, "I'll just follow the leader."

"No. You do it."

"To dreams."

I nodded. "To dreams."

As the melody to Alicia Keys' "Unbreakable" played inside my head, I felt we could be whoever we wanted to be in our little fantasy world. Rashad gazed into my eyes, trying to interpret my thoughts. I smiled. He smiled. The small tealight candle flickered on the table and ignited a flame to our joy.

As our conversation continued, he either studied the script as if for a final exam or he really cared about the drama on my job. By the time dinner came, we had drank two glasses of wine. Either I was intoxicated or happy as hell. I'd stop and chuckle in between sentences. When I smiled, he smiled and vice versa.

By the time we left the restaurant, I was quite inebriated. When I thanked him, he leaned in for a kiss and I tripped. He laughed. "Did I knock you off your feet?"

"No, it was the wine."

"Don't be so sassy or I'll do it again."

Please do. "What are your plans for the evening?"

"You."

Was he trying to say that he planned to do me for the evening? I covered my chest. Did he realize that I was a good Christian girl, who'd only been with one man my entire life? I gasped as if his comment was too much for my innocence. "What?"

"I'm just saying that I'm hanging out with you for the evening. Is that cool?"

"You want to go dancing?"

"Sure, why not?"

When we walked into a spot on 38th Street, the DJ played Salsa. I smirked. With his hand on my waist, he leaned in and asked, "What's the problem?"

"I bet you don't like this music."

Without answering my question, he dropped my bag on a seat and grabbed my arm. He led me to the dance floor. As he directed my steps, our bodies attuned to each other. His right leg forward. My left leg back. His hand guided my waist. My hand stroked his torso with each turn. Our movement translated the sexy Spanish lyrics. He danced into my heart, as our souls danced together. Suddenly, as if all the music stopped, we stood fused together, frozen in time in the middle of the dance floor.

My body was responding to this man in a way I never imagined. How could I extinguish the fire burning in my panties? I wanted him and, based on the sensual way in which he touched me, I knew he wanted me. Could this be right? As I battled with whether I was actually going to sex-up this stranger, we swayed from side to side and my pelvis felt like it would overflow. Well, it has been three years.

When we resumed dancing, he twirled me around in his rapture and dipped me down in lust. We breathed in unison at a hesitant, but affirmative pace. My anticipation increased as I resolved that I was going to make love to this man.

Scene 17

RASHAD

What are we going to do with all of this chemistry? Our bodies spoke volumes and our eyes were paralyzed in one another's gaze. I leaned my forehead into hers, "You want to get
out of here?"

Her eyes fluttered as she nodded. It confirmed that she felt
what I felt and neither of us could control it. When we hopped
into the taxi, I couldn't keep my hands from touching her and
her delicate fingers raked my face. My soldier stood armed and
ready to fire.

We inched toward one another and our lips locked. She held
me tightly while I stroked her back. Her hands inched up my
shirt and we moaned. Our reason left us and we steamed up the
windows. When we finally pulled up to Fatima's house, I tossed
the driver a twenty.

The fearless gaze that we'd maintained throughout the
evening escaped us as it took moments for her to retrieve the
keys from her purse. When the door swung open, I pinned her
to the wall and kicked it closed with my foot. Her hands framed
my face as we kissed and I removed her top. She kicked off her
shoes without disconnecting with me. We moaned anxiously as
she began to unbutton my shirt. She lifted my wife-beater and
kissed me on my chest. I reached down to pull her skirt up. My
hand traveled slowly up her legs. I yanked at the slinky thong

covering her womanhood. Her inner thigh was soaked with her goodness. I couldn't resist the desire to touch her. It was so warm and snug. Her muscles contracted and sent sparks through me. I fumbled with my pants. Finally, my slacks dropped to my knees. I lifted her up and her thighs clamped around me. Her wetness dribbled on me as I rushed to the nearest chair.

Her skirt bunched around her waist as she straddled me. She looked down at my manhood and smiled. When I looked down to acknowledge her acknowledgment, I was covered with her love.

Not another second wasted, I lifted her hips and lowered her down onto me. She winced. I recoiled. "Are you okay?"

She nodded and I helped her glide down gently. She whimpered slightly when we united. My arms crisscrossed around her back and my hands rested on her shoulders. Her small waist snaked back and forth and her adorable face transposed graciously into a million expressions of appreciation.

I wiped sweat from her forehead as she whimpered desperately on me. I wanted to protect her. Why did this feel so right? Why did she feel so right? She nestled her head into my neck and bit softly. She purred and her pleasure brought me pleasure. My muscles cramped as I tried to restrain my satisfaction. I clutched her shoulders to fight the urge, but in the sweetest voice, she said, "Go ahead. It's okay."

All my lonely nights escaped me and I rested my head on her shoulders. How could I be so fortunate to get paid to feel this good? The dew on our skin pasted us together as we both exhaled sighs of gratification. Our heartthrobs conversed as we sat in silence for a ten-minute eternity.

She held my face in her hands and our foreheads knocked. Her lips grazing mine, she asked, "Are you okay?"

I traced her spine with the tips of my fingers. "Yes, are you?"

"I can't believe we're here."

I pierced into her eyes. "Me either, but it feels right. Doesn't it?"

We exchanged soft laughs and deep breaths. Finally, she asked, "Do you want to go downstairs?"

My back lifted from the chair and she climbed off of me. Her wrinkled skirt inched down. We both acknowledged that we forgot she was wearing it with a short chuckle. She reached out to help me from the couch.

My hands clung gently to her waist as we headed to her bedroom. A narrow hall led to a huge room that spanned the entire lower level. As I looked around in amazement, I slowly released her. I tried to calculate the square footage. The room was practically the size of my mother's two-bedroom apartment.

When she noticed I was in awe, she said, "Are you okay?"

I shook the shock. "Yeah, I'm fine. Your bedroom is amazing."

She mumbled, "Thanks."

"I've never seen a brownstone laid out like this."

Discomfort formed wrinkles in her forehead. "It was a wedding gift."

Trying to convince her that it was okay to discuss it, I grabbed her hand again and smiled. "This was a pretty nice gift."

She shrugged her shoulders. "My husband did it."

I tried to shake the thought that he miraculously gave her a room the size of Alabama in the heart of Harlem and said, "That's good."

She walked into her large walk-in closet. "Make yourself comfortable."

I was in another man's castle, trying to make his wife my queen. How the hell could I make myself comfortable? She stepped out of the closet wearing a pink negligee and I was suddenly at peace again. I reached for her hand and we two-stepped to the emotion vibrating in us.

When I woke up to a loud snore, I couldn't imagine it was the delicate little lady lying in my arms. How could something so beautiful sound like this? I peeked over at her alarm clock and realized she had another hour or so to sleep. I slithered from the bed, trying hard not to wake her. With the sunlight beaming in the room, I was able to scrutinize the details. My stomach began to somersault with envy.

I tiptoed into the bathroom and the cream ceramic tile

chilled my feet. I hopped onto the carpet and looked into the mirror. When will you be able to rent a room, nonetheless build one? Before I beat myself up too much, I stepped away from my reflection. The water drizzling in the garden tub helped drown my feelings of doubt.

After I looked in every cabinet for some ordinary soap, I finally showered in lilac shower gel. I smelled just like a chick as I crept back into the room and threw my dirty boxers back on.

She squirmed and I monitored her for a minute, but she drifted back into her coma. When I went upstairs into the kitchen, I searched high and low for breakfast food. What does this woman eat? I found multiple bags of coffee, but no food.

I noticed her house keys on the dining room table. *Should I?* I inched closer. Before I could rationalize my decision, I crept downstairs, put my clothes on, and headed to Pathmark.

I bought more than the bare necessities, so I ended up catching a taxi back. With each step toward the door, I prayed that she was still asleep. If breakfast was done when I explained that I stole her keys, I assumed she would digest it better. With three bags in each hand, I struggled to unlock the door. Just as it swung open, her home phone began to ring. Shit! Who is calling at six-forty-five in the morning? It finally stopped after almost six rings. I stood at the top of the stairs trying to see if she was awake. Dead silence, aside from her snore. Had it not been for that, I would have thought I killed her.

I rushed into the kitchen and mixed the eggs and cinnamon for my mother's famous French toast. Her pots and pans were meticulously stacked. I was afraid to destroy the work of art. In between the bacon and French toast, I brewed a pot of coffee. Just as I poured the eggs into the pan, her alarm clock sounded. My plan to have breakfast done and the kitchen clean by the time she saw it failed, as she stood in the doorway of the kitchen, bundled in her robe.

"Look at you."

While I made her plate, I looked up at her and smiled. "Look at you."

She curled her lips. "Went grocery shopping?"

I nodded.

"Thanks."

"Anything for the Teem."

She giggled. The twinkle in her eyes said she liked the twist that I put on her corny *little lady* line. I walked out into the living/dining room and put her plate on the table.

"Your coffee is coming." She began to speak, but I interrupted. "A lot of cream and more sugar."

"You're too much."

When I brought the coffee back, she stroked my forearm. "It's no fun eating alone."

"Okay, I'm coming."

After I scraped a few eggs onto my plate, I rushed back in to eat with her. She hadn't touched her food. I frowned. "Is everything okay?"

"Yes. I was just waiting for you."

I smiled at Fatima's softer morning personality. She raised her coffee cup. I raised my fist. She giggled and said, "To releasing control."

"To releasing, in general."

She curled her lips in embarrassment. I smiled. That statement applied to me as much as it applied to her. She set her coffee cup down and looked at me. "You're too funny."

Finally, she put a piece of French toast in her mouth and looked at me in admiration as pleasurable expressions rippled across her face. "This is so good. This is my favorite breakfast food."

I nodded. Why did she feel the need to reiterate everything that she'd already written down? Time ticked away as we had our morning bonding session, I peeked at my watch.

"Do you know what time it is?"

"I'll get there when I get there."

I nodded. "Okay, don't bite my head off when you're running late."

"Trust me. I don't bite."

"Okay. I trust you."

She winked and we enjoyed a peaceful morning. I was really feeling Fatima minus one decibel.

Scene 18

FATIMA

When I got into the taxi, I immediately called Mya. She picked up on the first ring. "Ho."

"No, I'm not the ho. He is . . ."

"Ooh."

I giggled and she joined me, but I don't think she really thought I'd done what I did. She asked, "What did y'all do yesterday? I guess you're enjoying his company, huh?"

I enjoyed something else, too. With my lips curled, I giggled again. "Mmm-hmm."

"Ho, stop withholding info. How was he at dinner? Did he stay the night?"

"Oh, girl."

"Tima, don't make me hurt you." She began to rattle off my evening. "I didn't hear from you after dinner. If it was bad, you would have called me. I called around seven this morning." I imagined her stretching her mouth, as she stressed. "No, you didn't."

"Did I?"

"Tima, you didn't."

"Well, hell. I haven't been that close to a man in three years. I couldn't resist."

"I knew that was going to happen. I want to hear every detail."

"Well, it probably would have never gotten to that point, had we not gone dancing."

"Dancing?"

"Salsa, at that."

"He likes Salsa."

"Girl, talk about Livin' La Vida Loca!"

"You're stupid. That was an added bonus, huh?"

"Pretty much. And he's really good at it. He swept me off my feet."

"So—the sex?"

"Excellente." I giggled. *"Muy bueno."*

"Well, I'm glad you got some sex therapy. Maybe now, I don't have to worry with admitting you to a psych ward."

I sucked my teeth. "Whatever."

"Three years without sex would drive any woman crazy and you've been tipping the insane scale a lot lately."

When I pulled up to my building, I rushed her off the phone. "Okay, we'll talk. I'm at work."

"I know you're not just getting to work."

"I'll call you later, honey."

When she continued to interrogate me, I said, "Smooches." Then, closed my phone.

I bounced into the office. Kia frowned before she greeted me. I smiled. An inquisitive stare covered her face as I waltzed into my office. When I sat down, I took a deep breath before turning on my computer. While my mind replayed the visions of last night, she stood in my doorway.

"What's up, honey?"

She snickered and mumbled, "Honey?"

"What's up?"

Finally, she got up the nerve and asked, "Fatima, are you okay?"

"Don't I look okay?"

She nodded and whispered, "Actually, you look like you had a drink this morning."

Boy, I wished I could share with her why I was intoxicated. Instead, I touched my chest like I was appalled. "Kia, I'm just in a good mood. Can't I be in a good mood?"

"Yeah. I guess." Still, she had a constipated look on her face. What the hell is her problem? Maybe she needs a piece, too. She pointed a folder in my direction and her words dragged out, "The art department sent over the cover for Tisha Blount's new release."

I reached out. "Well, let me see it then."

Like she expected me to explode, she crept over to me. When she got close, I growled and snapped my hands out with clawed fingers. "Boo!"

She flinched and her eyes bugged out. I laughed hysterically and said, "I'm just picking with you, loosen up."

She laughed with hesitation and studied me as I opened the folder. I said, "I love it. I absolutely love it."

"You do."

I nodded. "It's fabulous."

"But, you . . ."

"No, say it. I—what?"

"You always hate the covers where the female looks so desperate for the male."

"She doesn't look desperate."

She tapped on the young lady lying on the man's bare chest. "Look at her. Her hair is covering her face. Her head is down like she's praying on his stomach." She brushed her fingers over his face. "And, look. He's not even looking in her direction."

"You're absolutely right. I didn't even see it that way."

"Usually, you do. You always point that stuff out to me."

Depending on my mood, I might say anything. Too bad she was taking it all in. I chuckled. "Really."

"But it could be the Mimosa that you had this morning that's distorting your vision."

Shocked that my quiet assistant had blasted me, my mouth stretched open. She obviously paid more attention than I gave her credit for. Since her observation was so on target, I came clean. "Okay, okay. I went on a date last night with this amazing guy."

She smiled and gave me a hug. While I pushed her away, I said, "Okay, I said I went on a date. I didn't say I was getting married."

"I know. I'm just . . ."

"What?"

"I'm really happy for you. Is it someone from the dating service?"

My eyes twitched. "The dating service?"

"Yeah, remember you asked if I'd go through a dating service?"

"Oh yeah. I forgot. No, this is a guy that my friend Mya introduced me to."

"That's so good. I'm so happy for you." She hugged me again, leaving me baffled.

"Why do you keep hugging me?"

"I don't know. I think you deserve someone nice. You went through a lot."

She'd probably be really disappointed to hear that I actually had to pay for this nice guy. "That's so sweet of you."

"And you haven't dated since . . ." She paused as if she regretted her decision to bring up the death of my husband.

I smiled. "Nope, I haven't dated anyone since Derrick died."

My sexual drought must have been scribbled all over my face. She half-smiled at me and said, "Oh well, I have phone calls to make. Also, you have a meeting in a few minutes."

When she turned to leave the office rapidly after what I thought was a bonding moment, I turned my nose at her back. *Loosen up.*

Scene 19

RASHAD

Before last night, I assumed I would learn as much as I could about investing. Then I would see if I was interested in making a power move sometime in the future. Yet, jealousy sparked my ambition as I rushed home to print out the list of organizations that offer money to mid-income people to purchase houses in the city. I spent nearly two hours on the phone with people who pretty much explained that their organizations were hoaxes. City Props was the only organization that told me to come and fill out an application. As I darted out of my house and down to 114th and Frederick Douglass, I had become one of those people in a rush for time.

While I panted in front of the building, I took a moment to catch my breath and a second to pray. I opened the door and stepped up to the receptionist. As I looked around the small office, I said, "I'm here to fill out an application."

Her pupils danced as she asked, "Ah. For what?"

"I'm interested in applying for the grant to renovate vacant properties."

She raised her eyebrows. "See, we offer a bunch of programs. So, I just needed to make sure." She leaned toward the desk and whispered, "You don't look like the typical fixer-upper type."

As my forehead creased with curiosity, she added, "That's a good thing."

"Is it?"

"They're usually the contractor-type with the dirty fingernails, you know."

I nodded, but in my mind I was looking forward to getting my hands dirty. As she handed me the application, she explained, "Once you finish this, Monique will screen you."

After I filled out literally fifty pages, Monique stepped out from her small office wearing jeans and a City Props polo shirt. Her adorable smile made me smile as she said, "Mr. Watkins?"

Why does it turn me on when a woman says my name like that? When I stood up, I extended my hand. "Monique?"

"Monique Browne."

"Good to meet you."

I followed her into her office. The screening basically consisted of her telling me that my application would need to go through a million people before it was approved. Did she just say the mayor? You mean to tell me that Mayor Bloomberg decides if my black, broke ass is worthy of a grant. I don't know why I felt the need to rush this. It's not like I had registered for any of the contracting courses that I put on my to-do list. In less than twenty-four hours, envy had shifted me from a starving actor to an entrepreneur.

While I wondered what could expedite this process, Monique batted her eyes, "Mr. Watkins?"

I turned up my charm a few notches and smiled. "Yes, Ms. Browne."

"I will give you a call in about two weeks to schedule an interview."

Her attraction to me was obvious because she wouldn't look at me. I chased her roaming eyes and commanded them to pause. Before I spoke, she began to blush. "Why does it take so long?" She huffed. I said, "I'm sorry, am I getting on your nerves?"

"No, it's just that I have to go through this with every applicant that comes in here."

Her squeaky voice rippled through me, but I ignored it in my quest to get what I wanted. I shook my head. "I apologize. Those jerks shouldn't stress you out like that. Patience is a virtue."

"That needs to be this company's motto."

"So, be honest. What are the chances of actually getting this money?"

She curled her lips. "I'm not supposed to be telling you this, but since you won't go away . . ." She paused.

I mouthed, "I'm sorry." Simultaneously, I motioned for her to continue.

"New York is really funny. Either you're way over the income to get these grants or you're way under. And most people in the mid-income range really aren't interested in purchasing fixer-uppers." She shrugged her shoulders. "It's sad. Basically all you have to do is verify that your income is between seventy-five and one hundred and ten thousand per year and you can get a house. Granted, it's just a shell most of the time. People don't want to deal with all the permits and contractors. Although it's pretty much free money, renovating is a challenging process."

She looked down at my application. "When do you plan to bring last year's W2s or 1099s?"

"Ah . . ."

"The sooner you can get everything in, the faster we can process you." She winked. "Before the rush."

My raised eyebrows questioned the rush. She explained, "We get more apps in June than any other time of year. I think a lot of people are looking for apartments and they run across our agency and this seems like a better idea. Usually, by the time we call for the interview, they're no longer interested."

"Oh, that won't be me."

"Anyway, we'll need a letter of employment. Two pay stubs and last year's taxes."

"Does it matter that I wasn't in the range last year?"

"Oh no, it doesn't matter. As long as your current salary is in the range, you'll be fine." She winked again.

Was that her way of flirting or confirming that I had this grant guaranteed? Whatever her purpose, I stayed for an additional few minutes chatting about my chances.

My life had taken a turn for the better in less than seven days. What had I done to deserve this? My feet felt really light as I skipped to the train. Before I went uptown, I decided to call my favorite employer.

After being on hold for fifteen minutes, the same happy lady I'd parted with four hours ago answered, "Fatima Mayo."

I kidded, "Actually, I'm looking for Fatima Barnes. Do you happen to know where she is?"

"Oh yeah, sorry about that. I didn't know it was you."

"I guess I'm going to have to make it clear who I am when I call."

"That would be fine. What are you up to?"

"Just out, doing what I do."

"I wonder if I really want to know what that is."

"Nah, it's nothing major. I'm doing what everyone else does."

"Mmm-hmmm."

"So, what's your schedule like this evening?"

"I'm really backed up."

"I thought I took care of that last night."

"Stop. I'm at work."

"Me too."

She chuckled. "Rashad, you're a trip."

"So, what's up for the evening?"

My prayers were answered when she said, "Well, I have some reading to do this evening. So, I'll be home. You don't have to come over unless you want to."

It took me a second to decide if she was setting me up or not. So, I paused. "Ah . . ."

"Honestly, if you want to drop by later, you can. No pressure. Seriously."

"Well, I have something to do until nine. Would it be okay if I came over after that?"

"Call first."

"I certainly will. Have a good day."

It would make sense to just explain that I had to work at Tavern on the Green, but since their service was what sealed the deal, I thought it would be better left unsaid.

*   *   *

As I rolled into work around four-twenty my supervisor looked at the clock. "Rashad, you're pushing it. Every actor in New York wants your job."

"But can they do the job as well as me? Do you think you'll find another suave, black man like me?"

I knew she hated that I was so good at my job. My tardiness would have probably got me dismissed awhile ago otherwise. After my Fatima income rolls in, I planned to hand in my resignation anyway. So, her threat didn't faze me.

Unfortunately for me, starting time directly affects finishing time and I ended up leaving closer to nine-thirty. As I contemplated whether I should visit Fatima or not, I realized that I wanted to see her and share all I'd learned and the good news about the house. Shit! I'm obligated to learn this stuff. She won't be impressed. Still, I found myself in a rush to get home, in the shower, and to her house to be her willing and faithful servant.

By the time I called to say I was on my way, it was a quarter to eleven. My heart thumped before she picked up. Her voice sounded dry and sleepy. A part of me was disappointed. *Please still be awake.*

"You hungry?"

I expected her to curse me out; instead she said, "Yeah. I've been working all evening and haven't eaten anything."

"I'm on my way."

"Wait! You don't know what I want."

"I have an idea. I'm on my way."

Scene 20

FATIMA

I peeked at the time in the lower right hand of my computer screen. How did seven o'clock become eleven o'clock so fast? I had just looked at the time. If I had known it was this late, I would have told Rashad to forget it. I stormed into the kitchen to grab some crackers to hold me over until he got here. I'm going to grab my food and tell him to go home. He's taking this as a joke. How is he going to just casually roll up like he's on time?

As I ranted in the kitchen, the buzzer rang. I made him wait a few minutes before I opened the door. He handed me a pizza box and leaned in for a kiss. I turned my head. He gasped, "Are you mad at me?"

"No, I just know that you have time management issues that you need to work on."

"Issues?"

I dropped the pizza on the table and put my hand on my hip. "Yes, issues."

"If I'm not mistaken, we didn't confirm a time. I told you that I might stop by around nine."

"Well, do you realize that it's eleven o'clock? You're two hours late."

"The deal was that I would call you when I was on my way."

My pressure rose, as did the inflection in his voice. I huffed. "Are we arguing?"

"I'm not arguing, just pleading my case."

"Remember, you don't have a case."

He swallowed his pride and nodded. "You're absolutely right. I'm wrong." He took a deep breath. "Can we start over? I'm just happy to see you tonight."

I rolled my eyes and walked into the kitchen to grab paper plates. He followed and stood behind me as I reached up into the cabinet. His arms surrounded my waist and he leaned his head on my shoulder. "I missed you today."

When will I get over wondering if he's lying? Why do I even want it to be the truth? He kissed my neck and the nerves in my spine gravitated to him. I feared the connection between us.

He nibbled on my ear. "Don't be mad at me. I misspoke. I apologize."

"Yeah, whatever." I walked back into the dining room. He stood there and covered his face. I looked at him. "Are you eating, too?"

He slouched toward me. I put a slice on my plate and one on his. By the time I poured soda into the cups, his plate was clean and he reached for another slice. I frowned. "Did you inhale that slice?"

"I'm hungry."

Within seconds, the next slice was gone. He obviously hadn't taken anyone out to dinner. As it dawned on me why I was so angry, I blushed. When he caught me, he raked my forearm.

"Was the Teem mad at me?"

"Whatever."

"You know I didn't mean it." He puckered his lips and blew a kiss. "Sorry."

"Don't let it happen again."

"I won't. I don't like to see you go off like that."

"And I don't like to do it either."

I laughed because I meant it, but I think he laughed because he thought I wanted to act like that. I just wanted him to understand that timing is everything.

* * *

After a meeting, I walked into the office to a huge basket of spa treats. I anxiously opened the note: *Relax. I'm here to help. I hope our today can be better than yesterday.—Rash*

Did someone drop this man from heaven? I fanned myself with the card as I dialed his number. I left a message on his voicemail and he returned my call within minutes.

"Good afternoon, Ms. Barnes."

"How are you, Mr. Watkins?"

"I'm good now that I hear your smile."

"What if I said I wasn't smiling?"

"Then I would have to believe that you're lying to me."

"You're a clown."

"But I perform only for you."

I giggled. "You make me laugh."

"That's good, right?"

"I guess. Well, I'm calling to thank you for my lovely gift."

I unpacked my basket while we chatted. The cucumber melon scrub and lotion fit into the décor of my pastel office. I propped the products onto my trinket bookcase and positioned them just right. Rashad asked if he could take me out. I looked at the pile of work that I was trying to wrestle with on my desk and declined. His voice weakened, "Okay, I guess I'll just sit home and think about you."

"You're just trying to flatter me."

"I hope that I *am* flattering you."

"Okay. What are you trying to do?"

"I want to take you to a pool hall."

"Did I say I like pool? I can't play pool. What made you choose that?"

He sighed. "I think it's something you might enjoy."

"But I can't play."

"I'll teach you."

"It'll take too much time."

"You just have to take your time. It's about patience."

"And I don't have any."

"But I do and you're with me, so we'll figure it out, right?"

Scene 21

RASHAD

Just before Fatima pulled up in a taxi, I checked my watch. She was a half hour late. I started to feel like I'd been stood-up as my palms began to sweat. When the car door opened, the noise on the street silenced. She stepped one leg out and reached back for her change. Her smile illuminated and invoked a glow around her. I rubbed my eyes to make sure I wasn't hallucinating. Still, there was a radiance around her that perplexed me. She stood in front of me with her head tilted in confusion.

Finally, I leaned in for a kiss. "How are you this evening, Ms. Fatima?"

Her noise wrinkled. "How are you?"

"I'm fine, perfectly fine."

I opened the door to the Slate Bar, Restaurant & Billiards and we stood in front of the hostess. I said, "We'd like a table."

"Will it just be the two of you?"

I nodded and the hostess pulled out our pool equipment. "Here you go. You're downstairs at table eleven."

While we headed downstairs, Fatima grabbed my arm and asked, "Did you hear me say thank you?"

"No, but you're welcome."

"What did I do to deserve my surprise today?"

"Just being you."

I chuckled to myself. The anxiety attack that she had last night when she thought I was late is what sparked this date.

After I put the rack on the table, I grabbed Fatima's bag and set it on a chair. Just as I was about to explain a few techniques to Fatima, the waitress came over.

"Hey, guys, can I get you something?"

Fatima smiled. "Sure, you can get me a menu."

I frowned. "Just you."

"Well, you didn't act like you were hungry."

"How is a hungry person supposed to act?"

The waitress laughed. "I'll bring two menus. Would you like anything to drink?"

Fatima's mouth parted and I interrupted, "Merlot for her and a shot of Cuervo for me."

When she walked away, Fatima said, "What if I didn't want Merlot?"

I kissed her cheek and didn't answer her question. Her eyes slanted as I retreated. I stood the pool stick up in front of her. "Here, Teem. What do you know about pool?"

"Absolutely nothing, so I don't know why we're here."

I reminded her of a footnote in the script: "Not the typical date. Ones that make you think."

"Ah, yeah, and where does pool fall in?"

I lifted the rack from around the balls and she leaned impatiently on the other end of the table. "You'll see in just a second."

Her lips curled. "If you say so."

The waitress returned with our drinks and placed them on a nearby table. Fatima walked over and grabbed her glass as I continued with my instruction.

"The person that breaks, gets the first chance to determine which balls will be his."

"Sorry, Rashad, I don't want any balls."

My chin dropped and I shook my head. "Okay, either the high or the low."

"What's the difference?"

"The high numbers are stripped, low are solid."

She smirked. "Yeah, yeah, yeah, and the purpose is to finally hit the eight ball."

"But you have to get all of your balls in first."

"Okay, I got it. Can you get the waitress's attention?"

It wasn't until the waitress stood in front of us did she realize I hadn't looked at the menu. Just as she was about to part her mouth to order, her eyes shifted to me. "Do you know what you want?"

My hands folded on the top of my pool stick. "Actually, I never looked at the menu."

Her eyes lowered like she felt bad. "Do you want me to just order for you?"

"You may as well now since you've rushed the young lady over here."

Fatima huffed. "They have regular appetizers. Just tell me what you want."

"No, go ahead and order."

The waitress became amused with our little squabble. After Fatima ordered a grilled chicken club for me, a vegetable pizza for herself, and fried calamari for an appetizer, the waitress collected our menus. "You guys are so cute. How long have you been together?"

We both looked like she had shoved a pool stick up our behinds. Our eyes questioned what we should say. It was our first time on the spot. Fatima cleared her throat and said, "Nine months."

"You guys act like an old married couple."

She skedaddled away and left us with the discomfort of wondering what kind of vibes we were sending off. Fatima groaned, "That was weird."

"Who are you telling? Okay, now back to the game."

"Our cover was almost blown and you're back to the game."

I laughed. "So, do you want to retape that scene or can we just move to the next one?"

She sucked her teeth. "All right, go ahead and break the balls or whatever you do."

I leaned over the table and hit the balls. Several of the solid and striped balls dropped into the holes. She rolled her eyes. "See, now you're going to show off."

"Actually, I'm not. It's your turn and you get to pick which ones you're shooting for since I knocked both in."

"I want the solid ones."

I nodded. "Okay, do you know how to shoot?"

She bopped around the table with her lips curled. "Um-huh."

Her dress pants clung to her hips and her blouse gathered around her breasts as she overdramatized leaning over the table. She shoved the pool stick and barely even hit the white ball, which rolled approximately an inch. I grinned. "C'mon, let me show you."

"Why didn't it move? I thought I was supposed to hit it hard."

"It's about precision, not aggression. You have to concentrate on the target."

I wrapped my arms around her arms and we held the pool stick together. As I positioned her limbs, I said, "Angle yourself like this."

I leaned over her shoulders and the scent of her perfume distracted me so I could not remember where I was in my instructions. "Ah."

"So, do I just push it like this?"

Her eyes studied my profile as I continued the lesson. "Yeah, push it just like that. You ready to try?"

She tried and tried again. After almost ten tries, she finally hit the ball and the pride in her expression was priceless. She kissed me and cheered herself on, "Go Tima, it's your birthday."

The way little things excited her, everyday was her birthday. I nodded. "It certainly is . . ."

The waitress returned with our appetizer, but Fatima continued practicing. I admired the competitor in her. I grabbed the calamari and fed it to her as she became more confident in her shots.

When the stick would skid passed the ball or knock them off the table, I would repeat: "You've got to be patient. Concentrate and you'll hit your target."

She waved her hand. "Yeah, yeah, yeah. I got it. I got it."

When our food came, she sat down beside me and whispered in my ear, "I think I like pool."

"Why is that?"

"Because it's fun and it makes me think."

"Is that right?"

"Yes, that's right. You did a good job."

We played a few more rounds before fatigue got the best of both of us.

Scene 22

FATIMA

On the taxi ride home, I found myself caressing his leg for no reason. I was smitten with his aggressive nonchalance. He seemed fazed by nothing, but on point with everything. He stroked my hair but gazed out of the opposite window. I blushed just because. No, actually I blushed at my brilliance. How could I be so blessed to find the guy to act out my script so well?

Once we were in the house, we headed to my bedroom. He turned the cable station onto soft R&B and we sat on the bed holding hands. I mouthed the words to all the songs.

He chuckled. "You're so animated."

Just as I was about to respond, he leaned over and kissed me. My heart plummeted as if this was our first time. He hovered over when I laid down. Our eyes conversed, questioned, wondered, and anticipated. Without ending our gaze, we undressed. He stroked my hair delicately from my face, in the same motion that he loved me. Anxiety rippled through me and triggered my tear ducts to water. I took deep breaths to suppress the over-emotion. Gentle lovemaking combined with passion took us on a journey far away from Harlem. I was in paradise.

Maybe because he was the first man I'd been with in three years, but I felt hopelessly in love with him. As I fell asleep in his arms, I pleaded with myself not to surrender to this feeling.

* * *

After four weeks, Rashad was still full of surprises. I woke up to eggs, bacon, and coffee served on a tray. He stood over me in his boxers and undershirt. I said, "Good morning."

After setting the tray on my lap, he said, "Good morning, Sleeping Beauty. You didn't hear all that noise in the alley this morning?"

I shook my head and he walked over to the window and opened the blinds. "Yeah, someone must have been blocking the way and the trash truck kept beeping the horn."

"I didn't hear a thing. Where's your food?"

"Upstairs. I'm going to get it."

When he returned with his tray, he plopped down beside me. I covered my morning breath and leaned over to kiss his cheek. "Thanks for breakfast."

"No problem."

He handed me a small envelope that contained an index card with the following instruction: *A surprise awaits you at the end of this journey.* CLUE # 1—INSIDE THE BATHROOM, UNDER THE BLUE CANDLE.

I tapped my shoulder into his. "Rashad, what is this all about?"

"Fatima, it's just a game. You'll be done by the end of the day."

"What's the surprise?"

He hung his head. "It won't be a surprise if I tell you."

"It will, I promise."

"Just follow the clues. If you don't figure it out before the last clue, I'll tell you."

After I finished my breakfast, I sprung from the bed to find my first clue. I lifted the candle to find a small piece of paper with the number "5" on it. I stood in the doorway facing Rashad and said, "C'mon baby, can I get better clues than this?"

He laughed. "That is a good clue."

"Okay, so where's my next clue?"

"It's no fun to get all the clues at once."

I huffed. "Now, you got me all excited and I have to wait for the next clue. Can you at least give me a hint as to when I can expect it?"

His orange juice sprayed from his mouth as he laughed harder at me and made me laugh. "Okay, I guess I'll just have to be patient."

"Not patient, just not anxious."

I rolled my eyes in my head. "Okay, I guess I'll just have to wait."

I closed the bathroom door and looked at my first clue again. What does the number "5" describe? Hell, it could be anything.

On my taxi ride to work, I got a text-message: SECOND CLUE IS IN THE SIDE POCKET OF YOUR BACKPACK.

I quickly rummaged through my bag and found another sheet of paper with the clue: BOSTON. A big smile spread across my face as I knew I'd figured it out. I quickly called him, "Okay, Red Sox game, your favorite player wears the number five, or we're in the fifth row."

"Nope. That's not it."

"C'mon. Just tell me. Now, I'm going to have to go to work all day wondering what you have planned. Can you at least let me know when the surprise occurs?"

"You'll know soon enough . . ."

When I arrived at work, a small basket of chocolates sat on my desk. I opened the card: CLUE #3: CANDY.

How do the number "5", Boston, and candy relate? Now, I was baffled without a doubt. Kia came into the office saying, "You sure are getting a bunch of gifts."

I smiled. She handed me a large envelope. "He must be a really nice guy, huh?"

With my chin propped on my folded hands, I nodded. "Yes, he's extremely nice."

"It's so good to see you happy."

I sucked my teeth. "Are you saying I wasn't happy?"

"I mean you weren't unhappy. You were just really into work and you . . ."

"I . . . what?"

"You were just really pushy. You seem so much more relaxed the last few weeks."

My bottom lip hung. "I'm not pushy."

"It's not a bad thing, but I can tell a difference."

With the clues on the forefront of my mind, I didn't really have time to entertain my character flaws. I shooed her. "Whatever, Kia, I haven't changed at all." I opened the envelope. "What's this?"

"A submission from Serena McEnvoy. It's only the first three chapters."

"A new author?"

She nodded and I huffed. "Why does she insist on sending me the first three chapters when I keep telling her I need an entire manuscript for new authors?"

"I read it and I kinda like it."

I leaned back in my chair. "Maybe I'll take a look at it."

Kia laughed. I sat up to inquire what humored her. She said, "See, a few weeks ago, you would have just sent her a rejection letter."

"That's not true. I'm reading it because you said you liked it."

Her dancing eyes told me that her liking it never mattered before. I waved my hand. "Whatever. I'll check it out."

Shortly after Kia walked away, my phone buzzed with what I assumed to be my next clue. It was Mya asking to do Happy Hour. Depending on the result of this little game, I may not be able to make it, so I declined.

She promptly called to ask why. After I explained, she pointed out, "Tima, I think you have yourself a winner."

"Let's not lose focus."

She laughed. "Who? Me or you?"

"You!"

"I'm focused. I'm just saying he seems to be doing all the right things in the right ways."

"Yeah, yeah, yeah. It's still early."

"Don't even fake like you're not flattered."

I sucked my teeth. "I am flattered . . . and focused."

"And fake."

We laughed and chatted about miscellaneous things as I awaited my next clue. We tried to decipher the surprise based on the current clues. Two geniuses plus three clues equaled zero answers. She tried to hang on the line for the fourth clue, but it didn't seem to be coming anytime soon.

It was shortly after lunch when it arrived. He called and asked, "What year did Michael Jordan began playing in the NBA?"

"C'mon now, Rashad. You're pushing it."

"You don't have to answer right now, but the answer is your next clue."

This had become more like a job than a cute little game. I got on the Internet to find the answer. Now, it was 5, Boston, candy, and 1984. Tell me what this surprise could be.

Shortly after, he sent another text message: YOU'RE HOLDING IT IN YOUR HAND RIGHT NOW. How does he know what's in my hand? What does he mean? I text-messaged him back: DO YOU MEAN MY PHONE?

He responded: LOL. BINGO.

As I headed home, he called to remind me to check the mail. I kidded, "I guess my next clue is in there."

"Your last clue."

Suddenly, I was excited again. "Are you serious?"

"Yes, I'm surprised you didn't figure it out yet. I know how inquisitive you are."

"Yeah, but I'm no mind reader. Your clues are hard as hell."

He snickered, "I'm sorry."

"Okay, I'm almost home."

"I have some work to do, so if it's okay, I'll stop by a little later."

"Okay, I'll call you when I figure out the surprise."

"Make sure you do."

After I sifted through a bunch of other mail in my box, I found Rashad's letter. A Ticketmaster envelope fell out. I read his short note: CLUE #5: YOU'LL HAVE TO—COUNT ME OUT.

I frowned and pulled the tickets from the envelope: *New Edition Reunion Tour*. I laughed, because I, of all people, should have figured this out. Five members from Boston. They were at the height of their career in 1984: "Candy Girl"; "Mr. Telephone Man."

My head fell into my hands. I couldn't believe that he put so much energy into surprising me. How did he know I was a die-hard New Edition fan? When I called to tell him how happy I was, he didn't answer.

Scene 23

RASHAD

I felt my phone vibrate in my pocket as I chatted with an older couple sitting in my section. They were telling me how much they enjoyed my service and thanking me for a pleasant attitude. Of course, I had to seal the deal with, "You don't get great service every time you come here? That's unacceptable."

After stepping away from them, I rushed to the back to grab food for another table. The couple was gone when I returned. I delivered the food to the other table, and stopped to pick up the credit card folder. I was flattered to see a one hundred dollar tip when I opened it.

My smiled stiffened. I'm going to miss those occasional gifts when I turn in my letter. As much as it seemed like an easy decision to just walk away from an hourly job to a guaranteed salary, I struggled. What if I mess up somehow and Fatima decides that this is not what she wants to do anymore? Will I be S.O.I.?

As my phone vibrated in my pocket for the third time, it was clear what I had to do. Sure I have lucrative weeks here, but there are also slow weeks. Nothing can replace a consistent salary on a consistent basis. I still walk away with experience. If push comes to shove, I can always find another waiter job.

I snuck into the kitchen for a minute to call Fatima. She fake-cried on the phone. "Oh, Rashad. I was so surprised. I can't believe you took the time and energy to think of all those clues."

"It wasn't that hard."

"It was thoughtful though."

"Did you understand the last clue?" I asked.

"The last clue was the tickets."

"No, it was 'You'll Have to—Count Me Out.' Those are for you and Mya. I won't be able to make it Thursday."

A brief moment of silence broke the line. I was scheduled to work and couldn't find anyone to take my place. People were willing to trade weekend days with me, but I wasn't feeling that. Plus, I figured she'd want to go with Mya. She huffed. "I really wish you could go with me."

"I have a taping that night. It's nothing major, but I have to be there."

I looked up and realized that two of my tables were up. As she sighed on the other end, I said, "Sorry, Teem. We'll talk about it when I get there."

The decline in excitement in her voice made me uneasy. She sighed. "Okay, that's cool. Mya would love to go."

I looked around at the hustle and bustle in the kitchen and concluded it was time to give my supervisor my resignation letter. There is no way I can keep Fatima happy, hunt for a house, wait tables, and audition full-time. Something must give.

After my shift was over, I pulled my letter from my bag and asked my supervisor if I could speak to her privately. When I handed it to her, she joked, "I hope this isn't a resignation letter. I'm not accepting this."

"I thought you claimed you wanted to fire me anyway."

"I do, but like you always tell me, you're good at what you do."

"I'm sorry, but this is my two-weeks' notice."

Her eyes glossed. "Did you land a role?"

"Sorta."

"Where? What?"

"It's nothing major. I'm just an understudy."

She read over my letter. "You know this is one of the best waiter jobs you'll get. Do you really want to quit to be an understudy? That doesn't sound stable."

Maybe it wasn't, but my plans were much bigger than waiting tables or being an understudy. She continued, "You'll never make the kind of tips you earn here somewhere else."

With over four hundred dollars in tips floating in my pocket, I knew she was right. Still, I made it clear that I was done.

"Okay, I'll just sit around and wait for Rashad's call."

Her sarcasm tickled me, but I hoped I never had to make that phone call. When I stepped out of the restaurant, I was overwhelmed with confusion until I heard Fatima's voice. A small amount of excitement remained when she answered.

"What are you doing?" I asked.

She said, "Nothing. Rashad, how did you know I love New Edition?"

"Uh, the NE "HeartBreak" poster in your home office is a dead giveaway."

"Oh, I forgot about that."

"Did you talk to Mya about going?"

"She may not be able to go, but it's okay. I can go alone."

"We'll work something out."

"Don't worry. I'll be fine."

"Maybe I can pull a few strings and get the taping done earlier."

That's exactly what I did. Why be loyal to a job that I was seconds away from leaving? I called in sick early enough for them to find someone to replace me. When I told Fatima I could make it, she tried to convince me to do whatever I had planned. After I told her that it was canceled, she agreed to meet me in midtown after work.

I noticed her from a block away as she trotted toward me and fell into my arms. Judging from the euphoria on her face, she lied when she said she was fine with going alone. I said, "I'm happy to see you."

She pulled back. "I'm happier to see you."

"I bet."

She looked at me inquisitively. I put my arm around her shoulder and we strolled to Madison Square Garden.

From the moment New Edition stepped on the stage, Fatima

was no longer my partner. She was a member of the band. She knew every dance move by heart. She slid when they slid and turned when they turned. It was obvious that she needed no else to enjoy New Edition. My greatest reward for making arrangements to come to the show was witnessing Fatima completely lose herself in the music.

Scene 24

RASHAD

When I left Fatima, I rushed home to make sure my second pay stub was in the mail. When I first noticed I was being paid by Mayo Enterprises, a part of me wanted to quit, but as I checked my bank account, somehow my reservations disappeared. In a little over a month my account has gone from zip to fourteen thousand dollars. At that rate, I can cope with a little ego-bashing from time to time. Speaking of time, I studied my pay stub and wondered why it was fifty bucks more than the last one. As I scrutinized the stub, fourteen days worked and a deduction of three hours. I rushed into my bedroom and checked the previous one. That one deducted seven hours from my pay.

As I sat on my bed baffled, it dawned on me. I chuckled slightly and shook my head. I laughed harder when I calculated in my head the time I had been late. Collectively, it totaled three hours in a two-week period. I opted not to question her about it and just step up my time game. How do you question free money? Especially now that she has become my sole source of income.

When I sat at my computer to check email, I forgot that I had planned to send Fatima an evite for this evening. After shuffling through different invitations, I found the perfect one. A romantic night out. When she sent a response back of maybe, I was suddenly angered because I'd pulled a gang of strings to get these tickets. I sent an email back asking why in big, bold letters. After waiting five minutes for a response, I called the office.

Now that her assistant knows my voice, she puts me straight through. Fatima picked up. "Hey, Rashad."

I sighed. "So you're not sure if you can make it."

"Work is really stressing me out right now."

"When will you be able to give me a definite answer?"

"No later than three."

"Okay. Just keep me posted."

I thought for certain she'd be available. If she can't make it, I guess I can look at it as her waste of three hundred dollars, not mine. As I sulked in the destruction of my surprise, I checked the time. I hopped up. I had to schmooze my way into a course at the New York Real Estate Institute; I couldn't be late. Pacing through the apartment, I tried to decide if I should get dressed or just go with what I had on. Suddenly, I grabbed my backpack, jumped in a taxi and headed down to 35th Street. When I first called the school to inquire about this course, they claimed to be full until the end of the year. Determined not to take no for an answer, I went there in person and practically begged the administrator to make an exception for me. Though no one from City Props had called me back yet, I claimed I'd been given this grant and I desperately needed this course like yesterday. Once I agreed to pay seven hundred bucks, instead of the required three hundred and fifty for the Construction Project Management Certification course, somehow they had one extra seat. This course supposedly provides all the tools and information to put a construction management project into immediate action. Considering that I plan to take action immediately, I was determined to be here.

As I tried to sneak in the class five minutes late, the instructor looked up. "Welcome."

"Thanks."

He said, "You may as well keep standing and introduce yourself. Tell us a little about your experience and your goals as it pertains to construction management and what you expect from the course. We've already gone around the room."

How does my resume compare to everyone else's in here? I began, "Ah. My name is Rashad Watkins. I, ah, I have helped out on a few construction projects. Currently, I'm in the process of purchasing a fixer-upper and I hope this course will help me as I begin renovating the home. If this first project goes well, I plan to do many more."

"So, where's the house?"

Damn! Can a brother have a seat and collect his thoughts first? I said, "Harlem."

"Where in Harlem?"

"Actually, I haven't found the place, yet."

"SoHar is a goldmine."

My eyebrows rose. *SoHar?* Man, once they began to take over, they start changing names. This uncomfortable moment made me really appreciate City Props' goal of keeping Harlem in our hands. As he took in the look on my face, he added, "That's everything below a hundred and twenty-fifth."

"Yeah, I know."

As the course proceeded, my respect for him grew. He had nearly fifty large-scale renovation projects under his belt and I wanted to learn everything he already knew. After my tenth question, I noticed people becoming irritated, but I paid twice as much and I deserved twice as much attention. Toward the end of the class, the instructor announced that too many questions can prevent completing all the topics in the designated timeframe. As I frowned, he clarified, "I am more than willing to talk to any of you outside the course and you're more than welcome to visit me at different sites to gain hands-on experience."

While others gathered their things, I took his comment as a personal invitation. When the rest of the class left, I walked up to him and shook his hand. "Marty, I'm really enjoying the course."

"Yeah, you made it quite interesting today."

"Well, I definitely appreciate your thorough answers. I was curious when it would be appropriate for me to visit one of your sites."

He gave me his business card. "If I'm not teaching, I'm working. Call me and let me know when you'd like to get your hands dirty."

"I certainly will."

As I turned to walk away, he called my name. I spun around. He said, "I'll actually be onsite tomorrow."

Without a second thought, I got the details and told him that I would be there at eight sharp.

When I took my phone off of silent, it buzzed. Six voice messages. Two text messages. Fatima agreed to meet me at her house. As much as I hoped she would, I had yet to buy the dress I wanted her to wear. I eyed the dress in BCBG from the moment I first saw Fatima, imagining how it would complement her curves. While I attempted to text her to let her know I'd be there at six, my phone rang.

"Hello. Can I please speak with Rashad Watkins?"

"This is Rashad."

"This is Monique from City Props."

Her voice sounded optimistic. I crossed my fingers and said, "Hey, Monique. It's good to hear from you."

"Did you get the two messages I left today?"

"Nah. I've actually had my phone on silent for four hours. I'm just checking it. What's up?"

"You told me that you would bring the second pay stub to me today."

Damn! Here I am questioning why she hadn't called me and I'm the one holding up things. "How long will you be there?"

"I leave around five. What time can you get here?"

"I'll be there at five sharp."

I rushed into the BCBG store and didn't see the dress. My heart pounded. It was just here last week. As I spun in circles, a sales assistant walked up to me and asked if she could help.

My eyes pleaded with her to create a miracle. "I'm looking for this champagne halter dress. It's—."

"Oh, we moved those over here. They're on clearance."

I wanted to hug her. "Thank you."

"What size are you looking for?

"Eight."

She skipped over to the rack. "Guess what. You're in luck. This was just returned yesterday."

It had been reduced from two-ninety to two hundred dollars. My lucky streak was shining bright. When she explained that they accepted returns within fourteen days of purchase, it dawned on me that it could possibly not fit. What am I going to do? Oh well, we just won't be coordinated and she'll have to wear something in her closet.

By the time I got uptown to get my pay stubs and over to City Props, it was after five. I was practically out of breath when I rushed into the agency. The receptionist told me to go into Monique's office. As I stood in the doorway, she glanced at me. With the phone glued to her ear, she winked and gestured for me to sit.

I tapped my envelope on my knee and she continued to chat. My head nodded back and forth, inquiring if she could finish that call later. Finally, she said. "All right girl."

All right girl? She had me waiting while she talked to her home girl. I was slightly irritated until she looked at me and reached her hand out.

"Let me see your stubs."

The intensity in her eyes as she studied the pay stubs scared me. "Rashad, you're an actor, right?"

"Exactly."

"How long is this job?"

I scrounged for an explanation. "Well, this is an ongoing job. I perform a lot of business negotiations for Mayo."

My face crumbled. That wasn't exactly where I was trying to go with that. Then I smiled. She smiled back. "Okay, everything looks good. I'll set you up for an interview Monday."

"I thought it had to go through the mayor and all of that before the interview?"

"It does. It's already been approved by everyone. I just needed to verify your income."

"So, everything's good."

"Yes, Rashad." She winked at me. "You can actually begin looking for your place."

"My place, like my house."

"Yes. You're going into the interview highly recommended. So, I'm sure it will be okay."

I strained to contain my excitement. "Thank you, Monique. Thank you."

"No problem. Just trying to help a brother out."

"Yo. I really appreciate it. When I get my house, I'll have to take you out to dinner."

As if she awaited the offer, she scooted up in her chair. "I could actually help you look at some places this weekend."

"Uh, I don't want to start looking until the money is in my hands."

"How many times do I have to explain that I got you?"

I wanted to reciprocate her flirtation, but I struggled with mixing business with pleasure. Leading her on would assure my grant, but could possibly ruin my income. "I do understand, but my work schedule is hectic right now."

Disappointment covered her face. "Okay."

When I noticed the clock on the wall, I mouthed, "Shit."

She frowned. "What?"

"I have to get out of here. What time is my interview again?"

"Ten sharp. Don't be late."

When I stepped out, it had begun to drizzle. It took almost five minutes to get a taxi. My clothes were damp as I headed back to my mother's apartment to grab our clothes. Then, I headed to Fatima's house. When she didn't answer the door, I took a deep breath. It's better for me to wait on her than have her wait on me.

Scene 25

FATIMA

I sat at the kitchen table sipping coffee when Rashad decided six-fifteen was the same as six o'clock. My cell phone rang. I let it go to voicemail. Finally, I strolled to the door to find him sitting on a bucket that was in between the double doors.

My weight shifted to one leg as I propped my hand on my hip. I shook my head and mouthed, "Look at you."

He stood to his feet. His eyes begged me to rescue him. When I opened up, he asked, "Can I get a hug?"

"Can you tell me how you got in my front door?"

"Uh. I've been meaning to talk to you about that." He forced me to hug him. "Your lock is a little tricky. Depending on how you close it, it doesn't always lock."

"You think I don't know that?"

He shrugged his shoulders and I strutted into the living room. "Well, I do. I thought that my leading man would see it and fix it."

He froze. Finally, he took a deep breath and shook his head. "Already on it."

"So, what's in the garment bags?"

He hung one over the back of the chair and handed me a BCBG bag. "For me?"

"Yeah, I want you to wear it tonight."

When I pulled the gorgeous cocktail dress from the bag, I felt like I wasn't mentally prepared for wherever we were going. Then again, the McDonalds bag told me that dinner obviously wasn't included.

I touched the satin fabric. "Rashad, I absolutely love it. You have good taste."

"No, you have good taste. I just observe what I like to see you in."

"You sure know how to flatter a girl."

He pulled the food from the bag. "Here. Eat a little something, there won't be any food where we're going."

"How are you going to take me somewhere where I can't eat?"

He kissed me. "I'm sorry. We have to hurry up, though. So let's eat and get it moving."

After we ate, we both went downstairs to get dressed. While he showered, I arched my eyebrows and began to pluck the hair on my chin. When he stepped out, he grabbed the tweezers from me.

"What are you doing?"

"Getting the hair off of my chin."

"You don't have any hair."

I grabbed his hand and rubbed my chin. "Do you feel it?"

"Yes, I feel peach fuzz."

"It bothers me."

He pulled me to him and I wrapped my hands around his damp body. "Teem, it doesn't bother me."

"I want my face to be as smooth as your body."

He kissed my forehead. "It is."

I continued depilating when he left the bathroom. Minutes passed and he returend to the doorway. "C'mon. We're going to be late."

"Look who's talking?"

"Okay, you're right. But can you at least try to hurry?"

"I don't feel comfortable when I'm all dressed up and I can feel hair—"

"That's not there."

"Leave me alone. I'll be ready in a minute."

When I stepped out of the bathroom, he was stretched out on the bed wearing his boxers and a champagne shirt. I sat beside him. "Wake up."

He opened his eyes. "I wasn't asleep. Just waiting for you. There's no reason for me to be dressed and ready to go when it's going to take you another thirty minutes." He looked at the time. "We're going to be late."

I tickled him. "Why can't we be late?"

"I'm just trying to work on being on time."

We laughed at his joke. He stood and stepped into his pants and adjusted his tie. When I slipped my dress on, I asked him to zip the side. He just looked at me.

"C'mon, baby, zip it."

He kissed my neckline. I huffed. "C'mon. Stop being so frisky."

"I'm not. I just think you're the most beautiful woman in the world."

Although I asked him to do it, I hated that he used that line. It made me question me. Am I really as beautiful as he claims or does he say this stuff to fulfill my requirements? The look in his eye and intense arch in his brow told me he was sincere. What should I go on?

As I fumbled in the bathroom with the final touches, he stood behind me. We looked like we were headed to the Academy Awards and he was nominated for Best Actor. He wrapped his arm around my shoulder. "Let's get out of here."

My buzzer rang. "Who could that be?"

"The limo."

"The limo?"

As he trampled up the steps, he said. "Yeah, the limo."

I made sure the lights were out and rushed upstairs. Rashad was at the front door waiting. He kissed me as I walked passed. The limo held up traffic. My heart raced as cars beeped their horns and I skipped down the steps. The driver held the door open and I slid in. I peeked out and watched Rashad ease down the steps and into the car like he owned the world. An opened chilled bottle of Moët sat in a bucket of ice.

When he got in, he pinched my cheek and said, "Happy?"

I nodded and he continued, "I love making you happy."

Isn't that the same as saying he loves me? As I overexaggerated his words, he poured the champagne into the flute glasses. When I swallowed, he smirked. I apologized. He raised his glass. "Can we toast, Woodrow the Wino?"

"It was spilling over."

"To loving each other's company."

There he goes with the love word again. I was happier than I'd been in a long time. When the limo pulled up in front of the Broadway theater, I kissed his cheek. "I knew we were going to see *The Color Purple*."

"You think you know everything?"

When the driver came to open our door, Rashad held my hand and we stepped into the line. When we got into the theater, I asked for a hug.

He bent down and asked, "What's up?"

"I just wanted to let you know that I'm really happy."

"I'm happy, too."

When the usher directed us to our seats, I squeezed his hand. He half-smiled at my excitement. I covered my smile, as we took our seats in the private orchestra for six. I peeked over the brass rails and wiggled in my chair. He leaned over and whispered, "I love how the smallest things bring you joy."

Okay, in less than an hour, the word love has been used to describe four situations. I curled my lips. *Oh, I think he likes me.*

As I rambled on about how many times I had watched the movie, he asked me to do the part when Sofia approached Celie in the field. My eyes shifted. "Ah, I dunno know that part."

He laughed. "Fatima, don't tell anyone else that you've seen *The Color Purple* a million times and you don't know that part."

I pouted. "Well, I remember it, but not verbatim."

"Tell me what you remember."

I rolled my neck. "Tell me what you remember."

"I didn't proclaim I saw the movie a million times."

I lowered my voice, "You told Harpo to beat me."

He laughed and wrapped his arm around my shoulder. "You are one funny lady."

My giggle tapered off as I felt his gaze on my profile. I turned slowly and touched his smooth, intense face. He grabbed my hand and kissed it. The lights flickered and we smiled. He nodded to the stage, "It's about to start."

Scene 26

RASHAD

Fatima had a smile plastered on her face from the moment we got to the theater. It was a pleasure to be in the company of a woman that respected art. I watched her as she watched the play. If I didn't know better, I would have thought this was her first live show. Her excitement brought me joy. I found myself humming the songs along with the crew.

When tears rolled down her eyes and interrupted her joyous expression, I frowned. Then, I concentrated on the scene where Celie and her sister were being forced apart. Fatima mocked the hand movements of the actors. She sniffed and mouthed, "Nothing but death."

Her pain permeated through her tense muscles. I massaged her shoulders. I assumed that thoughts of her husband upset her. Shortly after the scene, intermission gave her a moment to recuperate. I leaned over and asked, "Are you okay? Do you need anything?"

When her smile greeted my concern, I was relieved. She chuckled. "That part reminds me of me and my cousin. We were inseparable when we were kids. We would act that part out."

Why was I happy to know that her tears weren't about her husband? I smiled. "Really. Are you two still close?"

She shrugged her shoulders. "Not really. She's in Alabama. I'm here. I guess we grew apart."

"How old is she?"

"My age."

She stared into space and I stared at her. She spoke of Alabama like it was on the other side of the world. It was as if she'd left it behind. Did she think she was better than her family? What's up with her and Alabama? My mother and her sisters go to Trinidad two or three times a year. They refuse to lose that connection. What made her feel that family was disposable?

We stood outside of the theater as I tried to pull something from my trick bag. When she folded her arms over her chest, I removed my suit jacket and put it around her. She batted her eyes. "Thank you, handsome."

"No problem, gorgeous."

After a few minutes, she said, "Let's just get pizza."

"I can't take you for pizza looking like this."

She rolled her neck. "Why not?"

Whenever I was slightly convinced that she was uppity, she'd do something like this. "No. We're going somewhere nice."

"Nothing's better than pizza."

I chuckled. "I forgot."

We walked to the nearest pizzeria. Before I could grab napkins and have a seat, she had folded her slice and tilted her head back.

In between chewing, she asked, "What are you laughing at?"

I shrugged my shoulders. She said, "You're always laughing at nothing. I got a feeling that you think I'm silly."

"I think you're cute."

"Be honest with me."

"Fatima, I *am* being honest."

It was as if someone had written a script for her as well. She laughed on point. She knew how far to push it and she knew just how to show her appreciation. I meant everything I said to her. It disturbed me to think that she thought it was all an act.

We sat in the greasy pizzeria in our black tie attire like we had on jeans and tennis shoes. I appreciated her style. She was a rare treat.

When we walked into her house, we kissed for an eternity. I

told her how much joy she had brought me and she told me the same in the midst of our embrace. We made love in the middle of her living room floor. While we united as one, thoughts filled my head. *I could be here. I could fall in love.*

I collapsed on her and rested my head next to her silky mane. Suddenly, I felt like I heard someone say, "Yo. How are you going to disrespect me like that?"

My head popped up and frowned. Her husband frowned back at me, snapping me back into reality. I ran my hand down my face and rolled over. I took a deep breath and digested the discomfort. She rose on one elbow and rubbed my chest. "What happened?"

"Nothing."

"Something happened."

I raked her hair. "I'm fine, baby. You know how men get after sex."

"No."

Was that her way of saying that I wasn't allowed to be a man after sex, because she was paying me? My mind was filled with all sorts of questions. How have I succumbed to this?

I asked, "Do you want to go downstairs?" I began gathering our things. "Let's go."

She followed, but I could see she wanted to decipher my thoughts. Downstairs in her room, she begged for an explanation for my change of mood. Committed to staying in character, I kissed her forehead. "Baby, I'm fine."

She huffed. "If you say so."

As we showered, she scrutinized my actions. I joked and made idle conversation. When we lay in her bed, I thanked her again. She rubbed my face. "Thank you, Rashad."

Scene 27

FATIMA

When I walked upstairs, I discovered surprisingly that Rashad was already gone. Assuming he'd gone to get breakfast, I walked into the kitchen to put on a pot of coffee. A bag with a bagel and a note attached sat on the table: *Coffee in microwave.—Rash*

My temples throbbed. *Where are you?* After six weeks, disappearing in the morning is definitely out of character. After I called him several times and received no answer, I stormed through the house spitting obscenities. Finally, I called Mya.

"Mya, I need help."

She giggled. "Ah, yeah."

"Stop. I'm not playing. I thought this would be easy, but . . ."

"You're catching feelings."

I sighed. "No, I mean. Maybe. How long do you think I can do this?"

"Tima, I really don't know. It's taken away some of the loneliness. Right?"

"Yeah, but if I end it now, then I'm going to miss him."

"Why do you want to end it?"

"Because I didn't expect to feel like this?"

"How do you think he feels?"

"I think he's just in it for the money."

"And you're just in it for the company."

My phone beeped. Before checking the ID, I quickly clicked over. "Hello."

"Hi, Fatima."

I mouthed, "Damn!"

It was my tenant on the third floor. "Hi, Kelli."

"Remember I told you that my faucet has been leaking."

"Yeah."

"Um. I thought you were going to have someone fix it?"

Here I was falling for the damn man that I hired to take care of these types of things and neglecting to enforce his chores. At least this was an issue that I knew how to fix myself.

"Kelli, I can fix it. I'll be up in about thirty minutes."

When I clicked over, Mya giggled. "I guess that was Rashad."

"No, it was a reminder that Rashad is getting paid for nothing."

"Fatima, I think you're tripping."

"Why would you think that?"

"Yesterday, when we talked, you were happy as a bug in a rug. Now, you're talking like you don't want to do this anymore. What happened?"

"We went out last night. Had a wonderful time. After we had sex, he all of a sudden got distant. Then, I wake up this morning. He's gone. He's not answering his phone. Kelli just called. Her sink is broke. So, I have to fix it myself, because he's nowhere to be found."

"If I'm not mistaken, he's just supposed to treat you well and be there when you need him. You're not supposed to know where he is every second of the day. You need to figure out want you want. You can't have it all."

"How many times do you have to tell me that?"

"As many times as it takes for it to sink in."

"All right, Ms. Know-it-all. I have to go fix Kelli's sink. Maybe we'll hook up later."

I threw on some sweats and grabbed the toolbox from the kitchen. Before I left, I tried Rashad again. It went straight to voicemail. After slamming the phone down, I looked at the picture of Derrick and sucked my teeth and yelled, "Who told you to die?"

I stomped upstairs to Kelli's apartment. Uncertain if I was more pissed that I forgot to tell Rashad to fix this weeks ago or my inability to locate him this morning, I tapped on her door. Just as I entered, her boyfriend was leaving. As if it were his responsibility, I thought why can't he fix it? I mumbled, "Hey."

Knowing her rent is way below market value, she blushed. "I didn't want to worry you. It's just been awhile."

"I'm sorry."

Standing in her bathroom, I tried to recollect how I'd done this previously. After opening the pack of new washers, I grabbed the wrench and began loosening the faucet. This is ridiculous. *Why am I doing this myself? What the hell am I paying Rashad for?*

Out of nowhere, water spurted out and smacked me in the face as I complained. I tried to cover the continuous surge with my hand. It spewed through my fingers. After my face and my clothes were soaked, I suppressed my pride and yelled out for Kelli. She rushed in to witness the geyser in her bathroom. "Oh my goodness. Do you know what you're doing?"

In the middle of being hosed down, I had to stop and roll my eyes. "What do you think?"

She scurried around the apartment. "What are we supposed to do?"

I yelled, "Call somebody!"

The water was practically up to my ankles; still I tried to decrease the pressure by covering it with both hands.

She screamed, "Who?"

"Any damn body. Call somebody."

After close to ten minutes and a two-foot flood, her boyfriend returned. He rushed in, opened the cabinet and turned the water off. He smirked. "Don't you know you're supposed to turn the water off before you do anything?"

Oh yeah, I forgot that part of the instructions. Kelli stood at the bathroom door. "Everything's wet." She looked at her fully loaded makeup case. "All my makeup is ruined."

"Kelli, I'm sorry. I'll replace everything."

She huffed. Afraid to continue with my maintenance respon-
sibilities, I batted my eyes at her boyfriend. "Can you do this? I'll
pay you."

He sucked his teeth. I frowned. *No his lazy ass isn't acting irritated.* He should have offered to do it anyway. I'm just a poor
little widow. As we debated with our body language, Kelli
whined about how I drenched everything she owned. Once he
agreed to change the washer, I stepped out of the pond and into
the hall. Water gushed from my shoes. My pants legs flapped
around my ankles. "Kelli, I'll be back with the wet vac."

Still hysterical about her stuff, she ignored me. I hung my
head and slouched down to my apartment. Suddenly, I was overwhelmed and wanted to cry. Before going backup stairs, I
checked the caller ID on my phones. Rashad still hadn't called.

As I pulled the heavy vacuum up three flights of stairs, the
tears fell. I stood outside Kelli's door and eavesdropped. They
called me every ditsy, spoiled-brat in the book, which triggered
more tears. It's not my fault that I was left with all this. I never
wanted to be a landlord. After taking a deep breath, I tapped
softly on the door.

"Come in," Kelli said.

Before turning the knob, I dabbed beneath my eyes with my
fingertips. When I walked in, they both wore smirks of curiosity.
Could it be possible that I heard everything? I curled my lips to
confirm that I did.

I proceeded with my cleanup duties. After sucking up an entire five gallons of water, I prayed that her boyfriend would help
me empty the water in the tub. Unfortunately, he didn't. I was
forced to tilt the heavy bucket alone. My constant grunts didn't
trigger any sympathy.

I pulled two hundred bucks from my damp pocket. Soggy
money is better than no money at all. Obviously they agreed as
they both reached out for it. I pulled it back to my chest. "Kelli,
one-fifty is for you for your inconvenience. Fifty dollars is for you
for fixing the sink." I looked at Kelli. "If you need more, let me
know."

Although I knew I was setting myself up to be played, I didn't care. She nodded. "I'll let you know."

I struggled out of the door and down the stairs with my vacuum. Seconds after I closed my front door, my phone rang. It was my tenant on the second floor. She was a middle-aged lady that never caused much trouble. I took a breath before answering.

"Fatima, I have a leak."

I covered the receiver and mouthed, "Shit!" Then, I moved my hand. "Ms. Harris, Kelli had a flood in her apartment. Where's your leak?"

"In the bathroom."

I huffed. "Yeah, I'll have someone look at it. I'll see if they can come out today. Will that be okay?"

"Yes, honey. Just let me know."

"Okay, I will."

After I peeled off my damp clothes, I plopped on my bed and sank my face in my hands.

Scene 28

RASHAD

I left Fatima's house at six in the morning to get her breakfast and to get home to change into some old clothes. When I crept into the apartment at the crack of dawn, I heard my mother's television, so I tiptoed around. I was nearly out the door in a ragged T-shirt, old jeans, and Timberlands when my mother called my name. I stood in the hallway. "What's up?"

"I don't want nothing. I wanted to make sure it was you."

"Yeah, it's me. I'm about to leave, though."

"Where are you going?"

"I'll be back."

I darted from the house before she had more questions. I arrived at the worksite at seven-forty-five. The contractors were already there moving and shaking. I watched the orchestrated operation for several minutes before Marty arrived. He pulled up in a Benz CLS and parked it on the dusty street. He grabbed two hard hats from his trunk. I stood up and shook his hand.

"Glad that you could make it this morning."

"Oh, I wouldn't miss it. I'm really excited."

"Yeah, it's exciting. I want to walk you through one of the houses that are almost done."

He instructed me to put on the hard hat and we headed to a house at the end of the block. He asked, "You've done some rehabbing before, right?"

"Uh, I've done a little." I chuckled. "When I was a teenager."

"Okay, that's fine. If you follow my lead, you'll never have to get down on your hands and knees with a hammer again."

I frowned. He clarified, "Managing construction projects is the way to go. As a worker, you can only perform one job at a time, right?" I nodded. He said, "Exactly, but if you know how to manage your contractors and can identify the shortcuts that they try to take, you can manage multiple projects at the same time."

He opened the door. "For your sake, I'm going to go through this apartment with a fine-tooth comb. You'll see why managing this stuff is important."

There was orange tape on various things. The apartment looked flawless to me. Marty pointed to one of the pieces of tape. "What do you think is wrong there?"

"Ah?"

He showed me how the contractors painted over a crack in the drywall instead of spackling it. Then we went into the kitchen, and he pointed to the ceiling. "Do you see the huge gap in the crown molding? These are the things you have to worry about."

He opened up the cabinet. "Look in there, what do you see?"

I joked, "Another piece of orange tape."

"No, actually the cabinet is cracked in there and that's a path for mice to get through."

He explained the importance of identifying all these things before the contractors are gone. We left that house and went into another one. It was practically still a shell with some of the framing done.

"You want to make sure that the electrician, the plumber, and the other contractors are all in sync. Timing is everything. This comes with experience, but if you shadow me, you'll get it down."

"What do you mean by timing?"

"You need to estimate how long your contractors need to frame, before you have the electrician and plumber come in.

What happens if the framing is wrong and you've already brought the electrician in? You have problems."

"Yeah, I can imagine."

My head throbbed. This was a lot to master, but as long as he was willing to counsel me, I would be here.

"But it's almost like science after awhile. Managing construction is all about knowing what has to be done, not necessarily knowing how to do it." He chuckled. "Do you know how to learn that?" Judging from the bewildered look on my face, he answered, "Read."

I agreed, "Well, I've been doing that."

"And there's a certain confidence that hands-on provides as well."

"What do you think the chances of me being able to manage my first project without a lot of prior management experience?"

"I'm not going to say you won't have any pitfalls, but everyone has to start somewhere."

I couldn't afford any pitfalls. This would be my home. He noticed my disappointment and said, "Some people manage to get this done without even attempting to take a course. My course should make sure you're well prepared. If not, I promise to help you as much as I can."

Somehow, I believed him. This seemed like it was his passion. How could his five-foot-five body hold all the energy he possessed? Some of it transferred to me. My mind traveled at the speed of light as I imagined how I would get this done.

Marty dropped me off at my mother's apartment. I rushed in like a big kid. Everything seemed within reach. I dashed into the shower. I couldn't wait to go back to Fatima's. Maybe we could do something like take a walk in the park, shop a little. The sun was shining and I wanted to have a nice, relaxing day.

It was around one, after I chatted with my mother and finally got dressed. I rushed to the pizzeria, because I knew Fatima would be hungry. On my way to her house, I called. She picked up and didn't say anything.

I said, "What's up with my Teem?"

"What is the purpose of our agreement?"

"What? What are you talking about?"

"Whenever I need you, you're never around."

"Fatima, don't start it."

"I thought you were supposed to help me."

Though the frustrated tremble in her voice told me otherwise, I said, "You're joking. Right?"

"You're not on your job."

My excitement quickly evaporated, but for my sanity, I said, "Tell me you're playing."

"Do I sound like I'm playing?"

As the attitude and inflection in her voice traveled through the phone, crushing my pride, all I could do was say, "Fatima, I'm out."

I hung up the phone. I will not have a woman yell at me. I'm a man's man. I can't do it anymore. As much as I enjoy being around her, it's these times when the bad drowns the good. The money is not worth disrespect. She can take this role and stuff it.

As I sprinted down her street, suddenly I remembered the good things, the way we laugh together, and how much fun we have and I questioned my decision to let it all go. Yet, my anger told me my fear to let this go wasn't about Fatima, it was just the loss of a companion. *Let it go, Rashad. Find a woman that isn't paying you.*

I pounded on her buzzer. When she opened the door, I stormed in and yelled, "What happened between last night and this morning?"

Her neck twirled with each syllable. "You weren't here."

It angered me that I was doing everything she asked me to do and more, yet she still wasn't satisfied. "What the hell do you want from me?"

"I want you to do your damn job!"

I walked up into her face. "My job? My job?" Her eyes blinked rapidly. I huffed. "All I think about is this damn job. All I do is think about ways to make you happy."

She sucked her teeth. "That's what you get paid for."

"I don't get paid to genuinely care about you. I get paid to act like I give a damn." I huffed. "This dumbass script."

Her mouth hung open. "What did you just say?"

"You heard me."

"When did it become a dumbass script? You're getting paid for that dumbass script. My money isn't dumb."

"Teem, you know what's sad. Everything I do for you is because I want to. That's why it's a dumbass script. Do you understand that?"

Her eyes lowered. Suddenly, I wasn't as pissed. Fear was written all over her face as she shrugged her shoulders. A strong desire to make her secure and to let her know that I wouldn't leave her too overwhelmed me. Her arms locked tightly around my torso. I kissed her forehead and said, "Attraction can't be bought. I would be here for free. You know that, right?" She shrugged her shoulders and I said, "Believe me."

She nodded on my chest. "Are you sure?"

"Yes, I'm sure."

She sighed, but I knew she thought I was here primarily for the money. Five weeks ago, she would have been absolutely right. Even I am tripping on how my feelings are traveling so rapidly. I spend hours wondering what it is about her that has me so caught up.

She looked up at me and pushed her finger in my chest. "Do you know what I've been through today?"

"Why don't we sit down, have a slice of pizza, and talk about it."

She sucked her teeth and slouched in the chair. Her eyes rolled in her head as she released a disgruntled sigh. "The chick upstairs called me about her leaky faucet, and . . ." she curled her lips, "somebody wasn't here."

I chuckled. "So, it's my fault. Huh?"

"No, but I had to go fix it myself."

"A leaky faucet is no emergency. Why didn't you just wait?"

"Because . . ."

I softly knocked on her forehead. "Because you have a hard head."

"Well my hard head landed me in a damn puddle of water."

"What happened?"

"I forgot to turn the water off."

"No."

"Yeah. And it took damn near ten minutes before Kelli's boyfriend rescued me." She giggled. "Water was everywhere. We could have gone swimming."

The harder I laughed the worst she made it sound. "The ceiling was wet. All of Kelli's toiletries were soaked. I felt so stupid."

I stood up, huddled over her, and wrapped my arms around her. "Is that why you wanted to fire me?"

"Oh, you were fired! I was so pissed."

"Why were you mad at me?"

"Because I woke up to an empty bed. Then, you didn't answer your phone. Had you answered your phone, I wouldn't have felt so helpless."

I stroked her hair and reassured her. "You know I'm not going anywhere."

She pushed me away. "You know you're on probation."

I fell back into my chair. "Probation?"

"Mmm-huh. Three strikes you're out."

"How many strikes do I have now?"

"One and a half."

We burst out laughing. I shook my head. "Teem, you are a trip. I guess this will be a deduction from my pay?"

As her chin dropped, she snickered. "You noticed?"

"It's not heavy."

"It must be if you noticed."

"Fatima, look, it's really okay."

When she realized that I was not concerned, she lifted her head. "Oh, by the way, can you go upstairs to check out Ms. Harris's ceiling?"

"Don't tell me the water seeped through?"

With her lips poked out for my sympathy, she nodded. I shook my head. "I see why you were tripping."

She rolled her eyes. "Why didn't you tell me you were leaving?"

"You sleep like a damn rock. Even if I wanted to wake you up, I couldn't." I stood up. "Where are the tools?"

"Sitting at the door where I left them."

I glanced around to the front door and noticed the large tool-box in the middle of the floor. "A'ight. Is Ms. Harris expecting me?"

She grabbed the phone and lifted her index finger. "Let me call her first."

After she spoke to Ms. Harris, I headed up to the second floor. She opened up. "Hello, young man."

"How are you today?"

"I was fine until it started raining in my bathroom."

I laughed. "Let me check it out for you."

She ushered me to the bathroom and pointed to the ceiling. The drywall looked pretty saturated. I gasped. "Wow. That's bad."

Inwardly, I laughed as I imagined Fatima when the water began gushing out. She nodded. "Yeah, I'm afraid it will fall in."

"I'm going to carve it out and put some plastic up there today. I'll come back tomorrow or Monday to put up a new piece of drywall."

She huffed. "Okay."

I bent down to open the toolbox. When I noticed DM engraved in the handle, I immediately felt the need to get my own tools. But with this sweet lady standing patiently in the hall, I figured it wasn't the time to be petty. I took a deep breath and found the saw.

When I climbed up on the sink, Ms. Harris thought it would be a good time to start a casual conversation.

"So, are you the super?"

"Ah, I'm just helping Fatima out."

"I've seen you around frequently. Are you a good friend of Fatima's?"

I nodded as I began to cut out her ceiling.

"That's good. She hasn't had a man around here since Mr. Mayo."

"Yeah, I know."

"So, are you her boyfriend?"

Ironically, I didn't know the answer to her question. Before responding, I cleared my throat. "We're good friends."

"I don't know how she survived his death. She went on with her life without missing a beat. I don't even remember her mourning."

I grunted because I felt like Fatima was still in mourning. Ms. Harris continued, "He definitely took care of her."

Like I need to hear that again. Hoping that my lack of response would send her away, I pretended to be preoccupied. Unfortunately, she didn't get the memo. "They were so close."

I huffed like I struggled with the cutting. "Ms. Harris, do you have a bucket?"

"Sure, let me get it."

When she returned, I put the bucket up to the hole I'd cut for the water to drain. As it trickled into the bucket, Ms. Harris stood at the door with her arms folded. *Lady, isn't there a Lifetime movie on or something?*

When the water became a slow drip, I reached for the saw and cut away a large square and covered the hole with a plastic bag. Before I left, Ms. Harris said, "She's a sweetheart. I've been praying for someone to come along."

She winked at me and I nodded. "All right. I'll have Fatima give you a call to let you know when I'm coming to patch up the ceiling."

When I returned to the apartment, Fatima giggled. "White powder is all over your face and hair." She kissed me. "It's sexy, though."

Ms. Harris comments played in my head as I looked at Fatima prance around, concealing the obvious. This poor girl is in pain.

Scene 29

RASHAD

Marty gave me all the information I could ever need about managing the renovation project. What happened to the part about finding the property? When I started this house-hunting, I was so pumped with adrenaline that I didn't realize how hard it would be. Each time I stepped into a vacant or condemned home, I become more and more discouraged. How can I make a dump into a castle? The cracked walls, nasty wallpaper, sunken floors, and missing steps overwhelmed me. How does a house ever get in this condition? The smell of mold and dust make my stomach somersault in disgust.

I roamed Harlem on my twenty-eighth birthday looking at dumps. Had it not been for the birthday card that Fatima gave me this morning, today would have completely passed me by. The weeks have been zooming by as well. In between searching for this house, studying renovating the house, interviewing contractors, and not to mention taking care of Fatima, I'm about to lose my mind.

If nothing pans out by the weekend, I may be forced to give up. When Monique told me that so many people think they can do this, but even when they have the money in hand, many come back and say forget it, I laughed, but now I'm thinking about how I'm going to join the crew of quitters.

My broker and I walked up to a house on 127th Street. Before we walked in, he confirmed, "You're going to love this place."

When the door swung open, the rotted smell made my nose wrinkle and forced me to squint. After I opened my eyes, what I had envisioned was before me. I hung my head. "This is unbe-lievable."

"Yeah, it has some structural issues, but the frame is great. The stairs to the basement have collapsed, but from this floor up, you're good."

I nodded. He continued, "What makes this place a jewel is that all you're doing is renovating versus gutting it out and de-signing an entire architecture. This is the first time I've shown this place. I can't believe it sat for so long. This is definitely a diamond in the rough."

My smile stretched wider and wider as we toured the safe parts of the home. It felt like this was my place. Before I became overly confident, I asked, "What are my chances?"

"There were no contracts on this place this morning. If you want to put a contract down, we can head over to the office now."

When we left the house, I could have skipped down the steps. Suddenly, my negative feelings were gone. After we fin-ished the paperwork, my anxiety level increased. I crossed my fingers, my legs, and prayed for all the luck in the world.

"So, how long does it take for them to accept the contract?"

"It usually takes about a week. You know City Props will have an inspector come out before the contract is actually approved. They have a vested interest."

"Yeah. I know."

"So, you'll know something by next week."

How was I going to contain my excitement for so long? Not to mention, I'd rather be disappointed immediately rather than wait seven days.

Trying to assure my chances, I decided to go over to City Props myself, just to warn Monique to look out for my contract. When I showed up, she blushed like I was just the person she wanted to see.

"Hello, Rashad."

"Hey, Mo."

She snickered. "When did I become Mo?"

I raised my hand for a high-five. Without knowing why, she slapped my hand. "You became Mo when I found my house."

"Oh, I'm so happy to hear that."

"Yeah, it's been almost a month since I started looking. I was about to give up.

"Most people do."

I smiled and her eyes gravitated to my pearly whites. Her head tilted. "I'm really happy for you."

"Thank you."

"No, it was all you."

"You pushed it through for me."

"Yeah, but . . ."

I squinted. "Are you okay?"

"Yeah, I'm going to miss you popping in here worrying me."

I chuckled, but she didn't so much as crack a smile. "I'll still come to visit."

"No, you won't. But anyway, are you going to take me to see the house?"

"Don't you have to see it before everything is approved?"

"No, it's above me now. The inspectors make the decisions from here."

"I can schedule an appointment with my broker for us to see the inside."

"That's cool. I'd definitely like to see it. Schedule an appointment and get back to me."

I thanked God for the best birthday present of all time and rushed home to get ready for my date with Fatima. She demanded that I meet her at her house at seven sharp.

Scene 30

FATIMA

When I walked into my office, Kia wore a look of fear. I smiled. "What's wrong?"

She shook her head. "Alana Lynch's book has gone to print and she called yelling. There are tons of errors."

My heart dropped and I winced. "What kind of errors?"

"Misspellings. Punctuation." She shrugged her shoulders. "It's bad."

I stormed into my office. "Get Alana on the phone."

Before I could drop my bag, Kia buzzed: "Fatima, she's on line one."

After several deep breaths, I picked up the receiver. "Alana, what happened?"

"You tell me what happened?"

"We're not going to get anywhere with all the yelling."

"I returned my corrections a week late and was told that it had already gone to press."

"So let me understand this. When you returned the final proofs, they were late?"

"Don't make this my fault."

"Trust me. I'm not making this your fault. I just want to know where the breakdown occurred."

As she sniffled on the other end, I frowned at the receiver. Her voice trembled, "I feel humiliated."

"Let me speak to my production editor and I'll give you a call back."

She slammed the phone down. Why am I even here? Egos take the fun out of everything. It made Derrick proud to say that his wife was slated to be one of the youngest editorial directors in the business. As I stood up to go to the production department, I began to wonder if I was here just to pay tribute to him.

When I walked out of my office, Kia shrugged her shoulders and I curled my lips. To calm her frazzled expression, I waved my hand. "Don't sweat it."

When I walked into the production editor's office, she sighed. "Fatima, what should I have done?"

"How many errors is she talking about?"

"It's a good number."

She flipped through the proofs and showed me several errors. I cringed. "Those should have been caught before it even went to her."

"Fatima, it slipped through the cracks."

"The cracks? This is an embarrassment."

"Yeah, but it doesn't justify reprinting. It's just not worth it."

As I looked over the errors, they were so blatant. How could this have happened? As tears welled in my eyes, she patted my arm. "Fatima, I'm sorry."

"I guess I'll have to copyedit everything that comes through here because I can't depend on you guys to hire competent freelancers."

"She edited several of our books in the past. I don't know what happened."

"She'll never edit anything else."

"Fatima, calm down."

"Calm down? It's my reputation on the line. Not yours. Not the freelancer's. Mine." I turned to the acknowledgments. "Look whose name is here, mine. That's what everyone will see when they read this trash."

I dropped the proofs and the pages sprawled all over the floor. As I stormed out, she said, "It can be corrected in the second printing."

I shouted, "That's too late."

Tears rolled down my face and I left the building to get myself together. I went to get a caramel macchiato with a triple shot of espresso. I needed support when I talked to Alana. She didn't deserve this and neither did I.

After several deep breaths, I got the courage to call her back. She pretty much called me incompetent and threatened to go to another house. I fought to restore her faith in me and promised to edit personally all her future works. After all of my pleading, we ended the conversation on an amicable note.

I lay my head on my desk. Kia came in and asked if I was okay. I propped my face up on my folded hands. "I need a vacation."

"Take me with you."

It hit me—I felt responsible for all of my authors. I looked at my pile that was headed to production for copyediting and knew I couldn't survive another slip through the cracks. After organizing the pile by release date, I buried my head into the pages. I scrutinized every word. It was the least I could do.

When Kia came in to tell me she was gone for the day, I told her to send all calls to voicemail. I was so entrenched that when I looked up twenty minutes after she walked out, it had actually been two hours. My head collapsed on the desk. When I awoke from my nap, it was ten o'clock. I jumped up. Oh my God! It's Rashad's birthday. I'm late. I scurried around, piling stuff in my bag. How did time get away from me?

Ten missed calls, all from Rashad. I quickly called back. He didn't answer. I sent him a text message. He didn't respond. I rushed home. When I jumped from the taxi, he was on the steps with a bottle of Cuervo in his hand. I ran up the steps. "I'm so sorry. I—"

He kissed me. "It's cool. Don't sweat it. I was worried about you. Are you okay?"

"But—"

"All that matters is that you're here now."

"I—"

"Teem, I'm just happy to see you."

"I feel horrible. How could I mess up on your birthday?"

"You're human."

Still, I felt the need to explain. "I had a terrible day at work and I just felt overwhelmed, laid my head down, and had the calls sent to voicemail, so I never heard the phone ring once. How long have you been here?"

"Since seven."

My eyes watered. "No."

"Teem, it's not heavy. I've been sitting here, thinking about life." He raised the half-full bottle. "Drinking Cuervo and just enjoying nature."

"Really?"

"Really."

"Why didn't you answer the phone?"

He chuckled and held his phone by the antenna. "My battery died after I called you a million times."

I felt like I should tell him that I loved him or should I say that I loved his patience.

"I had reservation at—"

"We'll just have to do something else."

"I don't know—"

"That's what you pay me for . . ."

When we walked into the house, I sat on the couch. "Rashad, let's celebrate tomorrow."

"We can still hang out tonight. Let me make some calls."

How could he be so considerate, even when I was inconsiderate? My head hung as I watched him plan his own party. I was completely exhausted and really didn't have the energy to do anything. I'm sure he thought I was a self-centered witch, so I just pretended I was wide awake.

He looked at me. "You ready?"

"As ready as I'm going to be. Where are we going?"

"To this karaoke spot."

Couldn't he have picked a place that I could lay low? I felt trifling for not being enthused and I felt even worst that I didn't as much as have a cake for him after all the days he made me feel special.

When we walked into the club, the hostess led us to a private room. I wanted to curl up on the couch, but Rashad shoved a huge book of song selections in my face. I flipped through the pages while Rashad ordered the food and drinks, and wasn't inspired to sing anything.

He chuckled and by the time I looked up to see what humored him, he had programmed a song. He stood in front of me with the microphone in his hand. The speakers blasted: "Solid as a rock . . ."

Suddenly, I felt like I'd overdosed on caffeine. I popped up. My parents' theme song was on. He reached out for my hand. I danced to him. How did he know that I loved this song? It's like one of my family's heirlooms. As we glided to the old school beat, I felt a closeness that frightened me. He sang in my ear: "'And for love's sake. Each mistake, you forgave.'"

I sang back: "'And soon both of us learned to trust . . .' "

We danced in our own universe until the waitress came to summon us back to earth. "Your food will be here soon."

She handed me an Apple Martini and gave Rashad a shot of Cuervo. While I took a sip of my drink, he swallowed his entire shot. He squinted and smacked his lips. I stood there and admired him. I wiped his mouth with my thumb. "You are so sweet."

He leaned in for a kiss. We swayed to silence. Then, he said, "Okay, we're going to select a few duets. If you want, you can sing some songs alone." He shrugged his shoulders. "It's whatever. We're gonna party like it's my birthday." He kissed me again. "Okay."

"Thank you, Rashad."

"For what?"

"Not making me feel like shit."

"Baby, you need to stop being so hard on yourself. You need to stop being hard on everybody. People mess up, but it doesn't mean anything."

I tried to digest his wisdom, as we went through the song list again. He pointed. "We can sing 'Make It Last Forever'?"

Why is he putting thoughts in my head? I shrugged my shoulders. "Why don't you find a song to sing to me?"

He agreed. After a few pages, he nodded. "Okay, I got one."

He programmed the song in and the music began. Although I couldn't make out the melody, I bobbed my head. The song title appeared on the screen: "You Are My Lady" by Freddie Jackson. Before my time, but still I blushed. As the lyrics displayed, my smile got wider. He serenaded me with a rock and snap. Soon, I was eager to sing to him. I chose Whitney Houston's "You Give Good Love."

His eyes got glossy as I sang the song. Okay, either he should be in Hollywood or he's feeling me too. I reprimanded my suspicious thoughts.

After a few more drinks and several more songs, I took a moment to realize how happy I'd been over the last few months. I wrapped my arms around his neck and leaned in to stare into his eyes. Seconds passed, finally I said, "I haven't been this happy since . . ."

His eyes dimmed like he knew I would mention Derrick, but I paused because I honestly could not remember ever feeling so free. I smiled. He slightly smirked and I kissed it away. "Rashad, I can't ever remember being this happy."

Immediately, his glow reappeared and I felt guilty for admitting that he possibly made me as happy as I was with Derrick. He caressed my back. "Teem, thank you. Thank you for changing my life."

My eyebrows gathered. "Huh?"

He chuckled and tapped his forehead into mine. "I love your personality." He laughed harder. "You sure can mess up the moment."

"No, you just threw me off."

He rubbed my face with the back of his hand to calm my giggles. "You've helped me see life totally different."

"And you have done the same for me."

Scene 31

FATIMA

My body hadn't had a moments rest and two days after Rashad's birthday, I was pegged to make the cheese tray for Mya's engagement party. After working until ten two days straight, I decided to leave work early. I caught the train up to 125th, so I could drop into H&M to get something cheap and cute and then catch a taxi to Fairway grocery store. After I spent thirty minutes or more there, I traveled down the street headed to the MAC store. I called Mya to see if she needed anything.

As soon as she answered, I looked across the street and saw Rashad standing on the corner. He must be leaving the gym. Why is he just standing there looking into space? Who is he waiting for? Distracted by his presence, I failed to say anything as Mya yelled into my ear, "Did you call me or did I call you?"

"I called you. I'm sorry; I was headed to the MAC store and wanted to . . ."

"What, Tima?"

On the opposite corner from where I stood, an attractive young lady hopped off the bus and into Rashad's arms. As Mya begged me to speak, I mouthed, "Oh my God."

Her face lit up as Rashad stroked her shoulder. My heart sank deeper and deeper until my knees buckled. Quickly, I found myself stooping behind an earring vendor's stand. Could she be the reason that nothing I did wrong upset him? Still I held my phone up to my ear. As the street vendor urged me to look at his merchandise, Mya shouted on the other end. I remained speechless.

Her eyes batted at him and Rashad's attraction to her was just as obvious. She was young, plain, petite; everything opposite of me. I judged maybe no more than twenty-four years old. He ran his hand over her limp ponytail and she looked up to him in admiration. I envied their interaction. He adored her just because. And here, I'm paying him to spoil some other chick. Why was my heart pounding so hard? My eyes filled. This is just a job for him. I've confused fantasy with reality. Who thought this was a brilliant idea?

They crossed the street together and looked like they had so much to talk about. I wondered if she knew about me. How had he explained our situation to her?

As their backs got farther away from me, my phone that was already up to my ear rang and startled me. Mya shouted on the other end, "Tima, are you okay?"

"I just saw Rashad with another woman."

To my surprise, I heard sympathy in her voice. "No! Tima. Where?"

"I'm on a hundred and twenty-fifth."

"Are you sure it wasn't just a friend?"

"It didn't look like a friend. It just didn't feel right."

"So, what are you going to do?"

"Maybe I should just tell him I don't need him anymore."

"Didn't you tell him if he began developing feelings for someone else, he had to quit?"

"Maybe he thinks I won't find out and he'll play the situation until he's busted. Why give up the money too soon?"

"Do you really think he would do that?"

"He's an actor. I don't know anything about him."

"Tima, you have to go with your gut. What do you feel about him?"

Still standing on the same corner stunned, I looked up Frederick Douglass, wondering where they were headed, hoping they'd return so he would know I saw him.

I was no longer in the mood to shop for makeup, so I hopped in a taxi and went to the grocery store. Mya tried to encourage me to look at both sides, but the attraction between them was too magnetic to ignore. We concluded that I should just probe him about his other relationship. If it turns out that there is something there, I'd give him his two-weeks' notice.

When Rashad arrived at my house on time, my heart ached. I flip-flopped with how to confront him. As I stood behind the door, I took deep breaths. He came in and hugged me. Half-heartedly, I hugged him back. My anxiety converted to anger, as the same I'm-happy-to-see-you grin that he had when he met his girlfriend earlier spread across his face. I wanted to claw his eyes out because they were the ones lying to me.

When I turned to walk in the kitchen, he followed. "You look lovely this evening."

"Yeah, right."

He chuckled. I shoved the cheese tray into his chest. "Here, hold this."

"Do I get a kiss or something?"

"Haven't you had enough kisses today?"

"Girl, stop playin'." He kissed me and I turned my face. "Why are you acting shady?" he asked.

"No reason. Are you ready?"

He put the tray on the table and grabbed my arm. "C'mon, baby. Give me a hug. I had a good day."

"I bet."

He ignored my insinuation that I knew he'd been with another woman, which frustrated me more. "Rashad, let's go."

He tossed his hands up in the air and grabbed the tray from the table. "A'ight, Teem. Whatever."

He stomped to the front door, and his frustration forced me to become defensive. "Why are you tripping?"

He held the front door open and raised his eyebrows. He chuckled in between short pauses. "You . . . think . . . I'm . . . tripping?"

I strutted past him. "Yes."

On the taxi ride to Mya's house, he massaged my knee. "Have you ever been diagnosed with schizophrenia?"

I punched him in his arm. "Only Mya can joke like that."

"I'm just saying, we had a great morning and now you have an attitude. I just don't get it."

I gasped and stared out the window. Feeling the need to approach him about what I'd witnessed, but afraid to admit to myself that he'd become more than a stand-in agitated me. Finally, I turned to face him again. "Do you remember your termination policy?"

"Are you trying to fire me?"

"Are you trying to quit?"

His silence scared me. I wasn't sure if I wanted to know anymore. Still, I asked again, "Are you?"

"How many times have I told you that I'm here for you? Not for the money. Even if you fire me, I'll still ring your doorbell every morning."

I sucked my teeth. "You need to be on the big screen."

"I'm serious."

We walked into the party among a group of film industry friends. Some recognized Rashad and that made me uncomfortable. How had I downgraded to a starving actor? He couldn't be the mysterious entrepreneur among them because they knew him and many of them had rejected him. My head hung slightly. Rashad wrapped his arm around my shoulder and we headed into the kitchen to greet Mya and Frankie.

Mya looked up inquisitively. "Hey, Rashad."

We hugged and she whispered, "Everything okay?"

I rolled my eyes at Rashad. She repeated my actions. Rashad shook Frankie's hand. "Man, how do you deal with these two?"

Frankie looked at us. "Man, they sucked me in. I got tricked."

I grabbed a paper cup and poured a drink from the pitcher labeled "Commitment." After taking a swallow, I asked, "Mya, what's in here?"

"Girl, that's a Cosmo. I was just trying to label the drinks something associated with engagement or commitment, you know?"

I poured another cup and handed it to Rashad. "Here, have some commitment."

He laughed and left us in the kitchen. With Rashad less than two steps out of the room, Mya said, "Did you ask him if he was falling for someone else?"

"No, I asked him if he wanted to quit. He claims he'd be here even if I wasn't paying him."

"He's full of it."

I poured my second cup and sipped. "Who thought this script was a great idea?"

"Don't even play, Tima."

My drink sprinkled out when I laughed. Mya rolled her eyes. "You are so crazy."

When I left the kitchen to mingle with the crowd, I chatted with several of Mya's colleagues and prayed no one would ask how I got hooked up with Rashad.

Standing merely steps away from him, I eavesdropped. He spoke to a gentleman that I didn't know. "Yeah, I just put a contract on a brownstone today. I'm thinking I'll fix it up and flip it."

The guy engaged him in his lie. Rashad continued, "Yeah, there are actually grants you can apply for that will give you money to fix up abandoned properties. People have no clue how much money's out there. You just have to get it. They just need to make sure you're financially stable."

The guy listened intently. I was impressed. At least he sounded logical and the thought that he could manipulate people who knew he was a starving actor turned me on. Then, on the other hand, it reminded me how well he could act.

To alleviate the confusion smothering me, I snuck back into the kitchen to pour another drink. Mya came in behind me. "Girl, Rashad is in there working the crowd."

"He's such a good actor."

"Funny, I never knew that."

We burst into laughter. She warned, "You better stop drinking. You know you can't handle too much alcohol."

After swallowing what was left in my cup, I quickly poured drink number four. Mya tried to grab my drink. After a silly tussle, she surrendered.

"Don't get drunk and mess up my engagement party."

I shooed her away. "Whatever. I'm fine."

When I returned to the other room, Frankie had begun separating the crowd into two groups to play Taboo. Caught off-guard when he pointed at me, I followed the count and said, "Two."

Rashad reached over and grabbed my arm. I stumbled over to him and he turned my back to him. He wrapped his arms around me and nestled his chin in my neck. I ducked and he kissed my cheek. We giggled and others around us watched our interaction.

Throughout the game, I had several more drinks and we became increasingly—and openly—flirtatious. My admiration for him grew as the night grew older.

Scene 32

RASHAD

Fatima swayed back and forth beside me. She had clearly had too much to drink. We raised our cups for a toast almost ten times throughout the evening. I celebrated my transition in life and God only knows what she celebrated, but we looked more like the engaged couple than Mya and Frankie. I was the only actor in a room full of film and casting directors. The connections I made were priceless.

Though neo-soul music played in the background, Fatima and I danced as if hip-hop blasted through the speakers. When her speech began to slur, I rubbed her back. My eyes directed Mya to assist me in detoxing my date. Mya rolled her eyes in her head and walked into the kitchen. She returned with a cup of ice water, while I tried to convince Fatima to have a seat. I attempted to put a piece of ice in her mouth and she pinched my chin, "Kiss me."

I leaned in for a wet kiss. Her vulnerability forced me to suppress my ambitions and stay beside her despite several career opportunities rolling out the front door. As I waved at my new contacts, I patted my pocket to assure all the business cards I collected were secure.

While I sat there massaging her back, suddenly her loud snoring drowned out the music. Mya laughed. "She's out."

"Yeah, I'll have to carry her home."

After I helped Frankie and Mya straighten up a little, I cradled Fatima in my arms and left. I hoped by the time we reached outside, she'd wake up. Instead she rested her head on my shoulder and snuggled closer. I hailed a taxi, stuffed her inside, pulled her out, and when I tried to get her house key from her purse, she decided to wake up.

She clutched her purse. "Give me that."

I let it go. "Okay, be my guest."

She opened the door and staggered in front of me. In her mind, I believe she thought she was switching. Watching her intoxicated strut cracked me up.

"Teem, do you know you only have one shoe on?"

She sucked her teeth, plopped on the couch, and kicked off her other shoe. "Not anymore."

I stood in front of her and reached for her hand. "Do you want to go downstairs?"

She pointed. "No, we need to talk."

"Talk?"

"I'll talk when I feel like it."

"No, baby. I was asking you a question."

"Well, ask me then."

Her incoherence tickled me. "Why don't you go first?"

She yanked my arm. "Sit down."

I fell beside her and stroked her face. "What's up?"

"What does your girlfriend think about us?"

I laughed. "You tell me."

"You tell me. I don't know her."

"Fatima, the only girlfriend I have is you."

"I saw her."

I laughed harder. "Who did you see?"

"Your girlfriend. I saw her today."

Before it dawned on me, I laughed hysterically, but my smile quickly turned into dismay. Could it really be possible that the only day I hang out casually with another woman, she saw me? I winced. "Have you been following me?"

She stabbed her index finger into my chest. "I didn't have to follow you. God put it right in my face. I walked down a Hundred and twenty-fifth Street, minding my own business, and there you were with that girl."

"Why didn't you say anything when you saw me?"

She pretended to cry. "Because I couldn't remember what the contract said. I know you're supposed to tell me when you have feelings for someone else, but am I supposed to approach you when I see you with another woman?"

"Fatima, I have nothing to hide. I'm a one-woman man. I would have to quit if I had a girl. What woman do you know would allow me to spend so much time with you?"

"You're not always with me."

Before I could continue to defend myself, she started snoring. Hoping that once she woke up sober, this argument would be over, I lifted her from the couch and carried her downstairs to the bedroom. She slung her arm around my neck and appeared so helpless. When I lay her down, I landed a soft kiss on her forehead before removing her clothes.

As I struggled to remove her pants, she whimpered and lay delicately in a posed position. I stood over her and admired how eloquent she remained despite her inebriation. I climbed in beside her. Facing her, I wrapped my arms around her waist. I spoke to her unconscious mind, "I'm so glad I met you."

Then, I kissed her. We lay face-to-face, breathing each other's breath. Ten minutes passed and she responded, "I'm glad I met you too."

Scene 33

FATIMA

When I squirmed, Rashad's arms surrounded me. I tried to recollect how we transitioned from Mya's house to my bedroom. Suddenly, I felt slightly embarrassed. Could I have been that drunk?

"Yes, you were that drunk."

When he answered my thoughts, I realized I'd spoken aloud. I turned to face him. "What?"

He brushed back the strands of hair hanging in my face. "You were messed up. I had to carry you out of Mya's house."

As I attempted to sit up, my head felt like a watermelon. "You're lying. Did people see you carry me out?"

"You know we have to save face for the Teem. I waited until everyone left."

"Was Mya mad?"

"No, she thought you were funny."

I exhaled because I wouldn't live it down if I ruined her party. He massaged the small of my back with the ball of his thumbs. "What do you want for breakfast?"

"Toast and water."

He laughed. "Do you need any aspirin?"

With my hands cupping my head, I nodded. "Was I that bad?"

"You were just having a good time."

"Thanks for the encouragement."

Rashad climbed out of the bed and went upstairs. Fragments of last night replayed in my memory. Not only had I gotten carried from the party, I'd lost my cool, too. I huffed and puffed and grunted like that would erase my actions.

He returned with toast, coffee, and a tall glass of water. After setting up the food tray, he helped me sit up. When I apologized, he frowned. I explained, "I asked you some questions last night that I shouldn't have."

"We don't have to discuss it anymore, not unless you want to discuss."

Hoping I didn't lose too much dignity, I smiled. "I don't want to discuss it anymore."

He put his thumb up and I returned the gesture. We were in agreement. Last night's scene was never intended for the script.

When Rashad got in the shower, I immediately called Mya to apologize. She giggled in my ear. "Tima, people have been calling me all morning talking about how much you glowed last night."

"Girl, whatever. I was drunk."

"Frankie kept telling me how much he thinks Rashad is in love with you."

I sucked my teeth.

She continued, "Everyone says it's all in his eyes. He looked like Prince Charming and you were his Sleeping Beauty when y'all left here. Frankie is so happy for you. I couldn't bear to tell him that this is all a hoax."

"I hope you never do."

"If I tell anyone, that would make me just as crazy as you."

After we chatted for a few more minutes, her tone became more serious. "Honestly, Tima. You guys looked like you're madly in love."

"Maybe I should audition for your next casting."

"So, are you telling me this is really all an act to you?"

Wearing nothing but a towel wrapped around his waist, Rashad opened the bathroom door and winked at me. A slight flutter rippled through my belly. Still, I said, "Yes."

While he shaved, I watched him from behind. His muscular arms and defined shoulder blades hypnotized me as Mya continued to quiz me about the nature of our relationship. The buzzing from his clippers drowned my remarks.

"Mya, this is what it is. Nothing more and nothing less."

"So, yesterday when you saw him with the girl and I thought you had had a heart attack, what about that?"

"I lost focus. That's all."

"Tima, we've been through wilder things and somehow you still manage to come out on top. I'm not going to worry about it."

"Thank you."

"You still looked happy as hell and everyone agrees."

My eyes rolled in my head. "Uh, I think that was the purpose."

When the noise in the bathroom stopped, it was time to get off the phone. Mya and I agreed to hook up later.

With the fresh smell of Acqua di Gio aftershave, Rashad plopped on the bed and propped his head up on my thighs. As I stroked his freshly shaven face, he raked my forearm.

"What are you doing today?" I asked.

"I'm free today. Whatever you want to do."

I whispered, "I want to have a black love story marathon."

His head sprung up. "What?"

"You know, watch all the black love stories."

I pointed to the extensive DVD collection on my bookcase. He wrapped his arms around my waist. "You really do live in a fantasy world."

My eyes shifted. "Duh?"

We laughed and he stumbled out of the bed. "Which one do you want to see first?"

I sighed. "Let's start with *Boomerang*."

He pulled the DVD from the shelf and popped it in. After grabbing the remote, he jumped back in the bed beside me. "Do you need popcorn?" he asked.

I kissed his forehead. "Not yet."

"Just let me know."

He folded a pillow under his neck and pressed play with the remote control. He chuckled. "This used to be my favorite movie."

His enthusiastic cooperation jogged my heart and we began our marathon.

Scene 34

RASHAD

The title guy read over each document, but I scribbled my signature before he could thoroughly explain. I was in a rush to get inside of my dry-rotted house and began carting stuff away. I'd already reserved a dump truck and a crew of guys for eight in the morning.

When the key to the padlock was placed in my hand, it felt like I was given a free diamond. Monique and another representative from City Props were there. Before I left the conference room, I hugged Monique and thanked her again. Her eyes slightly dimmed as our handshake broke. For a moment, I contemplated inviting her out, but didn't want to risk the chance of running into Fatima again. Over the last few weeks, her roller-coaster ride at work has triggered highs and lows in our relationship. The last thing I need is for her to terminate my employment when I need it most.

Monique folded her lips tightly as though she expected an invitation. Then, she said, "Make sure you stop by and visit." She winked. "Sometimes contracts fall through and we'll give the money to someone with a proven success track."

"Thank you. I will do that."

Finally, all parties left and I jogged to the train; then, from the train to my house. After struggling with the rusty padlock for five minutes, the rickety door creaked open. Unlike before, the rotten smell was inviting. It belonged to me. I again walked through the safe parts of the house.

My imagination ran wild as ideas filled my head: *A fireplace could go here. Leave this space wide open. Make this window larger.* Dust floated around me, while I floated away.

My anxiety wouldn't let me rest as I went home and began booking appointments in order—architect, electrician, plumber, and carpenter. I planned to be an intricate part of each phase. While I sat mapping out my house to completion, my mother walked in. "Hey, stranger."

"Hey, Ma."

She gave me a hug and I asked, "How proud would you be if you knew I purchased a brownstone?"

"More proud than I've been in a long time."

I dangled my key in front of her. She raised her eyebrows. "That key doesn't mean anything."

I pulled out my settlement papers and handed them to her. She looked them over and her eyes watered. "Rashad, how were you able to do this?"

"I told you that assistant job that I have pays pretty well."

Tears formed in her eyes as she nodded. "I'm so proud of you. I've been praying that something wonderful would break-through for you and look at this." She hugged me. "Now, this is the man I raised."

"I've always been the man you raised."

She sighed and said, "I lost you for a minute."

"You thought you lost me? I've always been focused."

"I couldn't tell."

"When it's all done, you can have one of the apartments rent-free."

"I've been waiting for the day that my only boy would take care of me."

"It's coming. That day is coming."

She held my face in her hands. "Is this why I've only seen you two times in the last four months?"

"Actually, my job is why you haven't seen me."

"Okay. Okay. When do I get to see the place?"

"It's just a shell now, Ma. I want you to see it when it's done."

She sucked her teeth. "Rashad, just take me to see it."

I took a break from my planning to take my mother to the house. She hugged me over and over again. Her excitement brought tears to my eyes. Nothing could replace making the person that sacrifices everything for you proud. She asked, "How much is this assistant job paying?"

After I explained to her the help that City Props offered, I think she got a better understanding of how I could afford it. When we left the house, I decided to take her to eat, which I hadn't done since I met Fatima.

We took the train to midtown for Italian food. As we sat down to break bread, it was obvious how long it had been. We caught up on the latest in each other's life. She pressured me for more information about my job and my lack of a relationship. She would die if she knew that my job and relationship were one. I successfully skated around her inquiries. Then, she asked, "Have you given up on acting?"

"Nah. Why would you say that?"

"You haven't mentioned anything about castings and you're spending all of your time on this new job."

Her comment rattled me. Not only had I noticed my slippage, but so had she. My obsession to please Fatima and become financially free had stifled my dream. When I looked at my mother, I felt slightly ashamed. "Acting is my life. I have some things I'm trying to do so I won't be a broke actor, but I will never give up acting."

"That's smart. I've been trying to tell you this."

After we finished eating, we chatted for awhile longer. When my cell phone rang, I knew it was Fatima. As eager as I was to speak with her, I let it go to voicemail. My mother asked, "Who's that calling?"

When the phone rang again, she said, "Why don't you answer?"

When I picked up, Fatima said, "Hey, you."

"Hey, you."

"Where are you?"

I asked, "Where are you?"

"In the house waiting for you."

"Okay, I'll be there shortly."

"See you when you get here."

My mother raised an eyebrow. "Who was that?"

"My boss."

"Sure sounded touchy."

I chuckled. "It's not that serious."

Although I knew she wanted more information, I brushed her off and rushed her home.

As I headed to Fatima's house, my conversation with my mother replayed in my head. It was clear that I needed to redirect my focus on the bigger picture.

Scene 35

FATIMA

My wedding anniversary brought back so many memories. We were married on Labor Day six years ago and today was the hardest because not only was it another anniversary, it was Labor Day and living through this is surely hard work.

I lay in my bed alone and contemplated staying in all day, sipping wine, and willing Derrick back into existence. It was actually a blessing because I was drowning with work, but the day off gave me an opportunity to wallow in my pity all alone. The manuscripts scattered beside me would have to wait until I was done with my yearly depression ritual. Rashad had left at the crack of dawn to go where, I don't know, nor did I ask. He had been doing that for weeks now; it had become routine.

I popped in my wedding CD. Al Green blasted through my speakers: "Let's, let's stay together. Lovin' you whether, whether times are good or bad, happy or sad."

Tears welled in my eyes as my wedding day played in my head. I went into my closet and pulled out my wedding album. *Today, I married my best friend. September 4, 2000.* I flipped back and forth through the pages hoping to jump into the photos and relive each moment. My phone rang and interrupted my medium attempt.

Rashad's voice came through the phone, "What are you doing on a beautiful day like today?"

I sighed. "Rashad, I'm not in the mood."

"We're going to the Caribbean Day parade. How can you not be in the mood?"

"I'm not from the Caribbean."

"But I am. Get ready. I'm on my way with our Trinidad flags."

"Rashad. I—"

He hung up the phone and I looked down in my lap to Derrick smiling up at me. I patted the picture. *I love you, honey.*

For the first time since his death, I took a shower on our anniversary. I debated whether or not I should be hanging out with Rashad, but before I knew it, I was dressed and waiting in my living room.

When he came into the house, he wore his Trinidad soccer jacket and jeans. I giggled. "You're a real patriot."

"I have to be."

"What's up with the fake accent?"

He kissed me. "You don't like my accent."

"No, it sounds like you're trying too hard."

"Okay, I'll quit."

"Thank you."

"What have you done all day?"

"Nothing."

"Good. You'll have enough energy to get rowdy with me at the parade."

"I'm not getting rowdy."

When I was infused with the energy from the crowds of people that surrounded me, I was made a liar. We stood on the sidewalk on Utica Avenue in Brooklyn raising our hands to the roof and grinding to the island sounds of calypso and reggae. I'd even got the nerve to tie the Trinidad flag bandanna around my head. Vendors lined the streets with ethnic foods and drinks. Rashad had poured enough Caribbean rum down my throat to last me until the New Year. As each elaborately decorated truck passed, I raised my flag like I was born in the islands. Rashad lifted me up on this back so that I wouldn't miss anything. Dancers marched behind the trucks with flamboyant costumes. Different celebrities surprised the crowd by popping up from their country's float. I bounced on Rashad's back and waved my arms in the air to the eclectic sounds that vibrated through me.

Rashad appreciated my enthusiasm. He would look up and smile sporadically. His muscles would bulge each time he hiked me up higher to protect me from sliding down his back. I leaned over his shoulder. "I'm glad you forced me to come out."

"Forced?"

"Yeah. I didn't want to come out today."

"You sure didn't fight hard."

I chuckled. "Whatever."

People cheered for their countries, yet we were all family. This was my first parade since I've been in New York, but it sure wouldn't be my last.

With one arm wrapped around Rashad's neck, I rested the side of my head on the side of his. My eyes closed in the midst of the commotion and I smiled. My meditation was disrupted when someone yanked my arm. I flinched and prayed that the feminine hands that I saw before I looked into her face were not those of Rashad's woman.

When I looked into my sister-in-law's face, I wanted to revise my prayer. Her eyes scorned me as I leapt off of Rashad's back. She looked at me. I looked at her. Finally, she spoke, "Hey, Fatty."

My stomach rumbled. "Hey."

Rashad held my hand like he wanted me to introduce him, but I didn't know what to say.

She smiled. "How are you?"

"I'm good."

"I see."

I took a deep breath. "I mean, I'm doing better."

"I guess you're dating again."

I shrugged my shoulder. She was never a big fan of mine. She thought I was too young for her younger brother.

She snickered. "It's funny. I actually thought about you today, because you know today is . . ."

"Of course I know . . ."

"You don't come around anymore."

I assumed that she was the reason that I felt abandoned by his family after he died, but I didn't feel like explaining. Instead, I dropped my head. "It's too hard. You know?"

She nodded. "I know. So introduce me to your new friend."

When I introduced them, I inadvertently said she was my sister-in-law. Rashad eyes dimmed. She gave me a hug and walked away. Suddenly, despite all the festivities, I rewound to being consumed with my tragedy.

Rashad recognized my preoccupation. He leaned over and asked, "Are you ready to go?"

"No, I'm okay. You're having a good time. I don't want to ruin it."

"Teem, I'd rather we go home, than have you looking over your shoulder."

"What?"

"You're not ready for her to see you with someone else. I know."

"I—"

"I understand. Let's go."

I wrapped my arm around his waist. "Thank you. Thanks for understanding."

Though he claimed to understand, his attitude while we sat on the train told me otherwise. I massaged his leg. "Are you okay?"

He shrugged his shoulder. "I'm fine."

I intertwined my fingers in his and wondered if I should explain that today was my anniversary and that my public display of affection was inappropriate. My eyes tried to explain, but he stared out the window at a cement wall. I raked his evenly blended hairline.

"I'm sorry for ruining your day."

He shook his head. "My day isn't ruined. You know that I don't stress the little things."

When we got to my house, he told me that he had some things to do and he would be back. I thought about stopping him, but decided to let him have his moment, because I needed one too.

He called a few hours later, as if nothing ever happened. I

tried to apologize, but he stopped me and told me to come to the door. When I opened up, his smile told me that I was forgiven. Our embrace confirmed that he was an exceptional man who has total control of his emotions. As much as I appreciated it, I also questioned his ability to just let things go.

Scene 36

RASHAD

The summer had disappeared right before my very eyes. I woke up the morning after Labor Day trying to figure out where it had gone. Fatima and I were both working like we had something to prove. We would leave her house around seven and neither of us would return until close to eleven. Considering that I thought I should be hands-on with the renovations, the freedom gave me the opportunity to handle my business.

It took me nearly two months to actually trust my contractors. When the renovations first began, I would come in every morning prepared to steam off wallpaper, cart away junk, or strip floors. After going to a few auditions and being questioned if I'd been in fight because my knuckles were scrapped up, I decided to take Marty's advice and lay back and let the pros do their jobs. And that, they have done. The house is divided into five apartments; that includes a duplex, which is where I will reside. The second level has one two-bedroom. The third level has one one-bedroom and a studio. We also divided a portion of the lower-level duplex and made a small studio accessible from the outside.

Fatima assumed I'd just become a more punctual person as I rushed her out of the house each morning. I think it has finally registered that I have a life too. I sat on the bed as she stood in the bathroom mirror complaining about the hair on her face that no one can see.

Five minutes passed and now I stood at the bathroom door. "What are you doing?"

"What does it look like I'm doing?"

"It would be faster if you just shaved."

Her eyes opened wider. "Are you saying that I have that much hair?"

"No, I'm saying that it would be quicker if you shave. You're picking at nothing. Soon you'll be pulling off skin."

"I know what I feel."

"I know what I see. I think it's just become a nervous habit."

"You don't have to worry about it, so you don't care."

I slouched on the door. "Fatima, if it bothers you that bad, why don't you do something about it?"

"I am."

"Something more permanent, like laser or electrolysis."

"So, you do see it?"

"No, I see the time you waste picking at invisible hair. So, if it will save you twenty minutes a day, I think you should go for it."

"You're so punctual now. You make me sick."

She gathered her things and rushed out of the bathroom. Her eyes were dark from lack of sleep and her body was getting slimmer everyday. I sympathized with her because she had committed herself to be a one-man show at work. I prayed that one day I could alleviate her of that burden. One day soon, she'd only have to work if she wanted to.

Before we left the house, she asked, "Are you going to that party tonight?"

"Are you?"

"Mya said that everyone who's anyone should be there and that you should go."

"What about you?"

Her face sagged. "I can't. I have too much work. It will be another late one."

I hugged her and she leaned her head into my chest. I stroked her back with silent apologies.

After putting an exhausted Fatima into the taxi, I headed over to the house. When I got there, the electrician sat outside.

I asked, "No one's in there?"

"Nah, I've been here for thirty minutes."

"Why didn't you call me?"

"I figured you were on your way."

As we headed into the house, I told him, "Look, call me if you get here and no one's here."

The contractors also had a key and are scheduled to be here every morning by seven-thirty. As I wondered what the holdup could have been this morning, the team straggled in. The lead guy said, "What's up, Rash?"

While checking my watch, I said, "Nothing man. What's going on?"

"Yeah, we're running a little late this morning, but it's not every day."

I just nodded, because it wasn't as if their lateness delayed anything. In fact, they were ahead of schedule and had done a hell of a job so far. In less than three months, the place had been transformed into the castle I dreamed of.

Whenever I stepped into the house, it seemed that another room was completed or framed. I walked through the house and checked out the new installments and rechecked everything else.

The renovations ran so smoothly, I began to believe that I could purchase two or three homes a year. Within two years, I would be living large and be a ballin' actor, instead of a starving one. It amazed me how easily it was to rent out the apartments. People would literally walk up to the contractors asking when it would be done and if I were renting out rooms. I had four applicants lined up to move in and ten on the waiting list if anything fell through. If I had known three years ago, I would be King of New York by now. Then on the other hand, I wouldn't have had the pleasure of meeting my Teem.

I brought Fatima dinner at work before heading to the networking party of the year. When I got there, she looked at me and her eyes watered.

"What's wrong?"

"You look so good and I have to let you go to this party alone."

"Teem, leave this stuff for tomorrow. It will be here."

"But look at me."

"You look fine. You'll just be the classy lady among all the trashy ones."

We laughed and she said, "I really can't. Aside from all of this work, I'm sleepy. I don't know where I'll get the energy from."

"We'll get you a Red Bull and I'll give you all the extra energy you need."

"What are you going to do if I fall out at the party?"

"You're not going to fall out." After looking into her weary eyes, I changed my mind. "Okay, let me stop stressing you. When are you leaving?"

"In about an hour."

"Do you want me to stay here with you?"

"If you stay, it will take me longer than an hour. So, go on and go to your little party. I'll just be here, working."

I pried myself from her office and headed downtown to the party. When I walked in, I searched for Mya. At least I could have a piece of Fatima if she couldn't be here. After going up and down the stairs aimlessly, I decided to relax in the cut.

When I saw a chick that I used to date, I tried looking in the opposite direction. She walked up to me.

"Hey, Rashad."

I said, "Hey . . ."

"Deneen."

I knew her name but I wanted to knock her off her high-horse. She blushed. "So, what have you been up to?"

"Nothing much."

"Well, you look good."

"You, too."

"How's the acting career going?"

I shrugged my shoulders. "What about you?"

"Good. Work is picking up."

A year and a half ago, I thought this girl was the hottest thing

in the city. As she stood in front of me selling herself, I just
wanted her to disappear.

She rocked in front of me. I stood still. She continued to talk,
"You are so handsome."

I chuckled. Now I'm handsome. When I was sending her flowers and begging to take her out, she wasn't interested. I looked
at all the other fake chicks at the party and shook my head. It's
hard to tell the real from the fake. Despite all of Fatima's requirements, I know she's real.

"What are you doing later?" she asked.

"Ah, I have to meet my girl."

Her dancing came to a complete halt. Her eyes opened wider.
"Oh, Okay."

Trying not to come across too harsh, I asked, "What are you
doing later?"

She shrugged her shoulders and walked away shortly after.
Why do women think they can always use their sex appeal to get
you? I walked through the club, trying to see if I recognized anybody. After shaking hands with a few of my colleagues, I gathered that this was a networking event for starving actors to
network with starving actors. Mya or any of her director friends
were no where to be found. Maybe they were in VIP. If I can't get
to the important people, what the hell is the purpose? Since my
heart really wasn't in the club, but all the way in Harlem, I called
Fatima to see if she was home yet. When I told her I was on my
way, she asked, "What about the party?"

"I'd rather be with you."

Scene 37

FATIMA

What else can I do with my life? My heart used to be so deep into this job that it was all I thought about. As I sit here on hump day, counting the seconds to Friday, I'm wracking my brain with other possibilities. With one elbow propped on my desk and my hand on my head, I gazed out of the window.

When Kia buzzed and disturbed my daydream, I asked her to take a message. She agreed, but buzzed again. I didn't respond, so she came to my doorway. "Who is it?"

"It's Rashad. He said that it would be quick."

Suddenly, he became the target of my frustration. If I wasn't giving him the money that Derrick left me to live off, I could quit. Why should I be miserable working while he walks around like a king getting paid for love? When I picked up, his calm voice settled my anxiety. "Teem."

"Yes, Rashad."

"What are you doing?"

"Working, Rashad."

"Tell them you have to leave."

"Uh, it's not that simple, Rashad. I have work to do."

"Okay, you don't have to leave right now, but I'd appreciate if you tried to take off Thursday or Friday or both."

"For what?"

"I have all-day passes to the US Open."

"The Open?"

"Yes."

"How did you get tickets?"

"Anything for the Teem."

In a second, my mind was at the stadium watching the tennis matches, smiling at Rashad. I giggled. "I'll see what I can do. I'll shoot for both. If it's too much, I'll just take off on Friday."

"Okay, baby. I'll see you later."

I tied up some loose ends and piled a long list of things to do on Kia's desk. After apologizing for giving her added stress, I let her know that I'd be out for the next two days. She frowned. "Do you think it's a good idea considering the nature of the environment?"

Considering that Monday was a holiday, it probably wasn't smart of me to take off for the rest of the week, but life is too short. I'd begged Derrick to take me to the Open the entire time we were together, but we never got there. I attended as many Knicks' games and Giants' games that he had room in his schedule, but never the sport that I love.

In the script, the things I like to do stated that I enjoy going to sporting events, but it didn't specify the sport. How did he nail it straight on? I spent the entire day thinking about the next day. Technically, I was off today, too.

Rashad called shortly before I left work and told me he was in the neighborhood. I agreed to meet him outside of my office. When I stepped out of the building, it was just like seeing him for the first time. I blinked. He was the same man I'd parted with in the morning, but I was more drawn to him. He gave me a one-arm hug and kissed my forehead. Several shopping bags hung on his arm.

"What's all that stuff?"

"It's yours."

"Mine."

"Yeah, I noticed you don't have any sporty clothes. All you have is fly-girl clothes—stilettos and skirts and tight jeans."

Trying to separate our interlocked fingers, I pulled away from him. "So! Who needs sporty clothes?"

He squinted. "Ah. If you're planning on going to the Open, you do."

I chuckled and grabbed his hand again. He snatched it away, so I grabbed his forearm and snuggled close to him. "What did you get me?"

"I'll show you at dinner."

He wrapped his arm around my shoulder and I put mine around his waist. Though he spoke sensitively, he looked in an opposite direction. "Anything for the Teem."

Looking up at him inquisitively, I watched him as he daydreamed. Where had his mind wandered to in a matter of seconds?

We ended up at Negril on 22nd Street. After we sat down and ordered a few drinks, he pulled out my outfits. He bought a blue Polo shirt, the 2006 US Open Signature Edition, as he explained. In addition, he purchased a Nike baby-tee with TENNIS written on it. He bought me tennis shoes to match both. As I folded the clothes on my lap, I blew a kiss at him. "Thank you, baby."

His arrogant nod was his way of saying that I was welcome, but it made me chuckle.

When I woke up to the smell of bacon and footsteps pacing back and forth, I heard Rashad's voice on the phone. I lay still trying to eavesdrop on the intense conversation occurring upstairs.

"Look, three weeks and that's it."

After a short pause, he said, "Hell no, it has to be over in three weeks. This is taking up too much of my time. I need to put all my focus on acting."

He continued, "I know it's guaranteed money, but it has got to end at some point. If we keep on, this could go on forever. I got better things to do. Either you handle it or I'll have to do it."

My heart dropped. Was he planning to have his agent break up with me? I thought this had become real. In three weeks, my script comes to an end? After Derrick died, I promised myself not to worry about what the future held and live everyday for it's worth. Suddenly, all rational thought escaped me. I wanted to know today about my tomorrows.

When I stepped out of bed, I felt light-headed. My heart ached as I listened to Rashad wrap up plans to end our agreement. I sat on the toilet tempted to cry. It was only temporary from the start. How could I expect him to give up his dream to hang out with me forever? A part of me forgave him and appreciated his will to stay this long.

When I walked upstairs to candles flickering on the table, I was confused. Despite the frustration I heard on the phone, he still gave this role one hundred percent. As I entered the kitchen, he puckered for a kiss and then smiled. "Good morning, beautiful."

"Hey, Rashad."

"We can do better than that. Let's try again. Good morning, beautiful."

"Good morning."

With his hands on my shoulders, he turned me around. "Okay, have a seat and I'll bring the food in there."

"Can I get some orange juice?"

"I'll bring it to you. Now, go and relax. I put all the latest gossip magazines on the table."

"I didn't buy any magazines this week."

"I went to the newsstand this morning and bought them for you."

The latest copies of *inTouch*, *Us Weekly*, and *People* lay on the table. I hooted, "See, I knew you were into celebrity gossip."

He chuckled. "Nah. I figured I should start reading what they will be saying about me when I get to Hollywood."

In a blink, I was reminded of his real aspirations. This role would end in three weeks and he will be on to pursuing his dream. I'll be here alone again. Where else will I find an actor so perfect that he makes me forget this isn't real?

I wished I could support him, but I didn't want to accept that his dream would separate us. So, I slouched into the dining room and sat at the table. As I flipped through the magazines, the gossip didn't seem as steamy as usual. My mind wandered on to future cover stories: *Did Rashad Watkins play the role of a boy toy for a desperate widow before his big break?*

My head began to throb. The whole country would know about me. When he set the plate on the table, I looked down at his scrumptious French toast. He even took time to decorate the plate with garnish. When he sat down, he took my hand and prayed:

"Lord, we thank you for waking us up this morning. We ask that you bless us as we go about our day. We thank you for patience as we wait for the desires of our heart . . ."

My mind blocked out the rest of the prayer. What desires? Is he insinuating that when he quits, I'll find someone else? My eyes remained tightly closed as he shook my shoulder. "Amen."

I jumped and looked at him. "Yeah, Amen."

"I said, 'Amen' like five times. What were you doing? Saying your own prayer?"

I shrugged my shoulders. "I guess."

By the time we got to National Tennis Center, I had forced myself to get over that we only had three weeks left. He asked if I wanted a drink, I decided to shoot for draft beer. As he handed me a twenty-ounce cup, he joked, "Don't keep running back and forth to the bathroom."

"Nope. I'm not going to miss anything."

As I watched people hustle around me, the big screens and all the courts surrounding us, I still couldn't believe I was here. I tugged on Rashad's shirt. "What made you bring me to a tennis match?"

"I listen." He paused. "You told me that you hadn't played tennis since you came to New York."

"Okay, and?"

"It was the way you said it, like you missed the sport."

"I do."

"I know. That's why I purchased lessons for you at Harlem Tennis."

I shook his arm. "No you didn't!"

"Yes, I did."

My eyes watered. "Are you serious?"

"Yes, Teem."

I looked at him in amazement. "How did you know?"

"What? That you were the best player on your high school squad?"

My eyes shifted. "Rashad. Yes. Where did you get that from?"

He bent down and kissed me. "Good actors do their research."

"I guess it's that simple, huh?"

He nodded. A piece of me wanted to tell him that I was in love with him, but I didn't want to hinder his plans. He made it clear that he loved acting more than he loved the money I offered for his love. Maybe these tennis lessons were to fill the void of his absence.

Scene 38

RASHAD

As it all began to come together, I was certainly more proud of myself than I thought. In a little over a week, I will be receiving income from my tenants and I can tell Fatima to keep her money.

After the safety inspector approved the place, I needed to get the city's approval and the tenants I'd already lined up could move in. My adrenaline rushed a million miles a minute as I played the main character in all these different dramas.

To celebrate, I booked a secluded suite in a Vermont bed & breakfast where I planned to tell Fatima that I quit and offer her my love for free.

Before I picked up the rental car, I stopped by my mother's apartment. There were messages posted on my bedroom door: *Monique called 9/20. Monique called 9/21*. I frowned. Why didn't she just call me on my cell phone?

As I packed my clothes, I dialed City Props. When Monique came to the phone, she joked, "How are things, Mr. Landlord?"

"Wonderful. How are you?"

"I'm fine. I was calling because another house fell through and before I give it to the next person in line, I wanted to know if you felt like rehabbing another house."

I sighed. She continued, "We're really impressed with how quickly you got everything in motion with your house. And believe it or not, we hate to see our money go to waste. We'd rather give it to someone who's done this before."

"What about my income? Will the rent serve as my income?"

"No, we're hoping to go to settlement before you begin receiving rent. If we were to account for that, you'd be over the limit. So, I was hoping to use your current salary. Is that okay?"

This opportunity was screwing up my plan, but how could I say no to another practically free house. My ego expanded as I imagined eventually owning half of Harlem. Before I could evaluate the effects of my actions, I said, "Oh, that's not a problem. What do I need to do?"

"First you need to go check the house out. Let me know if you're really interested and we'll get the ball rolling."

"Okay. Where is it?"

"One hundred and twenty-ninth and Fifth."

"When can I see it?"

"Is today at two okay?"

Actually, I planned to pick up Fatima from work by three. Since she didn't know anything about the plans, I decided I could push that back.

"That's fine."

"Someone will meet you outside the house. Talk to you soon."

As I stood outside of the condemned house, the reservations that I had when I first started my search reappeared. There's no way in hell that I have the time to sacrifice fixing this house. Then I remembered why my house seemed to take all of my time. I was determined to have it done by an unreasonable deadline. This one could be on the slow track. One of the brokers for City Props walked up and shook my hand.

The dry-rotted smell that used to make me sick invoked an ambitious rumble in my stomach. We couldn't walk around much, but from a visual estimate, I could divide the place into five apartments. He continued his sales pitch, but I was already sold. I said, "Look man, I'm on my way out of town, but I want this place. What should I do?"

"Call Monique and let her know."

When I called Monique to give her the heads up, I also let her know that I wouldn't be available throughout the weekend. She asked, "So where are you going?"

"Just driving up to Vermont."

"Sure wish I could go."

I felt indebted to her as well. It took no scientist to figure out that she gave me the hookup. I said, "One day."

"What do you mean?"

"One day, you'll go to Vermont."

"But, what if I want to go with you?"

I ingored that and proceeded to discuss business. "You're funny. So, do I need to sign anything before Monday?"

"No, I can push it through with your old application. I'll probably need you to send your pay stubs in again."

"Okay, that's cool."

"Just call me Monday and we'll discuss what to do next."

"Okay, sweetheart."

She paused. "Don't make me smile."

"I aim to please."

"Okay, I'll talk to you Monday."

When I called to tell Fatima I'd be picking her up from work, she asked a million questions. Where are we going? Why are you picking me up? Why are you on your way now?

"I thought you liked surprises."

"I do, but I . . ."

"You like to know everything."

"I'm just curious."

I chuckled. "Whatever you want to call it. I'll be outside of your building in fifteen minutes. I'm in a blue Ford Taurus."

"I . . ."

"See you few minutes, baby."

Scene 39

FATIMA

My head spun faster than I could organize my desk. Knowing there was no way to accomplish all I needed to do before leaving, I decided to just leave. Monday is another day and I'll deal with it then.

When I rushed outside, I looked around and Rashad beeped the horn from the middle lane. After dodging traffic, I hopped in the car and kissed him. "What's this all about?"

"We're going out of town."

"I have a tennis lesson in the morning."

"You'll have to cancel."

As we passed 125th on the FDR, I asked, "When are we leaving?"

"Now."

"Rashad, I have to pack."

"Already did that."

"What did you pack for me?"

He sighed. "You need to learn to be relaxed and let me take control."

"I'm just curious."

"Didn't I promise to take care of you?"

"How long do you plan to take care of me?"

He chuckled, but didn't answer. Based on my estimation, it

was approximately seven more days. He rubbed my knee. "Take one day at a time, Teem."

I watched him from the corner of my eye. "Where are we going?"

"Vermont."

"Vermont? What the hell is in Vermont?"

"Teem, you'll like it."

"You could take me up there and leave me stranded."

"What makes you think I would want to leave you stranded?" I shrugged my shoulders and he massaged my knee. "I kinda like your company."

"I kinda like you too."

On the long ride, I kidded, "We could have driven to Alabama."

"Never satisfied, huh?"

"I am satisfied. I was just saying this is a long ride."

"Are you afraid to be locked in a small space with me for too long?" He paused. "Or are you afraid to deal with yourself?"

I frowned. "What are you trying to say? I don't have a problem with myself or you."

He smiled slyly. "I'm just wondering."

"Well, don't."

I stared out of the passenger side window at the beautiful scenery. As we drove farther north, Fall was a little more obvious. The trees and grass and peacefulness made me miss home. My sudden connection with Alabama startled me. When I had reached New York, I promised I'd never return, but as I admired the greenery I wasn't so sure that still held true. All of a sudden, I felt the need to pull out my cell phone and call my mother.

"Mama."

"Fatima?"

"Yeah, Ma."

"How are you, baby?"

"I'm pretty good. Work is a little hectic, but everything else is good."

"Have you decided whether you're coming home for the holidays?"

"I don't know, yet."

She went on to tell me all the family gossip. Finally she said, "You know I worry about you when you don't call."

"Ma, I talked to you last week."

"Fatima, I haven't talked to you in almost a month."

I sighed. "I'm sorry, Ma. I'll get better."

"I know you're busy; just try to give me a call sometimes."

"I will."

"I love you, Fatima."

"I love you, too."

As I closed my phone, Rashad reached over and rubbed my leg like he knew what I was thinking. "How often do you visit Alabama?"

"Like once a year." I paused. "If that."

"You should visit your family more."

I didn't feel the need to respond, but I pondered it. Ten minutes or so later, I nodded.

After a few rest stops and six hours later, we arrived at the Green Mountain Inn on Main Street in Stowe, Vermont. When he went to check-in, I sat in the car wondering what would make him select this place. The small little country town had completely shut down by nine o'clock. For a girl who likes adventure, this seemed a last resort. Maybe he got it for a reasonable price. At least I didn't have to worry what he decided to pack for me; no one around here would care. He hopped back into the car and pointed. "We have to go up here to the Chesterfield House."

"Okay. So, what will we eat tonight?"

"There's a restaurant up there."

When we got out of the car, he grabbed the luggage from the back and we headed into the building. There was a nice Victorian feel to the place. I looked around and nodded. "It's nice."

He frowned at me as if he never doubted it. He opened the hotel room door and let me walk in first. Classical music played in the huge suite. The fireplace crackled across from the king-size canopy bed. Chocolate-covered strawberries and wine sat on the table opposite the door. When he walked in behind me, he noticed my excitement.

He bent down to kiss me. "You like it?"

"I love it."

A Jacuzzi tub was beside the bed with all sorts of spa products decorating the ledge. He held me in his arms. "I love to make you happy."

My heart wanted to say, "I love you." Instead, I kissed him. As we stood in the middle of the floor, passionately kissing, I never imagined I'd feel so complete with another man. As I admitted my feelings to myself, I pushed away.

"What's wrong?"

"Nothing. I'm just . . ."

He pulled my head to his chest to let me know that he didn't need an explanation.

Scene 40

RASHAD

As I held her in my arms, I had so many things that I wanted to tell her and needed to tell her. I thought about telling the whole story, but decided it made better sense to explain it all when I no longer needed her income.

After I turned the fireplace off in the already warm room, I grabbed a chocolate-covered strawberry and fed it to her. I tasted the sweetness on her lips. She smiled.

"Are we going to eat?"

"Yes."

"I'm hungry."

She grabbed another strawberry and I poured wine into our glasses. I said, "To our future."

She sipped and added, "Together or apart."

A dart stabbed me in the heart. Afraid of what she meant, I didn't ask if it was a question or a statement. Instead, I stood up and asked if she was ready to have dinner. She popped up. "Yep."

We strolled out into the peaceful Vermont night. The air was clean and crisp. Bright stars shone down on us. They appeared close enough to touch. Our clasped hands swung back and forth. When we walked into the Main Street Grill, she kidded, "I wonder if we're the only black people here."

As I shrugged my shoulders, the black host walked up and said, "Ay, mon! What's good mon?"

Her eyes danced around. I smiled at him. "Hey, it's just the two of us."

"Right this way."

We followed and Fatima squeezed my hand. I tried to suppress my laughter. Her eyes bulged as she attempted to communicate with me.

The second he walked away, we burst into laughter. She said. "I didn't know black people lived in Vermont. Not to mention Jamaicans."

I put my finger over my mouth. She curled her lips. "He must be in protective custody."

"Fatima, stop being prejudiced."

He stepped back up to the table with a basket. "This is our signature bread, honey oatmeal."

We nodded. Before he finished talking about the specials, Fatima had broken a piece of the bread. Her expression told me it was good. I smiled at her. She nodded. "This is the best bread I've ever had."

"'Tis good, mon."

She chuckled, but I knew she was laughing at him and not about the bread. She nodded. "'Tis good."

When he walked away, she sucked her teeth. "He can cut it out with that Jamaican accent."

"Fatima, that's that man's culture."

"But he's in Vermont. He better assimilate. If they come looking for him, they will find his Jamaican butt in no time."

"What makes you think someone is looking for him?"

She giggled. "Because I know."

I sat there admiring the crazy thoughts that her mind conjured up. She was even funnier than I think she could ever imagine. I grabbed a piece of the bread and it melted in my mouth. By the time our dinner arrived, we'd devoured three baskets of honey oatmeal bread.

The food seemed wonderfully fresh as we barely talked during dinner, aside from Fatima kidding that they probably killed the cows out back.

When dinner was done, we decided to unwind with dessert and wine. After two bottles, Fatima was the loudest one in the restaurant. I kept hushing her, but her comedy made me laugh just as loud as she spoke. We literally closed the restaurant down.

Scene 41

FATIMA

When we got back to the room, we danced to silence. He massaged my shoulders and kissed my forehead. We undressed each other and the relit fire crackled as we tiptoed to the bed. Momentarily, he held me and stared into my eyes. I wondered about his hesitation. What was distracting him? He brushed my hair from my face and appeared like he wanted to talk. Instead, we kissed. Gently, he touched me almost as if he was afraid. Did he not have the courage to tell me this would be our last time together? Finally, he loved me sensually and I lay in the bed full of emotions. My eyes watered and I turned so he could hold me in the spoon position. Knowing he couldn't see, I let the tears fall as he rested his chin on my shoulder. I inconspicuously wiped my eyes and said, "Rashad."

He rose up. "Yeah, baby."

"Never mind."

He didn't pry for more as usual. Instead, he rolled onto his back and stared at the ceiling. Hoping that his thoughts would somehow transfer from his fingertips, I reached for his hand. He willingly offered. He raised our clasped hands up to his mouth and kissed my hand.

On my side, I turned to face him, scrutinizing his breathing. Then, I leaned over and lay my head on his chest. He stroked my back and we feel asleep.

*　*　*

The bright sun alarmed us at seven in the morning. I rubbed his chest. "Good morning."

"Good morning. We forgot to close the blinds last night."

"I know."

"Do you want to try and get some rest or do you want to go for breakfast? We're going kayaking at ten."

"Ten?" I huffed. "Well, I guess we have no choice."

"We can eat more of the honey oatmeal bread that you begged Peter for last night."

"I didn't beg him."

"Yeah, okay."

We got up and I pulled my clothes from the luggage. I selected an outfit. "Is this for today?"

He chuckled. "Baby, I just packed. You can wear whatever you want."

After we got ready, we headed to the Main Street Grill again. The smell of fresh biscuits and bacon filled the air. I looked at Rashad. He laughed. "I know. You can't wait to eat."

I pushed him. "Shut up."

We were greeted by Peter again. I kidded, "Did you stay the night here?"

He laughed. "I have a room at the hotel."

I nudged Rashad and nodded at Peter. "Oh, you live here?"

"Yeah, I come here six months and go back to my country for six months."

"Really? You go back to Jamaica?"

"Yah, mon."

"So, how did you arrange that?"

"I have an agent that gets me hospitality work at hotels in the states."

"Oh, wow. That's interesting. So you work for only six months?"

When we sat, Rashad tapped his knee against mine under the table, but Peter didn't seem to mind my interrogation.

He said, "Yeah, I work hard while I'm here and go home and relax."

"Must be nice. Do you have a family in Jamaica?"

Rashad's eyes cursed me. Peter said, "Yes, my wife is there."

Our conversation was interrupted by a couple waiting to be seated. Peter raised his finger. "I'll be back."

Rashad smirked at me. I giggled. "What?"

"You are a trip."

"Are you trying to tell me you didn't want to know how he got here?"

"No, Teem. I really don't care."

"You know, we've only seen like ten people that work here. We could be on the set of a murder mystery."

His eyes squinted as he laughed hysterically. "You are crazy. You have a thing for movie sets, huh?"

He stood and headed for the buffet. I sat stunned waiting for a fly to land on my tongue. Peter came back to the table. "Are you okay?" He poured my coffee. "You leaving tomorrow?"

I nodded suspiciously. It was okay to find out his story, but surely I didn't want him keeping track of me. "How did you know?"

"Breakfast is all-included. I have to check your room number."

My neck inched back. He laughed. "Your husband gave it to me last night."

"Oh, that's not my husband. He's just my—"

The proximity of the sound of Rashad's footsteps startled me. *Maybe I shouldn't have said it like that*. He chuckled. "I'm just her assistant."

My head jerked in his direction. His smile masked his discomfort. The muscle in his jawline pulsed, as he dropped his plate on the table. My shoulders slumped and I grimaced.

As my apologetic gestures tried to rewind the actions of my compulsive tongue, he tilted his head toward the buffet. "Get something to eat before there's nothing left."

Peter vanished during our silent altercation. Before I stood, I reached over to touch his arm. "Are you going to wait for me?"

"Of course I'll wait for you, Fatima."

I pouted my way to the buffet. *Fatima, you really don't know what the hell to say*. Why didn't I just say, you mean my boyfriend? It seems that the perfect words are always two steps behind. I stood in front of the most amazing breakfast spread that I've ever seen. Pastries, muffins, biscuits. My eyes popped out when I saw a fresh loaf of honey oatmeal bread. After piling three slices on my plate along with eggs and bacon and a cheese Danish, I bounced back to the table.

When I was greeted with a smile, I appreciated that he accepted that I never knew what to say and that he didn't take it personally.

Scene 42

RASHAD

It's times like this when I wonder. The way her head shook back and forth made it appear that she wanted to say, "Oh, hell no, that's not my husband."

It took every nerve in my body not to tell her to go dig her damn husband up from the grave. Instead, I squashed her comment with my compassion for her and her pain. She stared into my eyes and pouted. That look always triggered amnesia in me as she transformed back into the lady I wanted to spend the rest of my life with.

She tasted her food and squirmed. "Mmmm. This is so good."

I chuckled as I enjoyed her appreciation for new things. When we finished breakfast, we walked into the tea lounge. She tugged at my hand. I leaned in closer and she whispered, "Let's act like we're rich."

"What?"

"If you haven't noticed, we're the only black folks here."

"So."

Her pupils swirled. "So, we'll be a famous R&B couple, if they ask."

"You love to play games."

"We'll be Kindred."

I laughed. "Girl, you are funny."

"I just want to know if they—" Her nose wrinkled like she'd been confronted with a foul smell. "—would even know."

Just when I thought she was crazy, it was validated without a shadow of a doubt. We sat near an older white couple. The guy looked like a lumberjack, just like all the other men in town, and the lady looked like she was pulled straight from the pages of *The Happy Homemaker.* Fatima smiled at the couple and I followed her lead.

"It's so nice here."

Initially, the lady didn't seem receptive and I was surprised when the man chimed in, "Yeah, we love it here."

Fatima asked, "You come here often?"

He nodded. "Yep, 'bout five times a year."

"This is our first." She reached over and rested her hand atop mine. "We like it. Don't we, honey?"

I nodded. "Yeah, we like it."

The lady asked, "What brings you here?"

Fatima sighed. "Well, we just finished touring. So we're here to regroup and get some writing done for our third album."

Did she really just say that? The couple's jaws dropped. I wanted to burst out laughing, but I nodded in support of her fabricated plot.

"Singers?"

Fatima nodded. "Yeah, singers and songwriters."

After I got over the shock, I added, "She's the singer and songwriter. I just sing her songs."

The man laughed. "Well, you've got the answer to a happy marriage." He coughed. "Sing her song. I like that."

His wife rolled her eyes at him. "Can we buy your music from the store?"

Fatima smiled. "Yep, we're Kindred. Our first album is 'Surrender to Love' and the second is 'In This Life Together.'"

As they inquired further about our break into the industry, I was amazed at how well we fed off of one another and evaded having our cover blown. When we left the tea lounge, we had an adrenaline rush like we'd gotten away with a crime.

We laughed hysterically and she looked at me. "Why did we do that?"

"Why did *you* do it?"

We laughed harder. For the entire ride to Lake Elmore, we replayed what we said, what we should have said, what we planned to do if they wanted autographs.

When I opened the car door, she spilled out of the car still amused by our little skit. I caught her stumbling and wrapped my arms around her. The light fall breeze whirled around us, drawing us closer. I kissed her. "You make everything an adventure."

"We'll see how adventurous you think I am when I flip the kayak over."

Her hair fell through my fingers as I cupped her head in my hands. "Don't worry. I can handle it for the both of us."

She referenced the kayak and I referenced life. One day soon, she would have nothing to worry about. When we walked over to the trailer to get the equipment, she twiddled her thumbs. I asked, "Are you nervous?"

She shuddered. I laughed. "Don't be. I got you."

"You sure?"

"Positive."

Her eyes doubted me and I stepped up to the counter. After the boat keeper gave basic instructions and handed us life jackets, he walked with us to the kayaks. Fatima staggered behind.

I sat in the front of the kayak and Fatima reluctantly sat behind me. When the guys pushed us onto the lake, I explained the technique to Fatima. "It's best if we paddle in unison. If I'm moving too fast, let me know. To turn right, we paddle hard on the left and vice versa."

I looked back and she squinted like she really wanted to follow my instructions. Her bottom lip trembled. I rested the paddle on my lap and reached back and rubbed her leg. "Are you cold?"

She nodded.

"Once we start moving, you'll warm up."

She dipped her paddle in the water. I followed suit. "Now, left . . . and right."

When I turned to make sure we stroked at the same pace, she smiled.

"You like this, don't you?"

She nodded. "Yeah, it's really peaceful."

The sun beamed down on us, casting an orange shadow to the calm water. We coasted alongside a mountain and the leaves on the trees graced us with a multitude of fall color combinations. Neither of us spoke as we absorbed the great outdoors.

This sport can make or break a relationship. As we rowed in sync and she humbly followed my lead, I presumed it made us. These were the defining moments that made her. About a half mile away from the dock, Fatima complained about her arms tiring, but she didn't stop moving until I stopped.

When we positioned the kayak so that we wouldn't drift too far out, I grabbed her paddle and lay both on my lap and I leaned back to rest my head in between her legs. She ran her hands over my face and said, "I love it here."

"I know."

"What's this trip about?"

"Just a weekend getaway from all the drama in the city."

She inhaled the crisp air. "I just don't . . . I mean . . . Are you?"

Scene 43

FATIMA

I couldn't say it. How could I ask him if he was about to leave me? The words were stuck in my throat. I contemplated: What more could he give me? I asked him to facilitate a fantasy and he exceeded his performance in all areas.

As the authentic sounds of nature entertained us, it felt like time stood still. His raised eyebrows begged me to finish my sentence. I sighed. "Are you happy?"

"The happiest man in the world."

Why did his lines feel like lies? Could it be because they were my words and not his? I kissed away the uncertainty and wondered how I'd drifted so far away from reality.

"Do *I* make you happy?"

He rocked side to side. "Don't make me flip this boat over to get through to you. You know that you make me happy."

I laughed. "I just needed to know."

He sat up. "What's the title of our second album again?"

I frowned. Then it dawned on me, I laughed. "Oh! The title is 'In This Life together.'"

He smirked. "All right then."

My eyebrows rippled. All right then, what? Why was he pretending like he wasn't about to call it quits? He shook his head. "You're a trip. You came up with this whole fabricated story and

I have to remind you who we are. You have to stay in character, Teem."

His words stung. That's it. He planned to stay in character until the end. Then, he would step away from the script and stomp on my heart like this role never existed. He sat back up, lifted his paddle over his head, and gave me mine back.

"C'mon. Let's head back. I want to do more sightseeing."

I watched his broad shoulders seesaw as we headed back. Each stroke made him more and more attractive. I shook my head and pitied the way I would feel once he was gone.

By the time we got back to the hotel, the sun had gone down. We sat on the balcony with our jackets on until night fall. Before we got ready for dinner, we admired the stars. Why can't I predict the future? If the clarity of the sky has anything to do with an astrologist's accuracy, sign me up for a reading in this town as soon as possible.

When we returned from dinner, it was quite disheartening that we'd be returning to the city in less than twelve hours. I wanted to talk about his plans for us, but the mood was too perfect to ruin. So, I fell asleep with tons of unanswered questions and woke up with even more.

When would he turn in his resignation? Would he still want to be friends? Am I smitten with Rashad or the main character that I developed? Was he planning a clean break? Would he step out gradually?

Before he woke up, I practiced an array of lead-ins to inquire about the conversation that I overhead. Nothing seemed right. No matter which way I worded it, it made me sound as if I wasn't holding up to my end of the bargain. I propped my chin in my hand and watched him snake around. He flinched and his eyes popped. My eyes met his. He squinted. It was obvious my gaze startled him, so I smiled to calm him. "Good morning."

He wrapped his arm around my waist and laid his head in my lap. As I traced the definition in his back, my eyes rolled in my head. Boy, how I'm going to miss him.

While I showered, I concluded that I didn't want to force him to say what he wasn't ready to say. Maybe he had changed his mind. He brought me here to say something, but maybe he didn't have the heart to do it. When I stepped out of the bathroom, Rashad sat with his head in his hands. The shades that I pulled down now blocked the sun out. My heart raced. Maybe he was about to say it. I tiptoed toward him. He ran his hand over his face. "Whew! I'm tired."

My eyes asked if there was another reason that he looked distressed. I pretended to be protecting my towel from falling, but I held my heart in my hand. He smirked. "What's wrong with you?"

"Ah, I was just wondering if you were okay."

His face wrinkled and then he laughed. "Are *you* okay?"

Maybe I'm paranoid, but he looked like the one with the problem. I proceeded to get prepared.

Once we were both ready, Rashad took our bag to the car while I looked around at the room. This place was probably the beginning to the end. My eyes filled and I quickly dried them when Rashad came in. I presumed my stance asked for a hug. Instead, he stopped several feet away from me and said, "C'mon. We have to get back to the city."

"I don't want to go back."

He huffed. "We have to. I have an audition in the morning. I want to get back and relax."

I dragged from the room. When I sat in the car, I decided to suppress my insecurities with positive thoughts. At least I've been happy for almost six months.

When the engine shut off, my eyes popped open, and I was surprised to see we were on my street. After we'd stopped for lunch, I fell asleep, but I didn't realize I was out that long. I rubbed my eyes.

My hand rested on his leg. "Baby, I'm sorry. I didn't mean to sleep the whole ride."

"It's okay. I didn't mind. It gave me a chance to think."

To think? What is he thinking about? After we'd gotten the stuff in the house, I stood in the middle of the living room floor and he gave me a hug. As we rocked side to side, he asked, "Do you mind if I go home tonight?"

Although I did, I shook my head, no. He kissed my forehead and explained, "The audition is at six in the morning. Plus, I need to take this car back tonight."

I was certain—I didn't believe him. In all the years that Mya has been in the business, I never recall a casting at six in the morning. I shrugged my shoulders. "Okay, I'll talk to you later."

He kissed me again to prolong his departure. My eyes danced around the ceiling. He chuckled. "What's wrong?"

I smiled. "Nothing."

"Did you have a good time this weekend?"

I nodded. He kissed my forehead. "Me too."

"Okay. I need to get some rest," I said.

"Are you trying to put me out?"

"Ah. Yeah."

He laughed and kissed my cheek. With his hand still resting on my face, he stared into my eyes. "Good night, Teem."

I smirked. He kissed me once more and fled the scene. My hand gripped the knob and I touched the back of the door. Something told me this was our last night.

Scene 44

RASHAD

On the ride home, I began to wonder if I was really what Fatima needed and wanted. As my feelings sank deeper for her, the more I questioned transforming this into a real relationship. I was always told that if you want to know how something will end, look at how it began. How could Fatima and I ever have the wonderful relationship I imagined, considering it started with me being a male prostitute? Will she always think she can pimp me?

When my alarm went off at five in the morning, I hopped up and rushed through the apartment. Lucky thing I had organized everything last night. I was out and on the train by five-thirty. It was ten before six by the time I arrived at the audition. As I sat waiting in a crowded room, I dropped my head and prayed. Though my life as a landlord was looking positive, my heart was here awaiting stardom. This is what I was born to do.

My fist clinched tightly. It seemed it had been an eternity since I'd had the opportunity to audition for something other than a stand-in. As luck would have it, they were searching for a relatively unknown actor to play a major role in a blockbuster. Looking at the hundreds of dudes in the room with me, I wondered if this were a pipe dream.

They began by calling us in twenty at a time. My number being seventy-three, I was in the fourth round. A piece of me began to feel defeated. That was until the lead casting director introduced himself to the group. I smiled and hoped he recognized me. It was one of the guys I had met at Mya's house.

He announced that he planned to make a decision today. Then he said, "Does anyone have any issues that would prevent you from spending the night here?"

A few guys chuckled. He said, "Actually, I'm serious. For those of you who have worked with me before, you know that I give my all and I expect the same from you. That commitment begins the day you audition. If you can't spend the night, leave now."

It amazed me that several guys walked off the stage. They obviously hadn't been a part of the hustle as long as I had. Damn if I planned to go anywhere. The director continued, "Commitment means more to me than talent. You could be the best actor in the world, but if you're not committed, you'll never make it."

After the group audition, I made it to the individual audition. My fingers were crossed and nothing else mattered to me. I confirmed every ten minutes or so that my cell phone was definitely off. Several guys were cut just because their phones rang. Let my talent be the reason, because I would flip if it were something so stupid.

When I was called in, Steve, the director, greeted me, "Hey, Rashad. I thought that was you."

I walked over to shake his hand. He patted my back. "I'm glad to see you, man."

"Same here."

After I auditioned, Steve summoned me. His tone didn't sound too friendly. My eyes opened wide and he shook his head. "Nah, I just have a few questions for you, man."

I dramatically wiped my forehead. He and the others chuckled. After he told me that I had made it to the next round, he invited me into the coffee room. As he poured coffee, he asked, "How flexible are you?"

I frowned. He clarified, "I mean, at the party, you mentioned buying some property. I'm just curious how quickly you could pack up and be in LA. Or if you're even interested in being in LA."

As a goofy grin appeared on my face, he jumped in, "I'm not saying that you have the role. We have a few rounds left, but I just want to know your status."

"Look. I will drop everything and catch the first flight to LA if an opportunity comes through."

"That's what I like to hear." Then, his expression changed and he released a sympathetic sigh. "How's Mrs. Mayo?"

I cringed. "Fatima's fine."

"That's good. I've known her and Mya for a long time. I'm Mya's mentor."

I nodded, because he had shared that with me at the party. He continued, "Fatima was something else. I'm sure she still is." He sighed. "She's a hard woman to please. I always said I feel sorry for the man that had to replace Derrick."

He patted my back to alleviate the sting. Trying to shake it, I defended her: "She's not that bad."

"Fatima is a brat. Derrick knew how to manage her, but man, I wish you luck."

Since he had the upper hand on me at the moment, I couldn't hit him in his mouth like I was tempted. How could I be disrespected so easily? His comments were confirmation. I could never replace Derrick? Everyone, including Fatima speaks as if he were a god. I refuse to walk in his shadow.

Scene 45

FATIMA

When I woke up to no coffee or breakfast, it was obvious that Rashad was sleeping on the job or trying to quit.

By the time I got to work, it was close to noon. Kia blinked rapidly when I walked in. I smiled. "Hey, honey."

She whispered, "Mr. Lisbon called for you."

"Why are you whispering?"

She shrugged her shoulders. I asked, "What did he say?"

"He called at nine. Then again at ten and around eleven-thirty."

My eyes shifted and my heart dropped. "And what did he say?"

"He keeps saying for you to come to his office the moment you get in."

Her eyes told me she knew more, but I tried to think positive. It couldn't really be anything major. Before going to his office, I decided to do some investigation. No one that I tried to call picked up. Suddenly, I began to feel they were all trying to avoid me. I took a deep breath and stood proudly.

After ironing out my suit with my hands, I strutted out of the office. Kia whispered, "Good luck."

I waved my arm at her hoping to calm her concern. On the way to his office, I came up with a defense just in case. Finally, I stood outside of the president's office. The last time I'd gotten a personal call, it was when I was promoted to editorial director.

When his secretary noticed me, she tightened her lips. I responded with the same expression. After a few seconds of awkwardness, she said, "Fatima, you can go on in. He's expecting you."

With my head held high, I strutted into his office. Though he didn't greet me with a pleasant expression, I smiled. "Good morning."

"Good afternoon."

I nodded and folded my arms. He instructed me to have a seat as he stood up and walked to the door. As I lowered my bottom into the chair, my heart fell on the seat first.

When he finally sat across from me, his eyes scorned me. Mine lowered. He began, "You came to us straight out of college and you were a star for such a long time."

As he awaited a reaction, I just stared through him. I sighed deeply. He continued, "Over the last year or so . . ." He paused. "I just can't justify why you're here."

It took several seconds for his words to register. I squinted. Did he just tell me that he can't justify why I'm here? I mouthed, "What?"

"Everything you've acquired has been a flop. Money is going out and we're not getting a return. You've become a liability."

When I tasted my tears, I knew I couldn't sit there and humbly accept his verdict. I scooted to the edge of my chair. "Have you ever even considered that I've lost good authors to other houses because contracts are too slow or you're too cheap to approve my recommended advances? Have you ever thought about that? I've spent twelve hours a day here for the last three months because I can't depend on other people to hire qualified freelancers. What about them? Why is this all falling on me?"

"Fatima, we really like you and I didn't want it to get to this point. It's unfortunate for everyone, but I'm afraid we're going to have to let you go."

Now, my reputation was insulted and I disregarded my dignity as I shouted, "Let me go? Let me go? You couldn't even offer me the opportunity to resign?"

He muttered, "This way, at least you'll receive severance."

Now on my feet, I pointed. "I don't want your damn sever-ance. Keep it. I just want to keep my reputation." I spoke slowly. "Allow me to resign."

"I know you're upset right now, but maybe you should think about it. I'm offering you three months of pay."

I snickered. "I don't want your sympathy. Let me just quit and you don't owe me anything and I don't owe you anything."

He smirked and shrugged his shoulders. "It doesn't matter to me. Do what you feel is in your best interests. You don't have to walk out right now. If you would like to stay the remainder of the day to transfer responsibility, it's perfectly fine."

He must think I'm some sort of fool. What makes him think I'll transfer anything? I stormed from his office and jogged to mine. When I walked in, my runny eyeliner alarmed Kia. She stood up. "Fatima, what happened?"

"Type me a resignation letter effective immediately."

When I walked into my office, the room spun around me. I stood confused. The walls closed in on me as I absorbed what had just happened. I looked at all the things I needed to pack and began to wail. Kia rushed in with the resignation letter and asked, "Are you okay?"

"Kia, I needed a break anyway." I laughed in the midst of it all, because I subconsciously wanted this.

"It'll be okay. You know you'll find another job."

I sniffed. "You're right. Can you help me pack?"

We threw my stuff in trashbags and I called Rashad. His phone went directly to voicemail. Before I took the letter to Mr. Lis-bon's office, I tried again. Still no answer. In an attempt not to alarm him, I left calm messages.

Certain that the word had spread through the company sec-onds after it happened, I was offended that no one came in to say good-bye. That hurt more than the actual termination. Sec-onds before I walked out, I tried Rashad again. Then, it dawned on me, I had lost my job and Rashad was voluntarily quitting his.

As I sat in the taxi sniffling, I directed my anger at so many dif-ferent people. My industry contacts flooded my mind as I de-cided who and where I should send my resume. With my adrenaline rushing and anger exploding, I forgot how much I hated work anyway. Finally, I concluded that I would just stay still and decide what's next for Fatima. One week after Derrick's funeral I went back to work because I was on a path to success. And where has it led me? Crazy! Never once did I think about taking time for me. What about me?

My mind reverted to Rashad. The money I had always planned on using for a sabbatical was the money I'd been using to pay him. But now, there was more to this equation than me. What about him?

By the time I reached home, I had called him three more times. Already feeling like the victim, I refused to have two men in one day determine my future. It was best to end the relationship with Rashad.

Scene 46

RASHAD

When Steve asked if we were willing to stay the night, I honestly thought it was a joke. At 1:32 in the morning, I headed back home. He tested our endurance to a fault. As much as I want to succeed, I could have quit.

At a certain point, I couldn't even concentrate on the script. I wondered where Fatima was. How many times had she called? Was everything good with the new property?

When I walked out of the building, I was mentally and physically exhausted. Steve requested that we come back at eight in the morning. He must be on some kind of energy drug, because this was borderline hazing and he didn't seem affected.

I turned my cell phone on and there where eight messages. My mind was too drained to listen to them all, so I just called Fatima and gave her an update on her answering machine.

When I woke up at seven to go back to the audition, I checked my messages. My phone was on speaker as I prepared to leave. Fatima left a few messages for me to call. The intonation in her voice increased with each message. I chuckled slightly because I knew what she was thinking. Her final message started calmly.

"Rashad . . ." She took a long pause. "I just wanted to tell you that I will not be renewing your contract. As it stands now, your contract is due to end in two weeks and . . ." She sighed. "I'll pay you until then, but you don't have to show up anymore." She cleared her throat. "Have a good life."

Smoke blew from my ears. I dialed her number. She didn't answer. As I stormed around my room angry, I remembered that I had to get out of there. I refused to deal with it at the moment— I was so close to getting my breakthrough role. I heaved. How could she do this over the phone? What an insensitive woman. Here I am breaking my neck trying to be the man that she needed and she could just fire me over the phone. Did she even consider that I could have been hurt or in the hospital?

When I arrived at the audition, I was so distracted. Fatima became my enemy, because her inconsiderateness could possibly sabotage my future. I needed to wash my hands of it. After a moment of meditation to get my mind on my goal, I concluded that this was the answer I prayed for. I turned my phone off and prepared for another full day of hazing.

Scene 47

FATIMA

When I woke up and saw Rashad's number on the caller ID, I immediately called him back. His phone was off again. I wanted to scream, because I wasn't sure if he'd technically quit before I fired him.

Before I checked my messages, I opened another bottle of wine. My heart sank when the message date and time was stated. It was Rashad. Initially, I heard nothing but static. I prayed he had said something, anything. Finally, his distressed voice came through and I was able to make out only pieces of the message: "all day . . . quit . . . too much . . . won't talk . . . my life . . . future"

I choked on my tears. All day, he thought about quitting because this is too much and he won't talk to me for the rest of his life. Have a good future. Is that what he said? He agreed with my decision and he didn't feel the need to be on my doorstep everyday like he claimed. I thought we had something special. As I internalized the truth, I knew I'd made the right decision to let him go. He had this planned all along.

When I couldn't muster the courage to call Mya yesterday, I knew I'd reached an all-time low. She's been with me through it all. When she picked up, it pained me as I confessed my failure in everything. "Mya."

"What's wrong?"

"I got fired yesterday."

She chuckled. "Don't play with me, Tima."

"I wish I was playing."

"No! What happened?"

Feeling the need to laugh at the accusations, I snickered. "They claim I haven't acquired anything worth having in two years." I laughed at myself again. "They said I'm a liability."

"Screw them! You're the best thing that ever happened to them. The way you've been busting your ass lately. They have a nerve. Forget them. You can go to another house."

"Uh. I think I'm going to take a break." I paused so it could seep in. "I'm just not feeling this anymore."

"Tima, you love being an editor."

"I used to love it. I've been unhappy for a long time. It just doesn't make me as happy as it used to."

"Tima, maybe you should take a break. Make sure you're not letting them mess with your ego."

I sighed. "I don't know."

"So, are you straight financially?"

"Well, I've already told Rashad that I wouldn't renew his contract. So, that frees up all the money I'll need."

"You let him go just like that? What did he say? Are you guys still going to be together?"

"Well, we'd come to a crossroad anyway. I think I was taking too much time away from his life. He really wants to start focusing on his acting and . . ."

"Don't tell me he's going to leave you alone now that you can't pay him."

"He doesn't even know I got fired."

"Why didn't you tell him?"

"I think he planned to break it off anyway. I didn't talk to him all day yesterday and I—"

"So, did you guys break up while you were away this weekend?"

"Mya, I don't know. All I know is that I left him a message to tell him that I no longer needed his services—"

"You did what?"

"I told him that I didn't need him and he didn't have to come back."

"You left this on his answering machine?" Fatima, you know I've taught you better than that. When did you do this?"

"Yesterday."

She shouted, "Yesterday! Fatima, he was at a big audition yesterday. I haven't had a chance to talk to Steve to see how he made out, but one way or the other I'm sure he was stressed."

I huffed. "I don't care."

"What do you mean you don't care? The man had a busy day and you decided you want to break up with him over the phone."

"Well, it doesn't matter now, because he called back to say that he thought it was a good idea and he hopes I have a good life."

"Tima, are you kidding?"

"I wish I was."

"I don't want to jump to conclusions because I'm sure he had a pretty drilling day and it's possible that he just wasn't in the mood to deal with it."

"It doesn't matter. He agreed that we should be apart."

She sighed. "Well, he was just a stand-in anyway. Maybe it's best this way. He can pursue his dream and you can find real love."

Though I agreed, I yearned for Rashad. What was he thinking? How was this so easy to let go? What about all the love I felt when we were together? What about us? How was I supposed to handle another death?

"Fatima . . . Fatima . . ."

I sniffed. "I'm here."

"Honey, do you need me to come over there?"

"It just hurts so bad."

"Fatima, I think you should call him again."

"Mya, I can't keep throwing money away like that. At least when I had a job, I could justify tossing away a hundred and ten thousand dollars a year, but not now. Derrick would be so disappointed in me. I should be putting that money into something that's going to make money for me, because I'm not sure I'll ever go back to work."

"Why don't you call him and explain the situation? Let him make the decision."

"Mya, did you hear me when I said he made his decision? I will not call him and beg him to be my man. Bad enough, I paid for the relationship. Let me walk away with *some* pride left."

She sucked her teeth. "Okay, stubborn. You know him better than me."

She knew when to push and when to pull, because all of sudden, she had jumped on my side. After a brief silence, she said, "Screw him, Tima. If he doesn't want to be your man without the money, he's not worth it. This game has gone too far anyway. It was silly for us to think this would end smoothly."

As she sat on the phone damning the idea we conjured up, I needed to hear a voice of compassion.

I told her that I had to go and I called my mother. She instantly heard distress in my voice. "Fatima, you don't sound good."

My sniffle became a sob, as my mother pleaded with me to tell her everything. I decided not to share my relationship saga, but I told her how I was fired. Though the emotions I expressed were a result of Rashad, not my job.

"Come home for a few days, baby."

"I'll see. I don't know."

"You need to be with family right now."

As she continued to convince me, I logged on the Internet and searched for flights. Before I actually confirmed a reservation, I thought I should at least have a verbal exchange with Rashad. When I got off the phone, I called him again and his voicemail greeted me once more. I decided not to leave a message. If he had gone as far as cutting his phone off, he obviously didn't want to talk.

Sniffing all the way through the process, I bought my ticket to

Huntsville. Then, I curled up on my couch and reread old gossip magazines to submerge myself in other people's dramas.

It crossed my mind a few times that maybe I should start my own magazine. Derrick had already created the blueprint. All I needed to do was put as much energy as he put into it. I sucked my teeth. Then, I'll be dead, too.

Scene 48

RASHAD

Luckily, we were done by seven-thirty and Steve had narrowed it down to five soldiers, because this was clearly worse than boot camp. I'd pushed my own drama to the back of my mind, but as soon as I came back out of the building, I immediately wondered how Fatima could do what she'd done. After a few more random chats with Steve, I understood Fatima a little better and I felt I could never make her happy. It's funny, maybe she should pursue acting. I thought we were headed somewhere. But as I replayed her message for the twentieth time, it was obvious that I was the only happy one.

As much as I was angered about our break up, I guess she came into my life for a reason. I would have never believed I would own property in New York. Although I wanted more from her, she didn't owe me anything.

My mother looked shock when I walked in the house. She said, "It's good to see you."

I chuckled. "Good to see you, too."

As I kissed her cheek, she patted my back. Boxes lined the wall as she had already begun to pack her stuff to move into her newly renovated apartment. I sat down beside her. "You're ready to get out of here, huh?"

She nodded. "I'm ready. I can't wait."

"Access Hollywood" played on the television and I gazed at it. She laughed. "Why are you all into this trash?"

Instantly, that put Fatima to the forefront of my mind. Feeling the need to mend the ache in my heart, I chuckled and stood up. "I'm not watching this."

I headed to my room and checked my phone every five seconds. She hadn't called. She hadn't recanted her statement. I covered my face with my pillow. After evaluating where my life was headed, I realized Fatima was cheating herself out of the final product.

Scene 49

FATIMA

As I stood on the steps waiting for the car to take me to the airport, I looked up the street and saw Rashad. My heart smiled and I was so thankful that he'd come to question my irrational words. I had trotted down the stairs to meet him when I realized it was a bad look-alike. My head hung as the fake Rashad passed me.

When the car pulled up, I paused to look around. Maybe the real Rashad was near. I sat inside the car and hesitated closing the door. Then I knew—there was nothing keeping me in New York.

On the plane ride to Alabama, I was able to listen to my thoughts. I'd lost touch with Fatima and didn't know where to find her. How did I ever stoop so low as to pay for companionship? This is never where I expected to be. Derrick and I were supposed to build an empire. Now, I'm here, trying to fight the battle of this world alone.

When my mother came to the airport with almost the entire family packed in her minivan, I knew we were in for a celebration. My family should receive an honor for the Eleventh Hour Barbecue. They party for everything and, of course, there had to be a party for the return of the long-lost Fatima. Before we pulled up to the house, I could smell the grill.

"Who's coming?"

"Chile, everyone is already here. We ain't seen you in almost eighteen months."

I didn't realize it had been so long. I'd abandoned my roots. When I stepped out and onto my parents' two-acre lawn, I questioned why. I walked to the back of the house and my daddy wore his chef hat as he checked on the pig roast. I hugged him.

"Hey, Daddy. Thanks for doing all this for me."

"I know you don't eat like this in New York, so I got to take care of you."

I greeted all of my other relatives that came to celebrate my homecoming. How could I take this free love for granted? As my family and I exchanged stories, their dialect always made me giggle. I often had a Southern drawl again when I got back to New York. Being around all of my good country cousins made me want to stay in Alabama and escape the drama. They were just happy for the hell of it. We glided across the lawn doing the played-out "Booty-call" line dance. I drank nearly a keg of beer to numb my heart. By the time everyone began to leave, I was an Alabama girl again. I was fittin' to move back home as I walked around barefoot helping my mother straighten up.

When everyone was gone, my issues resurfaced. I checked my cell phone just in case Rashad had a change of heart, but I was terribly disappointed. My sister and my mother came into the house shortly after me. We sat in the living room with my grandmother and chatted.

Granny asked, "Tima, have you been with another man since Damon died?"

I chuckled. "Granny, his name was Derrick."

Granny curled her lips. "It don't matter what his name was. You ain't answer my question."

"Granny, I can't tell you that."

My sister said, "You know Granny thinks she's a sex therapist."

We all laughed longer than necessary. Granny huffed. "You got to get under a man to get over one."

I stretched my mouth open. "Granny."

She sucked her gums. "I haven't been old forever."

My mother chimed in, "Did you cheat on my father?"

"Nope."

Then, my mother said, "So, what do you know about getting under another man?"

"Your father died when I was fifty-nine. I still had a lot of iron in the fire." My grandmother giggled at her own joke and we shook our heads.

Suddenly all eyes were on me. My mother raised her eyebrows. "So, are you dating?"

I played up the lonely widow sigh. "It's just so hard to find someone comparable to Derrick. You know?"

Granny raised her eyebrow at my mother. "Huh?"

My mother clarified, "Someone that compares."

Granny laughed. "Fatima, you so siddity it's sickening. Ain't nobody going to compare. All mens is different."

She sure could slaughter the King's English. I giggled and my mother said it again to confirm that I got the message. "Fatima, nobody is going to compare. Everyone has their own special qualities. You can't make another man act like Derrick. What's most important is his character. As long as he respects you, is understanding, cares about you, and has his life together, that's what's important."

"I know."

Granny said, "Well have you slept with any other mens?"

"I told you."

"You said they ain't compare, but you didn't say you haven't slept with 'em."

"No, Granny. I haven't slept with another man."

She and my mother conversed with their eyes like this was something they had discussed. I tried to direct attention to the television. My twenty-year-old sister chimed in and confirmed they all had discussed my love life. "Tima, you have to stop looking at yourself as Derrick's wife. You're single now. You have to get back out there and look for the next man in line." She smiled. "It's been almost four years."

Granny chuckled. "Lawd, you musta been switched at birth cuz you sure ain't take after me."

My mother interrupted Granny's grunting. "Fatima, Felicia is right. You're too young to call it quits. It's not fair that you are a young widow, but you have to put that portion of your life behind. You still have time to have another fulfilling relationship."

I nodded and tried to understand what they were telling me. What did everyone else see that I didn't? How was I supposed to just forget all the dreams me and Derrick had shared?

Scene 50

RASHAD

As ready as my mother was to move, she seemed to have a hard time transitioning. More of her things were at the old apartment than the new. I stumbled into my new apartment carrying a heavy box when my cell phone rang. I was elated to hear Steve's voice.

"What's up, Rashad? It's Steve."

I crossed my fingers before responding. "Hey, Steve. Things are good."

"Are you sitting down?"

My heart jumped out of my chest and bobbled on the floor. I stared as my heart beat. "No, but I can be."

He laughed. "Well, sit down."

My knees trembled as I found a box. "Okay. I'm sitting."

"Pack your bags, buddy. You're about to be the hottest new actor in Hollywood."

As if my floor were a trampoline, I jumped up and down. I hit high-five with the door and the wall. What did I do to deserve this? Tears rolled from my eyes as I fought to catch my breath.

"Steve, man. Please tell me you're not playing with me."

"Look, man. I let agents handle rejections. If you didn't have the job, you definitely wouldn't hear it from me. Why don't you go out and celebrate tonight. We'll talk the specifics tomorrow. I just wanted to give you the good news."

"Man, you can give me the specifics now. I can be in LA in twenty-four hours."

He chuckled. "Look, man, you have about a week to make the move. Like I said, we'll talk tomorrow."

Still out of breath, I gasped, "All right, Steve, as long as you don't change your mind."

"Don't worry. It's sealed. I sent your tape to the producers and they loved you. It's your role, man."

Trying to express my deepest gratitude, I took a deep breath. "Steve, thanks for everything, man."

"Don't mention it."

I hung up the phone and jogged to the old apartment. When I announced the great news to my mother, we jumped around in circles. Though she'd told me to get a real job dozens of times, the tears in her eyes said she was glad that I never listened.

Monique happened to call in the midst of our celebration. She wanted to discuss the new property. Though I would have liked to be greedy and commit to doing everything, I told her that we needed to scrap the second property. I wouldn't have the time to manage the renovation. My head nodded to an internal beat as I explained that I was planning to be in LA.

Though I'm certain Monique was happy, she sounded disappointed. Now that we no longer had to do business, I thought it might be an ideal time for the dinner I promised her. I asked her to hold and covered my mouthpiece. I mouthed, "Do you mind if I take her out to celebrate?"

My mother shooed me. "Honey, I don't care. I'll celebrate on my own."

When I returned to the phone, I said, "Monique, I'd love to celebrate with you. If it's okay, I'd like to take you out this evening."

"Rashad, I would love to."

"I'll meet you at eight."

When I hung up the phone, my mother smiled. "Now, you can find yourself a woman."

I chuckled. "You've been trying to get me hitched since I graduated from college."

* * *

When I arrived at Monique's place, she was anxious and ready. She met me at the door and didn't invite me in. On the taxi ride to the restaurant, I asked her casual questions. She seemed to be in another world or at least not in this one. My ego longed for excitement, which she clearly lacked.

"Do you like to dance?"

She shrugged her shoulders. "Not really."

"Do you like comedy?"

"Sometimes."

I took a deep breath. Sometimes attraction is not enough. Finally, I just stared out of the window. When we arrived at the restaurant, I asked if she wanted a drink. She declined, "I don't drink."

Okay, Monique had officially blown my high. As I ordered a constant stream of Cuervo shots, I refused to grant her the authority. She could either join my party or watch it. Turns out, she chose the latter. After the taxi dropped her off, I told the driver to take me to Fatima's address. I'm now the man she wants me to be. I sang jingles as we headed uptown. "'If I have to beg and plead for your sympathy, I don't mind, because you mean that much to me."

I beat on the back of the driver's seat. When I stepped out of the taxi, I yelled, "Fatima!"

I jogged up her stairs and rang the bell. Her office light was on, so I tapped on the window. "Fatima. Open up. I want to be with you and I know you want to be with me. Fatima!"

I sang, "'Tell me when will I see you smile again.'"

Neighbors yelled from their windows, "Shut the hell up!"

Still, the lady I came for said nothing. She let me stand outside and make a fool of myself. I refused to go. She is the reason I am so happy. I loved her for making me worthy of her love. Like I couldn't go on without her, I yelled her name over and over again.

When the NYPD pulled up and escorted me from her door, stating they were called by the lady inside, I immediately sobered up. Well, almost, I yelled, "How can you do this, Fatima? We're better than this."

As the officers stuffed me into their cruiser, I sang Lenny Williams', " 'Cause I Love You": "I don't have much riches, but we gonna see it through. 'Cause I love you . . . and I need you.'"

The officers chuckled. One of them imitated a verse in the song: "'Lenny, you just oughta forget about her.'"

I laughed a bit. "'Maybe you've never been in love, like I've been in love.'" I sang loud enough for Fatima to hear.

He shook his head. "She just called the police on you, man. Let it go."

They slammed the door and I sang, "'I think I better let it go. Looks like another love TKO.'"

The officers laughed harder as the driver started the car. "Man, where do you live?"

As they mocked my desperate attempt to get my lady, I was disgraced. I stepped out of the house a man full of promise, and returned in a police car. When it sank in that Fatima could call the cops on me, I was determined to move to LA and forget she ever happened. Calling the cops on a black man for no reason is clear evidence that you couldn't give a damn about his future. As I fell asleep, I accepted that she could never be a part of my future.

Scene 51

FATIMA

New dreams replace old dreams. I sprung up in the middle of the night nine days later with the answer. Letting go of what Derrick and I shared meant letting a piece of myself die. I had yet to do that; instead I kept a piece of him alive and that has kept me from living. I thought I wasn't honoring his memory but I hadn't honored myself. How could he rest in peace if I'm fighting for his life? It was time to throw in the towel. I sat in the bed and pulled my wedding band from my right finger. Since nothing in my bedroom had changed since I went off to college, I thought this would be an ideal place to bury the band. I tiptoed to my trinket-like jewelry box and dropped it inside.

I tried to force myself back to sleep, but I couldn't help but think about Rashad. Could he see my reluctance to letting go? Is that why it was so easy for him to let go? I wanted to talk to him. I needed him to know. When I finally dozed off, my cell phone rang. I jumped up and assumed fate sent a subliminal message to Rashad.

I was disappointed to discover it was the doctor's office calling about a laser hair-removal appointment. As I rubbed my chin, I told them I'd try to make it. The receptionist reminded me of how long it took to get the appointment. If I missed this one, I could be looking at another two months. I took a deep breath and assumed this was the inspiration I needed to get back to New York and get everything off my chest.

When I called the airline to check on standby flights, I was told my best option would be at seven in the morning. The next day, I was packed and at the airport by five, praying that I could get on. My efforts weren't in vain as the flight attendant called for standby passenger, Fatima Mayo.

When I got off the plane, I checked my messages just in case there was a delay with me being in Alabama. There were no new messages. No one cared. My head drooped in disappointment. Suddenly, I was determined not to wallow in my pity. I had business to handle. I wanted to be with Rashad and a part of me knew he wanted me. I wanted to love him and build new dreams with him.

When the car pulled up to my house, I snapped. The light in my office had been on for ten days straight. Preoccupied with my irresponsibility, I almost forgot to pay the driver. I went into the house and the silence was too loud. I sat on the couch and stared at the portrait of Derrick and me. My family's advice was loud and clear. How could I ever move on if I couldn't let go?

I rushed downstairs, and changed my clothes. Wearing the tennis shoes Rashad had bought for me, I ran up to 148th Street to the address where I sent his pay stubs. I stood out of breath on his steps and smashed the bell. A lady said, "Yes."

I looked at the speaker and considered turning around, but I remembered his touch and the way he stared into my eyes. It had to be real. I didn't know who she was, but she was going to know who I was. I refused to let this love die. After clearing my throat, I said, "Hi. My name is Fatima Barnes. I'm looking for Rashad. Is this where he lives?"

She didn't respond, but the door buzzed. I opened up and headed for the second floor. The door opened and I was happy to see an older woman. My smile pleaded with her. "Is Rashad home?"

She looked confused. "He's at the new house."

"The new house?"

"Yeah, we're moving."

I nodded slowly. "Where's the new house?"

"On One hundred and twenty-seventh, sweetie. Aren't you the young lady that works with the company that helped him with the place?"

I had no idea what the hell she was talking about, but I nodded. "Yeah, but I forget the address."

She willingly told me the exact address and the cross streets. I dashed from the building and hopped into a taxi. I rang every bell on the door. Rashad appeared in the doorway and I pushed my way in. Boxes were sprawled around the apartment. We stood in the middle of the floor. Our emotions echoed as we stepped in circles around each other.

I said, "Hey."

With a blank look, he replied, "Hey."

Though I'd practiced my speech for nearly a day, I didn't know what to say. His stoic stance befuddled me. I asked, "Just moving in?"

"Well, my mother's going to move into this apartment now. I'm going to rent out the one that she had planned to live in."

"So, you own this place?"

"Yeah, I bought it awhile ago. But we just finished the renovation a week or so ago."

"So, why aren't you going to stay here?"

"Mya didn't tell you?"

"No, I haven't spoken to Mya. I just got back from Alabama about an hour ago."

"Well, I'm moving to LA tomorrow."

I gasped, "Tomorrow?"

He nodded.

"What's in LA?"

"I got the leading role in a new movie and we start taping this week."

"That's so wonderful. Ah . . . um . . ."

Confused, I didn't know why I was there. It was never about love for him. He had a dream and I was just a delay. I clapped my hands and nodded to avoid crying. "Bravo. I always knew you were a great actor."

My head hung and I reached out for a hug. He loosely slung his arm around me. As I fought my tears, I backed up to the door. "I'm glad I had a chance to wish you farewell."

"Teem." My eyes begged for something in his voice. He put one finger up. "Here, check this out when you get a chance."

He handed me a manila envelope with what appeared to be a manuscript inside. I smirked because he had no clue that I wasn't in that business anymore. When I put my hand on the door, I hoped he'd pull me back. I spoke slowly, "Maybe we'll hook up when I come to LA. Or when you come back."

He walked over and kissed my forehead. "Take care, Teem."

"You, too."

Afraid to end the scene, it took me nearly three minutes to exit the stage. My leading man never ran after me. I walked up the street at the pace of a turtle and peeked over my shoulder. Why didn't he rescue me?

I went back home and put the numbing cream on my face for my laser appointment as if I weren't already numb. I slouched to the train station. I never even felt the pinch that the doctor told me I should feel.

I sat in my living room sulking when the effects of the laser began. My skin started to sting and I tried to rub it away. Still, it hurt. Then, I was crying—my face burned and Rashad was on his way to Hollywood. Blowing my nose in her ear, I called Mya.

"Girl, your voicemail wasn't coming on while you were in Alabama."

I sniffed. "I know. My phone works sometimes down there and sometimes it doesn't."

"I thought you felt better the last time I talked to you."

"I just came from Rashad's place. I went there to confess my feelings, but he wasn't feeling it."

"What did he say?"

"Nothing. He didn't have to say anything. He looked at me like I didn't belong there."

"Did you get a chance to say anything?"

"No."

"Good."

"Why?"

" 'Cause he would probably think I told you that he's about to blow up."

"But you didn't."

"He doesn't know that. You fire him over the phone and show up two weeks later saying you changed your mind. He's not trying to hear that."

Spit bubbles lined my lips. "But, he has to know what I felt. I . . . He—"

"Honey, I don't know. Maybe you should go back and just get it off your chest."

"What if he doesn't want to hear it?"

"Can you handle that?"

"I don't think I can."

"Well, I think you did the right thing."

When my wailing became worse than when Derrick died, I pleaded, "Mya, let me go."

"I'll stop by when I get done, okay?"

When I hung up, I opened a bottle of wine. I decided to entertain myself while I got drunk, so I pulled out the manuscript from the envelope. It was titled: "The Perfect Script II" by Rashad Watkins.

My heart plummeted. Afraid to flip the page, I traced over the title. Would he describe a woman like me or someone else? I found the courage to read the summary of the characters. His words jumped off the page and pointed in my face. My shortcomings were all outlined in scenes: *Ability to love like she has never loved before. Cook for me as often as I cook for her. Treat me with as much consideration as I treat her. Never say goodbye over the phone.*

As I read on, I was shocked to see my positives as well as my negatives. His script stated that if the woman snores, she should wear nose strips. I'd asked him before if it bothered him, but, of course, he had said no. Damn it! I forced him to lie to me. His script showed that he saw the imperfect me as perfect.

My heart raced as I tried to think of ways to reverse this and really show him who I was. Getting fired and going home was the wakeup call that I needed. I'm alive. I didn't die with Derrick and Rashad made me see that. I have to go get him. I need to tell him that I'm ready to give love in return. I knew: Nothing in this house mattered. I could leave it all. It represented a life that was over.

My chin was covered with aloe as I ran around packing my things. In my quest to go get my man, I peeked in the mirror to see why my skin was still stinging. I screamed, "No!"

Dark polka-dot scabs covered my chin and neck. Oh my goodness, the laser singed me. Not today of all days. How can I convince him that I'm the girl for the script when I look like a leopard?

I called the doctor's office and yelled at the top of my lungs, "You burned me all up. What am I supposed to do?"

The nurse instructed me to continue using the damn aloe-vera. I shouted, "That's not going to make these scabs go away."

She said, "The scabs will go away in due time. Usually it's just the epidermis layer that is damaged and that sheds daily anyway. You'll be fine once it heals."

"I don't have time."

"I'm really sorry Mrs. Mayo. I think I explained to you extensively the side effects of laser on colored skin."

I slammed the phone down and called Mya. She told me to slow down as I rambled off my plans and my physical damage. I repeated, "Mya, he wrote a script describing his perfect woman and I want to audition for the role."

"Go get him, Tima. I knew he wanted you."

As she boosted me up, I paused, "There's one problem: I look like a leopard."

"From crying?"

"No, from the laser hair removal."

She gasped, "You're lying."

"Please, hurry up and get here. We have to do something."

"Okay, I'll be there soon."

I continued gathering my necessities while reading the script until Mya arrived. When I opened the door, her eyes watered. She covered her mouth. "Oh my god, Tima. It's really bad."

Her reaction scared me because I assumed that I was overre-acting. She stood beside me in the bathroom mirror and admitted, "You can't go get him like that."

"What am I going to do?"

"Just calm down. Maybe makeup can work."

We grabbed my makeup and she tried to apply concealer.

I winced.

"Does it hurt?"

"It still burns."

"Tima, we may have to wait until the morning."

"What if that's too late?"

"It won't be. Just get there bright and early."

"Can you go prep him for my arrival?"

She shook her head slowly. "Tima, that's not very grown up. Now, is it?"

"I just don't want to miss him."

"You won't. I'll ask Steve to come up with something to stall him until around ten. Is that good enough?"

"I should just go."

"Honey, trust me. You do not want to go like that."

Scene 52

RASHAD

When my mother arrived at the apartment, she asked, "Did that young lady find you?"

I frowned. She clarified, "She came to the house and I told her where you were. Did she know you were moving to LA?"

"Why?"

"It just looked like she was running out of time. Like she needed to see you immediately."

"Ma, how did you figure that all out?"

She put her hand on my shoulder. "Honey, I'm a woman. That girl really cares about you."

I chuckled. She continued, "Now you know people are on the waiting list for these grants for years. She got you in this place in less than a month. I think she likes you."

"Ma, that's someone different."

I laughed off the confusion. "What did she say when she came there?"

"That she was looking for you and I just gave her this address."

"Thanks."

She looked at all my scattered boxes. "What have you decided to take?"

"I'm going to take most of this stuff. I'm going to leave these boxes in the basement."

She sucked her teeth. "Don't leave me with a bunch of junk."

"Ma, I'm sure in between taping, I'll be coming back."

"It's just so funny that the day that this place comes together, you get your break."

I stretched out on the floor after helping my mother unpack and thought about Fatima. Why did she come here? What did she want? Each time I thought about how happy I was with her, I would remember the breakup over the phone and how the cops escorted me from her house. I never expected that my move to LA would be filled with so many unanswered questions. This is what I worked my entire life for, but something just didn't seem right.

When my phone alarm buzzed the next morning, it was time to finish loading up and head across country. During one of my trips out to the van, I looked up and was shocked to see Fatima walking down the street toward me. I was frozen by her humility. She wore a sweatsuit, no makeup; her eyes were puffy and red, but she was still the most beautiful thing I'd ever seen. I was confused by her presence. Especially the luggage she dragged behind her.

When she stood in front of me, I noticed strange-looking scabs all over her face. It looked as if it had been stonewashed. Was this a desperate plea for my sympathy? I frowned. "What happened to your face?"

The intensity in her face melted as she cracked a short grin. "We'll talk about that in a minute. But what I came to say is . . ."

My inquisitive stare forced her to pause. Finally, she cleared her throat and an urgent confidence spoke for her. "Rashad, I came here to tell that I love you." She took a deep breath. "I have loved you from almost the beginning, but I was afraid to admit it. I was afraid that if I loved you, I would lose control. I wanted to control the destiny of our relationship all because I was scared. I thought if I could protect myself from love, I would never lose it again."

She reached out for my folded, resistant arms. "You loved me in a way no one else would have, even with all the money in the world, and I'm not scared anymore. I had to choose between love and fear . . ."

I watched in shock as she continued, "I choose love, Rashad. I want to love you. I'm not ready to let you go. I want to give you everything you need."

"But why all of a sudden? A week ago you didn't want anything to do with me." I wondered if I could trust her again.

"Rashad, a week ago, I didn't want anything to do with me. I thought I had failed at being perfect. But now I know that being perfect doesn't make me worthy of love. Being open to love is what makes me worthy and I'm open. I see my mistakes and I hope you'll give me the chance to make things better."

"Have you really thought this out? You're standing here like you're ready to move across country with me and . . ."

She pulled a piece of paper from her purse. As she unfolded the page, I noticed it was from my script. She flipped it over and pointed to the third item: Be spontaneous.

My heart belonged to this woman in front of me and I owed her all my love for free. To relieve her of the burden of explaining further, I ripped the page, tossed it up in the air, and kissed her passionately to let her know I couldn't live without her either. Our hearts collided and I realized that love is not an accident—sometimes you have to write your own script.

A HIRE LOVE

CANDICE DOW

ABOUT THIS GUIDE

The suggested questions are intended
to enhance your group's reading
of Candice Dow's book.

DISCUSSION QUESTIONS

1. What was Fatima's baggage and how did it hinder her return to the dating scene?

2. How did Fatima compare to women who have been in the game longer?

3. Do you think her expectations were too high?

4. Did Fatima hold herself up to the same expectations?

5. In what situations did Fatima show her insecurities? And where did these insecurities stem from?

6. Do you think most people prefer to skip the get-to-know phase in relationships? Why or why not?

7. Would you have been able to trust anything Rashad said?

8. In Rashad's relationship with Fatima, what are some ways it affected him positively? And how did it affect him negatively?

9. In which ways do you think Rashad's relationship with his mother helped him to handle the relationship with Fatima? What similarities did Fatima and his mother share?

10. Do you think that most women really want the perfect mate?

11. How did Rashad's presence in Fatima's life cause her to reconnect with her roots and rediscover her zest for life?

12. Do you think the miscommunication between Rashad and Fatima plagues average relationships?

13. Do you think the script was a good idea? Why or why not?